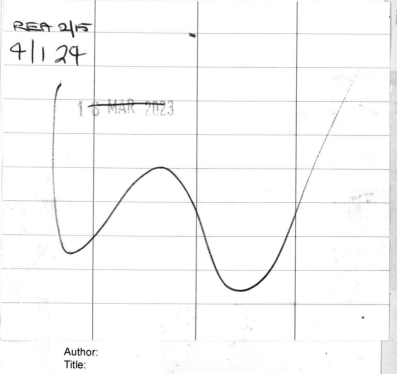

Also available by

Nora Roberts

Nora Roberts

Under Summer Skies

This edition published in Great Britain 2014
by Mills & Boon, an imprint of Harlequin (UK) Limited,
Eton House, 18-24 Paradise Road, Richmond, Surrey, TW9 1SR

Harlequin (UK) Limited's policy is to use papers that are natural, renewable and recyclable products and made from wood grown in sustainable forests. The logging and manufacturing processes conform to the legal environmental regulations of the country of origin.

Printed and bound by
CPI Group (UK) Ltd, Croydon, CR0 4YY

CONTENTS

From This Day

1

Spring comes late to New England. Snow lingers in isolated patches. Trees begin their greening hesitantly, tiny closed buds of leaves against naked branches. Early blooms of color burst from the earth's womb. The air is fresh with promise.

B.J. tossed open her window with a flourish and welcomed the early breeze into her room. *Saturday,* she thought with a grin, and began to braid her long, wheat-colored hair. The Lakeside Inn was half-full, the summer season three weeks away, and if all followed her well-ordered plans, her duties as manager would be light for the duration of the weekend.

Her staff was loyal, though somewhat temperamental. Like a large family, they squabbled, sulked, teased and stuck together like mortar and brick when the need arose. And I, she mused with a rueful grin, am head counselor.

Pulling on faded jeans, B.J. did not pause to consider the incongruity of the title. A small, childlike woman reflected in her glass, curves disguised by casual attire, braids hanging impishly astride a heart shaped, elfin face with huge smoky eyes dominant. Her only large feature, they swamped the tip-tilted nose and cupid's bow mouth and were prone to smolder or sparkle with the fluctuations of her mood. After lacing dilapidated sneakers, she jogged from the room, intending to check on breakfast preparations before stealing an hour for a solitary walk.

The main staircase of the inn was wide and uncarpeted, connecting its four sprawling stories without curve or angle, as straight and sturdy as the building itself. She saw with satisfaction the lobby was both tidy and deserted. The curtains were drawn to welcome the sun, needlepoint pillows plumped, and a vase of fresh wildflowers adorned the high, well-polished registration desk. The clatter of cutlery carried from the dining room as she passed through the downstairs hall, and she heard, with a long suffering sigh, the running argument between her two waitresses.

"If you really like a man with small, pig eyes, you should be very happy."

B.J. watched Dot shrug her thin shoulders with the words as she rolled a place setting in white linen.

"Wally does not have pig eyes," Maggie insisted.

"They're very intelligent. You're just jealous," she added with grim relish as she filled the sugar dispensers.

"Jealous! Ha! The day I'm jealous of a squinty-eyed little runt... Oh, hello, B.J."

"Good morning, Dot, Maggie. You rolled two spoons and a knife at that setting, Dot. I think a fork might be a nice touch."

Accompanied by her companion's snickers, Dot unrolled the linen. "Wally's taking me to a double feature at the drive-in tonight." Maggie's smug statement followed B.J. into the kitchen, and she allowed the door to swing shut on the ensuing retort.

Unlike the casual, old fashioned atmosphere of the remainder of the inn, the kitchen sparkled with twentieth century efficiency. Stainless steel glimmered everywhere in the oversized room, the huge stove attesting that the inn's main attraction was its menu. Cupboards and cabinets stood like veteran soldiers, walls and linoleum gleaming with fresh cleaning. B.J. smiled, pleased with the room's perfection and the drifting scent of coffee.

"Morning, Elsie." She received an absent mutter from the round woman working at a long, well-scrubbed counter. "If everything's under control, I'm going out for a couple of hours."

"Betty Jackson won't send any blackberry jelly."

"What? Well, for goodness sake why not?" Annoyed by the complication, B.J. plucked a fresh muffin from a basket and began to devour it. "Mr. Conners always asks for her jelly, and we're down to the last jar."

"She said if you couldn't be bothered to pay a lonely old woman a visit, she couldn't be bothered to part with any jelly."

"Lonely old woman?" B.J.'s exclamation was hampered by a mouthful of muffin. "She runs more news items through that house of hers than the Associated Press. Blast it, Elsie, I really need that jelly. I was too busy last week to go listen to the latest special bulletins."

"The new owner coming Monday got you worried?"

"Who's worried? I'm not worried." Scowling, she confiscated another muffin. "It's simply that as manager of the inn, I want everything to be in order."

"Eddie said you were muttering and slamming around your office after you got the letter saying he was coming."

"I was not…muttering…." Moving to the refrigerator, B.J. poured a glass of juice and spoke to Elsie's wide back. "Taylor Reynolds has a perfect right to inspect his property. It's just, blast it, Elsie, it was all those vague comments about modernizing. Mr. Taylor Reynolds better keep his hands off the Lakeside Inn and play with his other hotels. We don't need to be modernized," she continued, rapidly working herself up into a temper. "We're perfectly fine just the way we are. There's not a thing wrong with us, we don't need anything." She finished by folding her arms across her chest and glaring at the absent Taylor Reynolds.

"Except blackberry jelly," Elsie said mildly. B.J. blinked and brought herself back to the present.

"Oh, all right," she muttered and stalked toward the door. "I'll go get it. But if she tells me one more time that Howard Beall is a fine boy and good husband material, I'll scream. Right there in her living room with the doilies and chintz, I'll scream!"

Leaving this dire threat hanging in the air, B.J. stepped out into the soothing yellow sunlight.

"Blackberry jelly," she mumbled as she hopped on a battered red bike. "New owners with fancy notions...." Lifting her face to the sky, she tossed a pigtail behind her shoulder.

Pedaling down the maple lined drive, quicksilver temper ebbed, her resilient spirits were lifted with the beauty of the day. The valley was stirring with life. Small clusters of fragile violets and red clover dotted the rolling meadows. Lines of fresh laundry waved in the early breeze. The boundary of mountains was topped by a winter's coat, not yet the soft, lush green it would be in a month's time, but patched with stark black trees and the intermittent color of pines. Clouds scudded thin and white across the sky, chased by the teasing wind which whispered of spring and fresh blossoms.

Good humor restored, B.J. arrived in town with pink cheeks and a smile, waving to familiar faces along the route to Betty Jackson's jelly. It was a small town with tidy lawns, picket fences and old, well-kept homes. The dormers and gables were typical of New England. Nestled like a contented cat in the rolling valley, and the brilliant shimmer of Lake Champlain to the west, Lakeside remained serene and untouched by big city bustle. Having been raised on its outskirts had not dulled its magic for B.J.: she felt, as always when entering its limits, a gratitude that somewhere life remained simple.

Parking her bike in front of a small, green-shuttered house, B.J. swung through the gate and prepared to negotiate for her jelly supply.

"Well, B.J., what a surprise." Betty opened the door and patted her gray permanent. "I thought you'd gone back to New York."

"Things have been a bit hectic at the inn," she returned, striving for the proper humility.

"The new owner." Betty nodded with a fortune teller's wisdom and gestured B.J. inside. "I hear he wants to spruce things up."

Resigned that Betty Jackson's communications system was infallible, B.J. settled herself in the small living room.

"You know Tom Myers is adding another room to his house." Brushing off the seat of an overstuffed chair, Betty shifted her ample posterior and sat. "Seems Lois is in the family way again." She clucked her tongue over the Myers' profligacy. "Three babies in four years. But you like little ones, don't you, B.J.?"

"I've always been fond of children, Miss Jackson," B.J. acknowledged, wondering how to turn the conversation toward preserves.

"My nephew, Howard, just loves children."

B.J. braced herself not to scream and met the bland smile, calmly. "We've a couple at the inn now. Children do love to eat." Pleased with the maneuver, she pressed on. "They've simply devoured your jellies. I'm down to my last jar. Nobody has the touch you do with jellies, Miss Jackson; you'd put the big manufacturers out of business if you opened your own line."

"It's all in the timing," Betty preened under the praise, and B.J. tasted the hint of victory.

"I'd just have to close down if you didn't keep me supplied." Gray eyes fluttered ingenuously. "Mr. Conners would be crushed if I had to serve him store-bought goods. He simply raves about your blackberry jelly. *"Ambrosia,"* she added, relishing the word. "He says it's *ambrosia.*"

"Ambrosia." Betty nodded in self-satisfied agreement.

Ten minutes later, B.J. placed a box of a dozen jars of jelly in the basket of her bike and waved a cheerful goodbye.

"I came, I saw, I conquered," she told the sky with audacious pride. "And I did not scream."

"Hey, B.J.!"

She twisted her head at the sound of her name, waving
to the group playing sand lot ball as she pedaled to the
edge of the field. "What's the score?" she asked the
young boy who ran to her bike.

"Five to four. Junior's team's winning."

She glanced over to where Junior stood, tall and gangly
on the pitcher's mound, tossing a ball in his glove and
grinning.

"Little squirt," she mumbled with reluctant affection.
"Let me pinch hit once." Confiscating the boy's battered
cap, she secured it over her pigtails and walked onto the
field.

"You gonna play, B.J.?" Suddenly surrounded by
young bodies and adolescent faces, B.J. lifted a bat and
tested it.

"For a minute. I have to get back."

Junior approached, hands on hips, and grinned down
from his advantage of three inches. "Wanna bet I strike
you out?"

She spared him a brief glance and swung the bat to her
shoulder. "I don't want to take your money."

"If I strike you out," he yanked a pigtail with fifteen-
year-old audacity, "you gotta kiss me."

"Get on the mound, you apprentice lecher, and come
back in ten years."

His grin remained unabashed, as B.J. watched, sti-
fling a smile as he sauntered into position. He squinted,

nodded, wound up and pitched. B.J. swung a full circle.

"Strike one!"

She turned and scowled at Wilbur Hayes who stood as umpire. Stepping up to the plate again, the cheers and taunts grew in volume. She stuck out her tongue at Junior's wink.

"Strike two!" Wilbur announced as she watched the pitch sail by.

"Strike?" Turning, she placed her hands on her hips. "You're crazy, that was chin high. I'm going to tell your mother you need glasses."

"Strike two," Wilbur repeated and frowned with adolescent ferocity.

Muttering, B.J. stepped again into the batter's box.

"You might as well put the bat down," Junior shouted, cradling the ball in the mitt. "You're not even coming close to this one."

"Take a good look at the ball, Junior, 'cause it's the last time you'll see it." Shifting the hat lower on her head, B.J. clutched the bat. "It's going clear to New York."

She connected with a solid crack of bat and watched the ball begin its sail before she darted around the bases. Running full steam, head down, she heard the shouts and cheers to slide as she rounded third. Scott Temple crouched at the plate, mitt opened for reception, as she threw herself down, sliding into home in a cloud of dust and frenzied shouts.

"You're out!"

"Out!" Scrambling to her feet, she met Wilbur's bland blue stare, eye to eye and nose to nose. "Out, you little squirt, I was safe by a mile. I'm going to buy you some binoculars."

"Out," he repeated with great dignity, and folded his arms.

"What we need here is an umpire with two working eyes." She turned to her crowd of supporters and threw out her hands. "I demand a second opinion."

"You were out."

Spinning at the unfamiliar voice, B.J. frowned up at the stranger. He stood leaning on the backstop, a small lift to his well-formed mouth and amusement shining from his dark brown eyes. He pushed a lock of curling black hair from his brow and straightened a long, lean frame.

"You should have been content with a triple."

"I was safe," she retorted, rubbing more dirt on her nose. "Absolutely safe."

"Out," Wilbur repeated.

B.J. sent him a withering glance before turning back to the man who approached the heated debate between teams. She studied him with a mixture of resentment and curiosity.

His features were well defined, sculptured with planes and angles, the skin bronzed and smooth, the faintest hint of red in his dark hair where the sun caught it. She saw that though his buff-colored suit was casual, it was obviously well tailored and expensive. His teasing smile widened at her critical survey, and her resentment deepened.

"I've got to get back," she announced, brushing at her jeans. "And don't think I'm not going to mention an eye exam to your mother," she added, giving Wilbur a final glare.

"Hey, kid." She straddled her bike and looked around idly, then smiled as she realized the man had grouped her with the teenagers. Restraining her smile, she looked up with what she hoped was the insolence of youth.

"Yeah?"

"How far is it to the Lakeside Inn?"

"Look, mister, my mother told me not to talk to strange men."

"Very commendable. I'm not offering you candy and a ride."

"Well." She frowned as if debating pros and cons. "O.K. It's about three miles up the road." Making her gesture vague, she finished with the obligatory codicil. "You can't miss it."

He gave a long stare into her wide gray eyes, then shook his head. "That's a big help. Thanks."

"Any time." She watched him wander toward a silver-blue Mercedes and, unable to prevent herself, called after him. "And I was safe. Absolutely safe." Tossing the borrowed hat back to its owner, B.J. cut across the meadow and headed toward the inn.

The four stories of red brick, with their gabled roof and neat shutters, loomed ahead of her. Pedaling up the wide, curving drive, she noted with satisfaction that the short cut had brought her ahead of the Mercedes.

I wonder if he's looking for a room, she thought. Parking her bike, she hauled out her treasure of jellies from the basket. Maybe he's a salesman. No, she contradicted her own thoughts, *that was no salesman*. Well, if he wants a room, we'll oblige him, even if he is an interfering busybody with bad eyes.

"Good morning." B.J. smiled at the newlyweds who strolled across the lawn.

"Oh, good morning, Miss Clark. We're going for a walk by the lake," the groom answered politely.

"It's a lovely day for it," B.J. acknowledged, parking her bike by the entrance. She entered the small lobby, and moving behind the front desk, set down the crate of jelly and reached for the morning mail. Seeing a personal letter from her grandmother, she opened it and began to read with pleasure.

"Get around, don't you?"

Her absorption was rudely broken. Dropping the letter, she lifted her elbows from the counter and stared into dark brown eyes. "I took a short cut." Unwilling to be outmatched by his height or faultless attire, she straightened and lifted her chin. "May I help you?"

"I doubt it, unless you can tell me where to find the manager."

His dismissive tone fueled her annoyance. She struggled to remember her job and remain pleasant. "Is there some problem? There's a room available if you require one."

"Be a good girl and run along." His tone was patronizing. "And fetch the manager for me while you're about it. I'd like to see him."

Drawing herself to her full height she crossed her arms over her chest. "You're looking at her."

His dark brows rose in speculation as his eyes swept over her incredulously. "Do you manage the inn before school and on Saturdays?" he asked sarcastically.

B.J. flushed with anger. "I have been managing the Lakeside Inn for nearly four years. If there's a problem, I shall be delighted to take it up with you here, or in my office. If you require a room," she gestured toward the open register, "we'll be more than happy to oblige you."

"B.J. Clark?" he asked with a deepening frown.

"That's correct."

With a nod, he lifted a pen and signed the register. "I'm sure you'll understand," he began, raising his eyes again in fresh study. "Your morning activity on the baseball diamond and your rather juvenile appearance are deceptive."

"I had the morning free," she said crisply, "and my appearance in no way reflects on the inn's quality. I'm sure you'll see that for yourself during your stay, Mr...." Turning the register to face her, B.J.'s stomach lurched.

"Reynolds," he supplied, smiling at her astonished expression. "Taylor Reynolds."

Struggling for composure, B.J. lifted her face and assumed a businesslike veneer. "I'm afraid we weren't expecting you until Monday, Mr. Reynolds."

"I changed my plans," he countered, dropping the pen back in its holder.

"Yes, well…Welcome to Lakeside Inn," she said belatedly and flicked a pigtail behind her back.

"Thank you. I'll require an office during my stay. Can you arrange it?"

"Our office space is limited, Mr. Reynolds." Cursing Betty Jackson's blackberry jelly, she pulled down the key to the inn's best room and rounded the desk. "However, if you don't mind sharing mine, I'm sure you'll find it adequate."

"Let's take a look. I want to see the books and records anyway."

"Of course," she agreed, gritting her teeth at the stranger's hold over her inn. "If you'll just come with me."

"B.J., B.J." She watched with an inward shudder as Eddie hurtled down the stairs and into the lobby. His glasses were slipping down his nose, his brown hair was flopping around his ears.

"B.J.," he said again, breathless, "Mrs. Pierce-Lowell's T.V. went out right in the middle of her cartoons."

"Oh, blast. Take mine in to her and call Max for the repair."

"He's away for the weekend," Eddie reminded her.

"All right, I'll survive." Giving his shoulder an encouraging pat, she guided him to the door. "Leave me a memo to call him Monday and get mine in to her before she misses Bugs Bunny." Feeling the new owner's penetrating stare in the back of her head, B.J. explained apologetically. "I'm sorry, Eddie has a tendency toward the dramatic, and Mrs. Pierce-Lowell is addicted to Saturday morning cartoons. She's one of our regulars, and we make it a policy to provide our guests with what pleases them."

"I see," he replied, but she could find nothing in his expression to indicate that he did.

Moving quickly to the back of the first floor, B.J. opened the door to her office and gestured Taylor inside. "It's not very big," she began as he surveyed the small room with desk and file cabinets and bulletin board, "but I'm sure we can arrange it to suit your needs for the few days you will be here."

"Two weeks," he stated firmly. He strolled across the room, picking up a bronzed paperweight of a grinning turtle.

"Two weeks?" she repeated, and the alarm in her voice caused him to turn toward her.

"That's right, Miss Clark. Is that a problem?"

"No, no, of course not." Finding his direct stare unnerving, she lowered her eyes to the clutter on her desk.

"Do you play ball every Saturday, Miss Clark?" He

perched on the edge of the desk. Looking up, B.J. found her face only inches from his.

"No, certainly not," she answered with dignity. "I simply happened to be passing by, and—"

"A very courageous slide," he commented, shocking her by running a finger down her cheek. "And your face proves it."

Somewhat dazed, she glanced at the dust on his finger. "I was safe," she said in defense against a ridiculously speeding pulse. "Wilbur needs an optometrist."

"I wonder if you manage the inn with the same tenacity with which you play ball." He smiled, his eyes very intent on hers. "We'll have a look at the books this afternoon."

"I'm sure you'll find everything in order," she said stiffly. The effect was somewhat spoiled as she backed into the file cabinet. "The inn runs very smoothly, and as you know, makes a nice profit." She continued struggling to maintain her dignity.

"With a few changes, it should make a great deal more."

"Changes?" she echoed, apprehension in her voice. "What sort of changes?"

"I need to look over the place before I make any concrete decisions, but the location is perfect for a resort." Absently, he brushed the dust off his fingers on the windowsill and gazed out. "Pool, tennis courts, health club, a face lift for the building itself."

"There's nothing wrong with this building. We don't cater to the resort set, Mr. Reynolds." Furious, B.J. approached the desk again. "This is an inn, with all the connotations that includes. Family-style meals, comfortable lodgings and a quiet atmosphere. That's why our guests come back."

"The clientele would increase with a few modern attractions," he countered coolly. "Particularly with the proximity to Lake Champlain."

"Keep your hot tubs and disco lounges for your other acquisitions." B.J. bypassed simmer and went straight to boil. "This is Lakeside, Vermont, not L.A. I don't want any plastic surgery on my inn."

Brows rose, and his mouth curved in a grim smile. "Your inn, Miss Clark?"

"That's right," she retorted, "You may hold the purse strings, Mr. Reynolds, but I know this place, and our guests come back year after year because of what we represent. There's no way you're going to change one brick."

"Miss Clark." Taylor stood menacingly over her. "If I choose to tear down this inn brick by brick, that's precisely what I'll do. Whatever alterations I make or don't make, remain my decision, and my decision alone. Your position as manager does not entitle you to a vote."

"And your position as owner doesn't entitle you to brains!" she was unable to choke back as she stomped from the office in a flurry of flying braids.

2

With relish, B.J. slammed the door to her room. Arrogant, interfering, insufferable man. Why doesn't he go play Monopoly somewhere else? Doesn't he already have enough hotels to tinker with? There must be a hundred in the Reynolds chain in the states alone, plus all those elegant foreign resorts. Why doesn't he open one in Antarctica?

Abruptly, she caught sight of her reflection in the mirror and stared in disbelief. Her face was smudged. Dust clung to her sweatshirt and jeans. Her braids hung to her shoulders. All in all, she thought grimly, I look like a rather dim-witted ten-year-old. She suddenly noticed a line down her cheek, and lifting her hand, recalled Taylor's finger resting there.

"Oh, blast." Shaking her head, she began to quickly

unbind her hair. "I made a mess of it," she muttered and stripped off her morning uniform. "Looking like a grimy teenager and then losing my temper on top of it. Well, he's not going to fire me," she vowed fiercely and stalked to the shower. "I'll quit first! I'm not staying around and watching my inn mutilated."

Thirty minutes later, B.J. pulled a brush through her hair and studied the new reflection with satisfaction. Soft clouds of wheat floated on her shoulders. She wore an ivory dress, nipped at the waist, belted in scarlet to match tiny blazing rubies at her ears. Heels gave her height a slight advantage. She felt confident she could no longer be mistaken for sixteen. Lifting a neatly written page from her dresser, she moved purposefully from the room, prepared to confront the bear in his den.

After a brief excuse for a knock, B.J. pushed open the office door and slowly and purposefully advanced toward the man sitting behind the desk. Shoving the paper under his nose, she waited for his brown eyes to meet hers.

"Ah, B.J. Clark, I presume. This is quite a transfiguration." Leaning back in his chair, Taylor allowed his eyes to travel over the length of her. "Amazing," he smiled into her resentful gray eyes, "what can be concealed under a sweatshirt and baggy pants…. What's this?" He waved the paper idly, his eyes still appraising her.

"My resignation." Placing her palms on the desk, she leaned forward and prepared to give vent to her emotions. "And now that I am no longer in your employ, Mr. Reynolds, it'll give me a great deal of pleasure to tell you what I think. You are," she began as his brow rose at her tone, "a dictatorial, capitalistic opportunist. You've bought an inn which has for generations maintained its reputation for quality and personal service, and in order to make a few more annual dollars, you plan to turn it into a live-in amusement park. In doing so, you will not only have to let the current staff go, some of whom have worked here for twenty years, but you'll succeed in destroying the integrity of the entire district. This is not your average tourist town, it's a quiet, settled community. People come here for fresh air and quiet, not for a brisk tennis match or to sweat in a sauna, and—"

"Are you finished, Miss Clark?" Taylor questioned. Instinctively she recognized the danger in his lowered tones.

"No." Mustering her last resources of courage, she set her shoulders and sent him a lethal glare. "Go soak in your Jacuzzi!"

On her heel, she spun around and made for the door only to find her back pressed into it as she was whirled back into the room.

"Miss Clark," Taylor began, effectively holding her prisoner by leaning over her, arms at either side of her head. "I permitted you to clear your system for two reasons. First, you're quite a fabulous sight when your temper's in full gear. I noticed that even when I took you

for a rude teenager. A lot of it has to do with your eyes
going from mist to smoke, it's very impressive. That, of
course," he added as she stared up at him, unable to form
a sound, "is strictly on a personal level. Now on a professional plane, I am receptive to your opinions, if not to
your delivery."

Abruptly, the door swung open, dislodging B.J. and
tumbling her into a hard chest. "We found Julius's
lunch," Eddie announced cheerfully and disappeared.

"You have a very enthusiastic staff," Taylor commented dryly as his arms propped her up against him.
"Who the devil is Julius?"

"He's Mrs. Frank's Great Dane. She doesn't…she
won't go anywhere without him."

"Does he have his own room?" His tone was gently
mocking.

"No, he has a small run in the back."

Taylor smiled suddenly, his face close to hers. Power
shot through her system like a bolt of electricity down a
lightning rod. With a jerk, she pulled away and pushed
at her tumbled hair.

"Mr. Reynolds," she began, attempting to retrieve her
all too elusive dignity. He claimed her hand and pulled
her back toward the desk, then pushed her firmly down
on the chair.

"Do be quiet, Miss Clark," he told her in easy tones,
settling behind the desk. "It's my turn now." She stared
with a melding of astonishment and indignation.

"What I ultimately do with this inn is my decision. However, I will consider your opinion as you are intimate with this establishment and with the area and I, as yet, am not." Lifting B.J.'s resignation, Taylor tore it in half and dropped the pieces on the desk.

"You can't do that," she sputtered.

"I have just done it." The mild tone vibrated with authority.

B.J.'s eyes narrowed. "I can easily write another."

"Don't waste your paper," he advised, leaning back in his chair. "I have no intention of accepting your resignation at the moment. Later, I'll let you know. However," he added slowly, shrugging, "if you insist, I shall be forced to close down the inn for the next few months until I've found someone to replace you."

"It couldn't possibly take months to replace me," B.J. protested, but he was looking up at the ceiling as though lost in thought.

"Six months perhaps."

"Six months?" she frowned. "But you can't. We have reservations, it's nearly the summer season. All those people can't be disappointed. And the staff—the staff would be out of work."

"Yes." With an agreeable smile, he nodded and folded his hands on the desk.

Her eyes widened. "But—that's blackmail!"

"I think that term is quite correct." His amusement increased. "You catch on very quickly, Miss Clark."

"You can't be serious. You," she sputtered. "You wouldn't actually close the inn just because I quit."

"You don't know me well enough to be sure, do you?" His eyes were unfathomable and steady. "Do you want to chance it?"

Silence hung for a long moment, each measuring the other. "No," B.J. finally murmured, then repeated with more strength, "No, blast it, I can't! You know that already. But I certainly don't understand why."

"You don't have to know why," he interrupted with an imperious gesture of his hand.

Sighing, B.J. struggled not to permit temper to rule her tongue again. "Mr. Reynolds," she began in what she hoped was a reasonable tone, "I don't know why you find it so important for me to remain as manager of the inn, but—"

"How old are you, Miss Clark?" He cut her off again. She stared in perplexed annoyance.

"I hardly see…"

"Twenty, twenty-one?"

"Twenty-four," B.J. corrected, inexplicably compelled to defend herself. "But I don't see what that has to do with anything."

"Twenty-four," he repeated, obviously concluding she had finished one sentence and that was sufficient. "Chronologically, I have eight years on you, and professionally quite a bit more. I opened my first hotel when you were still leading cheers at Lakeside High."

"I never led cheers at Lakeside High," she said coldly.

"Be that as it may—" he gently inclined his head "—the arithmetic remains the same. My reason for wanting you to remain in your current position at the inn is quite simple. You know the staff, the clientele, the suppliers and so forth…during this transition period I need your particular expertise."

"All right, Mr. Reynolds." B.J. relaxed slightly, feeling the conversation had leveled off to a more professional plane. "But you should be aware, I will give you absolutely no cooperation in changing any aspect which I feel affects the inn's personality. In point of fact, I will do my best to be uncooperative."

"I'm sure you're quite skillful at that," Taylor said easily. B.J. was unsure whether the smile in his eyes was real or in her imagination. "Now that we understand each other, Miss Clark, I'd like to see the place and get an idea of how you run things. I should be fairly well briefed in two weeks."

"You can't possibly understand all I've been trying to tell you in that amount of time."

"I make up my mind quickly," he told her. Smiling, he studied her face. "When something's mine, I know what to do with it." His smile widened at her frown, and he rose. "If you want the inn to remain as is, you'd best stick around and make your sales pitch." Taking her arm, he hauled her up from the chair. "Let's take a look around."

With all the warmth of a January sky, B.J. took Taylor on a tour of the first floor, describing storage closets in minute detail. Throughout, he kept a hand firmly on her arm as if to remind her of his authority. The continued contact made her vaguely uneasy. His scent was musky and essentially male and he moved with a casualness which she felt was deceptive. His voice rolled deep and smooth, and several times, she found herself listening more to its cadence than to his words. Annoyed, she added to the layers of frost coating her tone.

It would be easier, she decided, if he were short and balding with a generous middle, or, perhaps, if he had a sturdy mole on his left cheek and a pair of chins. It's absolutely unfair for a man to look the way he does and have to fight him, she thought resentfully.

"Have I lost you, Miss Clark?"

"What?" Looking up, she collected her wits, inwardly cursing him again for possessing such dark, magnetic eyes. "No, I was thinking perhaps you'd like lunch." A very good improvisation, she congratulated herself.

"Fine." Agreeably, he allowed her to lead the way to the dining room.

It was a basic, rustic room, large and rectangular with beamed ceilings and gently faded wallpaper. Its charm was old and lasting; amber globed lamps, graceful antiques and old silver. Local stone dominated one wall in which a fireplace was set. Brass andirons guarded the empty hearth. Tables had been set to encourage sociability, with a few more secluded for intimate interludes. The air was humming with easy conversation and clattering dishes. A smell of fresh baking drifted toward them. In silence, Taylor studied the room, his eyes roaming from corner to corner until B.J. was certain he had figured the precise square footage.

"Very nice," he said simply.

A large, round man approached, lifting his head with a subtle dramatic flourish.

"'If music be the food of love, play on.'"

"'Give me excess of it, that, surfeiting, the appetite may sicken, and so die.'"

Chuckling at B.J.'s response, he rolled with a regal, if oversized, grace into the dining room.

"Shakespeare at lunch?" Taylor inquired. B.J. laughed; against her will her antagonism dissolved. "That was Mr. Leander. He's been coming to the inn twice a year for the past ten years. He used to tour with a low budget Shakespearean troupe, and he likes to toss lines at me for me to cap."

"And do you always have the correct response?"

"Luckily, I've always been fond of Shakespeare, and as insurance, I cram a bit when he makes his reservation."

"Just part of the service?" Taylor inquired, tilting his head to study her from a new angle.

"You could say that."

Prudently, B.J. scanned the room to see where the young Dobson twins were seated, then steered Taylor to a table as far distant as possible.

"B.J." Dot sidled to her side, eyes lighting on Taylor in pure feminine avarice. "Wilbur brought the eggs, and they're small again. Elsie's threatening to do permanent damage."

"All right, I'll take care of it." Ignoring Taylor's questioning stare, she turned to her waitress. "Dot, see to Mr. Reynold's lunch. Please excuse me, Mr. Reynolds, I'll have to tend to this. Just send for me if you have any questions or if something is not to your satisfaction. Enjoy your meal."

Seeing Wilbur's eggs as a lucky escape hatch, B.J. hurried to the kitchen.

"Wilbur," she said with wicked enjoyment as the door swung shut behind her. "This time, I'm umpire."

A myriad of small demands dominated B.J.'s afternoon. The art of diplomacy as well as the ability to delegate and make decisions was an intricate part of her job, and B.J. had honed her skills. She moved without breaking rhythm from a debate with the Dobson twins on the advisability of keeping a frog in their bathtub to a counseling service with one of the maids who was weeping into the fresh linen supply over the loss of a boyfriend. Through the hours of soothing and listening and laying down verdicts, she was still conscious of the presence of Taylor Reynolds. It was a simple matter to

avoid him physically, but his presence seemed to follow
her everywhere. He had made himself known, and she
could not forget about him. Perversely, she found herself
fretting to know where he was and what he was doing.
Probably, she thought with a fresh flash of resentment,
probably he's even now in my office poring over my
books with a microscope, deciding where to put in his
silly tennis courts or how to concrete the grove.

The dinner hour came and went. B.J. had decided to
forego supervising the dining room to have a few hours
of peace. When she came downstairs to the lounge the
lighting was muted, the hour late. The three-piece band
hired for the benefit of the Saturday crowd had already
packed their equipment. The music had been replaced
by the murmurs and clinking glasses of the handful of
people who remained. It was the quiet time of the evening, just before silence. B.J. allowed her thoughts to
drift back to Taylor.

I've got two weeks to make him see reason, she reminded herself, exchanging goodnights as stragglers
began to wander from the lounge. That should be plenty
of time to make even the most insensitive businessman
understand. I simply went about things in the wrong
way. Tomorrow, I'll start my campaign with a brand
new strategy. I'll keep my temper under control and use
a great many smiles. I'm good at smiling when I put my
mind to it.

Practicing her talent on the middle-aged occupant in

room 224, B.J.'s confidence grew at his rapidly blinking appreciation. Yes, she concluded, smiles are much better than claws at this stage. A few smiles, a more sophisticated appearance, and a brisk, businesslike approach, and I'll defeat the enemy before the war's declared. Rejuvenated, she turned to the bartender who was lackadaisically wiping the counter. "Go on home, Don, I'll clear up the rest."

"Thanks, B.J." Needing no second urging, he dropped his rag and disappeared through the door.

"It's no trouble at all," she told the empty space with a magnanimous gesture of one hand. "I really insist."

Crossing the room, she began to gather half filled baskets of peanuts and empty glasses, switching on the small eye-level television for company. Around her, the inn settled for sleep, the groans and creaks so familiar, they went unnoticed. Now that the day was over, B.J. found the solitude for which she yearned.

Low, eerie music poured out of the television, drifting and floating through the darkened room. Glancing up, B.J. was soon mesmerized by a horror film. Kicking off her shoes, she slid onto a stool. The story was old and well-worn, but she was caught by a shot of clouds drifting over a full moon. She reached one hand absently for a basket of peanuts, settling them into her lap as the fog began to clear on the set to reveal the unknown terror, preceded by the rustle of leaves, and heavy breathing. With a small moan at the stalking monster's distorted face, B.J. covered her eyes and waited for doom to claim the heroine.

"You'd see more without your hand in front of your eyes."

As the voice came, disembodied in the darkness, B.J. shrieked, dislodging a shower of peanuts from her lap. "Don't ever do that again!" she commanded, glaring up at Taylor's grinning face.

"Sorry." The apology lacked conviction. Leaning on the bar, he nodded toward the set. "Why do you have it on if you don't want to watch?"

"I can't help myself, it's an obsession. But I always watch with my eyes closed. Now look, watch this part, I've seen it before." She grabbed his sleeve with one hand and pointed with the other. "She's going to walk right outside like an idiot. I ask you, would anyone with a working brain cell walk out into the pitch darkness when they hear something scraping at the window? Of course not," she answered for him. "A smart person would be huddled under the bed waiting for it to go away. Oh." She pulled him closer, burying her face against his chest as the monster's face loomed in a close-up. "It's horrible, I can't watch. Tell me when it's over."

Slowly, it dawned on her that she was burrowing into his chest, his heartbeat steady against her ear. His fingers tangled in her hair, smoothing and soothing her as though comforting a child. She stiffened and started to pull back, but the hand in her hair kept her still.

"No, wait a minute, he's still stalking about and leering. There." He patted her shoulder and loosened his grip. "Saved by commercial television."

Set free, B.J. fumbled off the stool and began gathering scattered peanuts and composure. "I'm afraid things got rather out of hand this afternoon, Mr. Reynolds." Her voice was not quite steady, but she hoped he would attribute the waver to cowardice. "I must apologize for not completing your tour of the inn."

He watched as she scrambled over the floor on her hands and knees, a curtain of pale hair concealing her face. "That's all right. I wandered a bit on my own. I finally met Eddie when not in motion. He's a very intense young man."

She shifted away from him to search for more far reaching nuts. "He'll be good at hotel management in a couple years. He just needs a little more experience." Keeping her face averted, B.J. waited for the heat to cool from her cheeks.

"I met quite a few of the inn's guests today. Everyone seems very fond of B.J." He closed the distance between them and pushed back the hair which lay across her cheek. "Tell me, what does it stand for?"

"What?" Diverted by the fingers on her skin, she found it hard to concentrate on the conversation.

"B.J." He smiled into bemused eyes. "What does it stand for?"

"Oh." She returned the smile, stepping strategically

out of reach. "I'm afraid that's a closely guarded secret. I've never even told my mother."

Behind her, the heroine gave a high-pitched, lilting scream. Scattering nuts again, B.J. threw herself into Taylor's arms.

"Oh, I'm sorry, that caught me off guard." Mortified, she lifted her face and attempted to pull away.

"No, this is the third time in one day you've been in this position." One hand lifted, and traveled down the length of her hair as he held her still. "This time, I'm going to see what you taste like."

Before she could protest, his mouth lowered to hers, at once firm and possessing. His arm around her waist brought her close to mold against him. His tongue found hers, and she was unaware whether he had parted her lips or if they had done so of their own volition. He lingered over her mouth, savoring its softness, deepening the kiss until she clung to him for balance. She told herself the sudden spiraling of her heartbeat was a reaction to the horror movie, the quick dizziness, the result of a missed dinner. Then she told herself nothing and only experienced.

"Very nice." Taylor's murmured approval trailed along her cheekbone, moving back to tease the corner of her mouth. "Why don't we try it again?"

In instinctive defense, she pressed her hand into his chest to ward him off. *Lightly* she told herself, praying for the earth to stop trembling, *treat it lightly*. "I'm afraid I don't come in thirty-two flavors, Mr. Reynolds, and…"

"Taylor," he interrupted, smiling down at the hand which represented no more of an obstacle than a blade of grass. "I decided this morning, when you stalked me in the office, that we're going to know each other very well."

"Mr. Reynolds…"

"Taylor," he repeated, his eyes close and compelling. "And my decisions are always final."

"Taylor," she agreed, not wanting to debate a minor point when the distance between them was lessening despite the pressure against his chest. "Do you engage in this sort of activity with all the managers of your hotels?" Hoping to wound him with a scathing remark, B.J. was immediately disappointed when he tossed back his head and laughed.

"B.J., this current activity has nothing whatever to do with your position at the inn. I am merely indulging my weakness for women who look good in pigtails."

"Don't you kiss me again!" she ordered, struggling with a sudden desperation which surprised him into loosening his hold.

"You'll have to choose between being demure or being provocative, B.J." His tone was mild, but she saw as she backed away, his eyes had darkened with temper. "Either way we play, I'm going to win, but it would make the game easier to follow."

"I don't play this sort of game," she retorted, "and I am neither demure nor provocative."

"You're a bit of both." His hands slipped into his pockets, and he rocked gently on his heels as he studied her furious face. "It's an intriguing combination." His brow lifted in speculation. An expression of amusement flitted over his features. "But I suppose you already know that or you wouldn't be so good at it."

Forgetting her fears, B.J. took a step toward him. "The only thing I know is that I have absolutely no desire to intrigue you in any way. All that I want you to do is to keep your resort builder's hands off this inn." Her hands balled into tight fists. "I wish you'd go back to New York and sit in your penthouse."

Before he could answer, B.J. turned and darted from the room. She hurried through the darkened lobby without even a backward glance.

3

B.J. decided that making a fool of herself the previous evening had been entirely Taylor Reynolds' responsibility. Today, she resolved, slipping a gray blazer over a white silk shirt, I will be astringently businesslike. Nonetheless, she winced at the memory of her naive plea that he not kiss her again, the absurd way her voice had shaken with the words. *Why didn't I come up with some cool, sophisticated retort?* she asked herself. *Because I was too busy throwing peanuts around the room and making a fool of myself,* she answered the question to her frowning mirror image. *Why did a simple kiss cloak my brain with layers of cheesecloth?* The woman in the mirror stared back without answering.

He had caught her off guard, B.J. decided as she arranged her hair in a neat, businesslike roll at her neck's nape. It was so unexpected, she had overreacted. Despite herself, she relived the sensation of his mouth claiming hers, his breath warm on her cheek. The knee trembling, brain spinning feeling never before experienced, washed over her again, and briskly, she shook her head to dispel it. It was simply a matter of the unexpected creating a false intenseness, like pricking your thumb with a needle while sewing.

It was important, she knew, to refrain from thinking of Taylor Reynolds on a personal level, and to remember he held the fate of the Lakeside Inn in his hands.

Dirty pool, her mind muttered, recalling his easy threat to close the inn if she pressed her resignation. Emotional blackmail. He knew he held all the aces, and waited, with that damnably appealing smile, for her to fold or call. *Well*, she decided, and smoothed the charcoal material of her skirt, *I play a pretty mean game of poker myself, Taylor Reynolds.* After trying out several types of smiles in the mirror, polite, condescending, dispassionate, she left the room with brisk steps.

Sunday mornings were usually quiet. Most of the guests slept late, rising in dribbles to wander downstairs for breakfast. Traditionally, B.J. spent these quiet hours closeted in her office with whatever paperwork she felt merited attention. From experience, she had found this particular system worked well, being the least likely time for calamities, minor or major, to befall guests or staff.

She grabbed a quick coffee in the kitchen before plunging into the sea of invoices and account books.

"How providential." She jerked slightly as a hand captured her arm, and she found herself being led to the dining room. "Now, I won't have to have breakfast alone."

The dozens of flaming retorts which sprang to mind at Taylor's presumptuousness were dutifully banked down. B.J. answered with her seasoned polite smile. "How kind of you to ask. I hope you spent a pleasant night."

"As stated in your public relations campaign, the inn is conducive to restful nights."

Waving aside her hostess, B.J. moved through the empty tables to a corner booth. "I think you'll find all my publicity is based on fact, Mr. Reynolds." Sliding in, B.J. struggled to keep her voice light and marginally friendly. Remnants of their argument in her office and their more personal encounter in the lounge clung to her, and she attempted to erase both from her mind.

"So far I find no discrepancies."

Maggie hovered by the table, her smile dreamily absent. No doubt she was thinking of her date last night with Wally, B.J. thought. "Toast and coffee, Maggie," she said kindly, breaking the trance. The waitress scribbled on her pad, her cheeks flushed.

"You know," Taylor observed after giving his order, "you're very good at your job."

B.J. chided herself for her pleasure at the unexpected praise. "Why do you say that?"

"Not only are your books in perfect order, but you know your staff and handle them with unobtrusive deftness. You just managed to convey a five-minute lecture with one brief look."

"It makes it easier when you understand your staff and their habits." Her brows lifted in easy humor. "You see, I happen to know Maggie's mind is still focused on the double feature she and Wally didn't watch last night."

His grin flashed, boyish and quick.

"The staff is very much like a family." B.J. was careful to keep her tone casual, her hands busy pouring coffee. "The guests feel that. They enjoy the informality which is always accompanied by quality service. Our rules are flexible, and the staff is trained to adjust to the individual needs of the guests. The inn is a basic place, not for those who require formal entertainment or unlimited luxury. Fresh air, good food and a pleasant atmosphere are our enticements, and we deliver."

She paused as Maggie placed their breakfast order on the table.

"Do you have a moral objection to resorts, B.J.?"

The unexpectedness of Taylor's question put her off. Blinking in confusion at the long, lean fingers as they held a knife, spreading Betty Jackson jelly on toast, she stammered, "No…why of course not." Those fingers, she recalled irrelevantly, had tangled in her hair. "No," she repeated more firmly, meeting his eyes. "Resorts are fine if they are run correctly, as yours are. But their function is entirely different from ours. In a proper resort there's an activity for every minute of the day. Here, the atmosphere is more relaxed, a little fishing or boating, skiing, and above all the menu. The Lakeside Inn is perfect exactly as it is," she concluded more fiercely than she had intended and watched one brow rise, nearly meeting the curling thickness of his hair.

"That's yet to be determined." He lifted his cup to his lips.

His tone was mild, but B.J. recognized traces of anger in the disconcertingly direct eyes. She dropped her eyes to her own cup as if enticed by the rich, black liquid.

"'The gray-eyed morn smiles on the frowning night.'"

The quote brought her head up sharply, and looking into Mr. Leander's smiling, expectant face, B.J. searched her brain. "'Chequering the eastern clouds with streaks of light.'"

Thank goodness I've read *Romeo and Juliet* a dozen times, she thought, watching his pleased saunter as he moved to his table.

"One day, he's going to catch you, and you're going to draw a blank."

"Life's a series of risks," she returned flippantly. "Better to accept its challenges."

Reaching over, he tucked a stray lock behind her ear, and she jerked away from his touch, unexpectedly shy.

"For the most part," he drew the words out with infuriating emphasis, "I believe you do. It should make things very interesting. More coffee?" His question was pleasant and easy as if they had shared the morning meal on a regular basis. B.J. shook her head in refusal…. She felt uneasily inept at parrying words with this domineering, sophisticated man….

Sunlight poured through the many-paned windows, spilling in patchwork patterns on the floor, a lawn mower hummed along the outer edges of lawn, and somewhere close, a bird sang his enjoyment of a golden day. Closeted in the office with Taylor, B.J. tuned even these small pleasures out, keeping her mind firmly on the business at hand. Here, with the impersonal wedges of invoices and account books between them, she felt confident and assured. In discussing the inn's procedure, her feet were on solid ground. Honesty forced her to admit that Taylor Reynolds knew his profession down to the finest detail. He skimmed through her books with the sharp eye of an accountant, shifted and sorted invoices with the ease of a business manager.

At least, B.J. told herself, he doesn't treat me like an empty-headed imbecile who can't tally monthly accounts. Rather, she found him listening to her explanations with attentive respect. Soothed by his obvious appreciation of her intelligence B.J. decided if he did not yet look on the Lakeside Inn as she did, perhaps that too would come.

"I see you deal with a great many small businesses and local farms."

"That's right." She searched the bottom drawer of her desk for an ashtray as he lit a cigarette. "It's advantageous on all sides. We get more personal service and fresher produce, and it boosts local economy." Finding a small ceramic ashtray under a pile of personal correspondence, B.J. placed it on the desk. "The Lakeside Inn is essential to this district. We provide employment and a market for local products and services."

"Umm."

Finding his response less than illuminating, B.J. opened her mouth to continue when the door burst open.

"B.J." Eddie stood, bottom lip trembling. "It's the Bodwins."

"I'll be right there." Suppressing a sigh, she made a mental note to tell Eddie to knock during Taylor's stay.

"Is that a natural disaster or a plague?" Taylor asked, watching Eddie's speedy exit.

"It's nothing, really." She edged toward the door. "Excuse me, I'll just be a minute."

Shutting the door behind her, B.J. hurried to the lobby.

"Hello, Miss Patience, Miss Hope." She greeted the elderly Bodwin sisters with a wary smile.

Tall and lean as two aged willows, the Bodwins were long-standing guests.

"It's so nice to see you both again."

"It's always a pleasure to come back, Miss Clark," Miss Patience announced, and Miss Hope murmured in agreement. Habitually Miss Patience announced, and Miss Hope murmured. It was one of the few things which separated them. Over the years they had melded into mirror images from their identical wire rimmed spectacles to their identical orthopedic shoes.

"Eddie, see that the luggage is taken up, please." Miss Patience flashed a knowing smile which B.J. tried not to notice. B.J. saw her sharp-eyed glance drift over her head. Turning, she spotted Taylor.

"Miss Patience, Miss Hope, this is Taylor Reynolds, the owner of the inn." Miss Patience shot her a meaningful look.

"A pleasure, ladies." Gallantly, he took each thin-boned hand in his. A blush, dormant for twenty-five years, rose to Miss Hope's wrinkled cheek.

"You're a very fortunate young man." Miss Patience gave Taylor a thorough survey, then nodded as if satisfied. "I'm sure you know what a treasure you have in Miss Clark. I hope you appreciate her."

B.J. resisted grinding her teeth for fear the sound

would be audible. With a smile, Taylor laid a hand on her shoulder.

"I'm quite convinced Miss Clark is indispensable and my appreciation inadequate."

Satisfied, Miss Patience nodded.

B.J. shook the offending hand from her shoulder and assumed a coolly professional manner. "You have your regular table, number 2."

"Of course." Miss Patience moved her lips into a smile and patted B.J.'s cheek. "You're a good girl, Miss Clark." Smiling vaguely, the two ladies drifted away.

"Surely, B.J." Taylor turned to B.J. with an infuriating smile. "You're not going to give those two dotty old girls the second table?"

"The Lakeside Inn," she said coldly, turning to precede him to the office, "makes it a habit to please its guests. I see no reason why the Bodwins shouldn't sit wherever they want. Mr. Campbell always seated them at number 2."

"Mr. Campbell," Taylor countered with infuriating calm, "no longer owns the inn. I do."

"I'm well aware of that." Her chin tilted higher in defiance. "Do you want me to turn out the Bodwin sisters and place them at the table near the kitchen? Don't they look fancy enough for you? Why don't you think of them as people rather than little black numbers in the bloody account book?"

Her tirade was sharply cut off as he gripped her shoulders. She found she had swallowed the remaining words before she could prevent herself.

"You have," he began in an ominously low voice, "a very unfortunate temper and some very odd ideas. No one tells me how to run my business. Absolutely no one. Advice is accepted upon request, but I only make the decisions, and I alone give the orders."

He moved toward her. She could only stare, fascinated and faintly terrified.

"Do we understand each other?"

B.J. nodded, wide-eyed, then gathered courage to answer audibly. "Yes, perfectly. What would you like me to do about the Bodwins?"

"You've already done it. When you do something which displeases me, B.J., I'll let you know." The underlying threat brought storm warnings to her eyes. "Of course you know," Taylor continued, his tone softening, "you're a very ingenious lady. You've managed to share my breakfast table and work with me throughout the morning without once using my name. You've skirted around it, jumped over it and crawled under it, fascinating me with the acrobatics."

"That's ridiculous." She attempted to shrug, but his hands were firm on her shoulders. "Your imagination needs re-oiling."

"Then perhaps…" His arms moved to capture her waist. She arched away only to be brought steadily closer. "You'd say it now." His mouth hovered above hers. She felt the unfamiliar sweet flow of weakness, the trembling warmth just under her skin.

"Taylor." She failed to bring her voice above a whisper.

"Very good, you'll use it more often." His mouth curved, but she saw the smile only in his eyes. "Do I frighten you, B.J.?"

"No." Her denial was faint. "No," she repeated with more firmness.

"Liar." His laugh was both amused and pleased as his mouth teased hers. It rubbed lightly, holding back the promise until with a moan she drew him closer and took it.

Her breasts crushed against his chest, her lips instinctively found his. She felt herself tumbling in helpless cartwheels down an endless shaft where lights whirled in speeding colors. His hands moved from her waist to her hips, his strong fingers discovering the secrets of subtle curves as his mouth took everything she offered. Craving more, she strained against him until her sharpened senses began to dim, and the world spun hazily around her and vanished.

Fear rose like a phoenix from the flames of passion, and she struggled away, stunned and confused. "I...I need to check how lunch is going." She fumbled behind for the doorknob.

His hands in his pockets, Taylor rocked back on his heels and held her gaze with steady assurance. "Of course…. Now run away to your duties. But you understand, B.J., that I intend to have you sooner or later. I can be patient up to a point."

Her hand connected with the knob. She found her voice. "Of all the appalling nerve! I'm not a piece of property you can have your agent pick up for you."

"No, I'm handling this strictly on my own." He smiled at her. "I know when something's going to be mine. Acquiring it is simply a matter of timing."

"I'm not an it." More outraged than she had thought possible, she took a step toward him. "I have no intention of being acquired and added to your trophies! And timing will get you nowhere!"

His smile was maddeningly confident. B.J. slammed the door full force behind her.

4

Mondays always kept B.J. busy. She was convinced that if a major calamity were to fall, it would fall on a Monday simply because that would be the time she would be least able to cope with it. Taylor Reynolds' presence in her office was an additional Monday morning burden. His calm statement of the previous day was still fresh in her mind, and she was still seething with resentment. In an icy voice, she explained to him each phone call she made, each letter she wrote, each invoice she filed. He would not, she decided, accuse her of being uncooperative. Frigid perhaps, she thought with wicked pleasure, but not uncooperative.

Taylor's impeccable, businesslike attitude did nothing to endear him to her. She was well aware that her cold politeness bordered on the insulting.

Never had she met a man more in control or more annoying. Briefly, she considered pouring her coffee into his lap just to get a reaction. The thought was satisfying.

"Did I miss a joke?" Taylor asked as an involuntary smile flitted over B.J.'s face.

"What?" Realizing her lapse, B.J. struggled to compose her features. "No, I'm afraid my mind was wandering. You'll have to excuse me," she went on, "I have to make sure that all the rooms are made up by this time of day. Will you be wanting lunch in here or in the dining room?"

"I'll come to the dining room." Leaning back, Taylor studied her as he tapped his pencil against the corner of the desk. "Are you joining me?"

"Oh, I'm terribly sorry." B.J.'s tone was falsely saccharine. "I'm swamped today. I recommend the roast beef, though. I'm sure you'll find it satisfactory." Satisfied with her delivery, she closed the door quietly behind her.

With ingenuity and luck, B.J. managed to avoid Taylor throughout the afternoon. The inn was nearly empty as most of the guests were outdoors enjoying the mild spring weather. B.J. was able to slip down the quiet corridors without running into Taylor. She kept her antenna tuned for his presence, however. Though she knew it was childish, she found herself enjoying the one-way game of hide and seek. It became a self-imposed challenge that she keep out of his sight until nightfall.

★ ★ ★

In the pre-dinner lull, the inn was drowsy and silent. Humming to herself, B.J. carefully checked off linens in the third floor supply room. She was confident Taylor would not venture into that area of the inn, and relaxed her guard. Her mind traveled from her task, touching on pictures of boating on the lake, walks in the woods, and long summer evenings. Though her daydreams were pleasant, they were underlined by a nagging dissatisfaction. She tried to shrug it off but found it stubborn. There was something missing from the images, or rather someone. Whom would she be boating with on the lake? Whom would she be walking with in the woods? Who would be there to make the long summer evenings special? A distressing image began to form in B.J.'s brain, and she squeezed her eyes tight until it faded.

"I don't need him," she muttered, giving a pile of freshly laundered sheets a pat. "Absolutely not." B.J. backed from the tiny room and quietly pulled the door shut. When she backed into a solid object, she shrieked and fell forward against the closed door.

"Jumpy, aren't you?" Taylor took her shoulders and turned her to face him. His expression was amused. "Muttering to yourself, too. Maybe you need a vacation."

"I...I..."

"A long vacation," he concluded, giving her cheek a fatherly pat.

Finding her tongue, B.J. responded with reasonable calm. "You startled me, sneaking around that way."

"I thought it was a rule of the house," he countered as his grin broke out. "You've been doing it all afternoon."

Furious that her cunning had fallen short of the mark, she spoke with frosty dignity. "I have no idea what you're talking about. Now, if you'll excuse me…"

"Did you know you get a half-inch vertical line between your eyebrows when you're annoyed?"

"I'm very busy." She kept her voice cool as she did her best to keep the space between her brows smooth. *Blast the man!* she thought as his engaging smile began to have its effect on her. "Taylor, if there is something specific you want…" She stopped as she saw his grin widen until it nearly split his face. "If there's some business you want to discuss—" she amended.

"I took a message for you," he informed her, then lifted a finger to smooth away the crease between her brows. "A very intriguing message."

"Oh?" she said casually, wishing he would back up so that she did not feel so imprisoned between his body and the closed store-room door.

"Yes, I wrote it down so there'd be no mistake." He took a slip of paper from his pocket and read. "It's from a Miss Peabody. She wanted you to know that Cassandra had her babies. Four girls and two boys. Sextuplets."

Taylor lowered the paper and shook his head. "Quite an amazing feat."

"Not if you're a cat." B.J. felt the color lacing her cheeks. *Why would he have to be the one to take the message? Why couldn't Cassandra have waited?* "Miss Peabody is one of our oldest guests. She stays here twice a year."

"I see," said Taylor, his mouth twitching. "Well, now that I've done my duty, it's your turn to do yours." Taking her hand, Taylor began to lead her down the corridor. "This country air gives me quite an appetite. You know the menu, what do you recommend we have?"

"I can't possibly," she began.

"Of course you can," he interrupted mildly. "Just think of me as a guest. Inn policy is to give the guests what pleases them. It pleases me to have dinner with you."

Cornered by her own words, B.J. offered no argument. Within minutes, she found herself seated across from the man she had so successfully avoided during the afternoon.

B.J. thought dinner a relatively painless affair. She felt too, as it neared an end, that she had done her duty and done it superbly. It was, however, difficult to resist the pull of Taylor's charm when he chose to put it into use. The charm itself was so natural and understated that she often found herself captivated before she realized what was happening. Whenever she felt her walls of indifference crumbling, she retreated a step and shored up the holes. *What a shame he isn't someone else,* she mused as he recounted an anecdote. *It would be so nice to enjoy a quiet dinner with him if there weren't any boundaries. But there are,* she reminded herself, quickly pulling out of the range of his charm. *Very definite, very important boundaries. This is war,* she reflected, thinking of their conversation of the previous day. *I can't afford to get caught behind enemy lines.* As Taylor raised his glass and smiled at her, B.J. wondered if Mata Hari had ever been faced with a tougher assignment.

They had reached the coffee stage when Eddie approached their table. "Mr. Reynolds?" B.J. looked on with approval as Eddie neither fidgeted nor seemed ready to burst with the tidings he bore. "There's a phone call for you from New York."

"Thank you, Eddie. I'll take it in the office. I shouldn't be long," Taylor told her as he rose.

"Please, don't rush on my account." B.J. gave him a careful smile, resigning herself to the fact she was a coward. "I still have several things to see to this evening."

"I'll see you later," Taylor returned in a tone that brooked no argument. Their eyes met in a quick clash of wills. In a swift change of mood, Taylor laughed and bent down to kiss B.J. on the forehead before he strolled away.

Mouth agape, B.J. rubbed the spot with her fingertips, wondering why she suddenly felt lightheaded. Forcing herself back to earth, she drank her coffee and hurried off to the lounge.

Monday nights at the inn were an old tradition. The lounge was the center of activity for the weekly event. As B.J. paused in the doorway, she ran a critical eye over the room. The candles had been lit inside each of the coach lanterns which sat on the huddled tables. The lights flickered against the wood. Scents of polish, old wood and smoke melded. The dance floor was gently lit with amber spotlights. Satisfied that the mood was set, B.J. crossed the room and halted next to an ancient Victrola. The faithful mechanism was housed in a rich mahogany cabinet. With affection, B.J. trailed a finger over the smooth lid before opening it.

People began to wander in as she sorted through the collection of old 78s. The hum of conversation behind her was so familiar, it barely tickled her consciousness. Glasses chinked, ice rattled, and an occasional laugh echoed along the walls. With the absentminded skill of an expert, B.J. wound the Victrola into life and set a thick, black record on the turntable. The music which drifted out was scratchy, tinny and charming. Before the record was half over, three couples were on the dance floor. Another Monday night was launched.

During the next half hour, B.J. played an unbroken stream of nineteen-thirty tunes. Over the years, she had noted that no matter what the mean age of the audience, the response to a trip through the past was positive.

Perhaps, she mused, *it's because the simplicity of the music suits the simplicity of the inn.* With a shrug, she abandoned her analysis and grinned at a couple fox-trotting over the dance floor to the strains of "Tea For Two."

"What the devil is going on in here?"

B.J. heard the demanding question close to her ear and whirled to find herself face to face with Taylor. "Oh, I see you're finished with your call. I hope there isn't any trouble?"

"Nothing important." He waited until she had switched records before he asked again, "B.J., I asked you what's going on in here?"

"Why, just what it looks like," she answered vaguely, hearing from the tone of the record that it was time to replace the needle. "Sit down, Taylor, I'll have Don mix you a drink. You know I'd swear there hasn't been time for this needle to wear out." Delving into her spares, B.J. began the task of changing needles.

"When you're finished, perhaps you'd take a look at my carburetor."

Engrossed in the intricacies of her job, B.J. remained untouched by Taylor's mockery. "We'll see," she murmured, then carefully placed the new needle on the record. "What would you like, Taylor?" As she straightened, she glanced toward the bar.

"Initially, an explanation."

"An explanation?" she repeated, finally giving him her full attention. "An explanation about what?"

"B.J." Impatience was beginning to thread through his tone. "Are you being deliberately dense?"

Liking neither his tone nor his question, B.J. stiffened. "Perhaps if you would be a bit more specific, I would be a bit less dense."

"I was under the impression that this lounge possessed a functional P.A. system."

"Well, of course it does." As she became more confused, B.J. pushed away the thought that perhaps she actually was dense. "What does that have to do with anything?"

"Why isn't it being used?" He glanced down at the Victrola. "And why are you using this archaic piece of equipment?"

"The P.A. system isn't being used," she explained in calm, reasonable tones, "because it's Monday."

"I see." Taylor glanced toward the dance floor where one couple was instructing another on the proper moves of a two step. "That, of course, explains everything."

His sarcasm caused indignation to flood through her. Clamping her teeth on a stream of unwise remarks, B.J. began to sift rapidly through records. "On Monday nights, we use the Victrola and play old records. And it is not an archaic piece of equipment," she added, unable to prevent herself. "It's an antique, a museum quality antique."

"B.J." Taylor spoke to the top of her head as she bent to change records. "Why?"

"Why what?" she snapped, furious with his ambiguity.

"Why do you use the Victrola and play old records on Monday nights?" He spoke very clearly, spacing his words as if speaking to someone whose brain was not fully operative.

"Because," B.J. began, her eyes flowing, her fists clenching.

Taylor held up a hand to halt the ensuing explanation. "Wait." After the one word command, he crossed the room and spoke to one of the guests. Seething, B.J. watched him use his most charming smile. It faded as he moved back to join her. "You're being relieved of Victrola duty for a bit. Outside." With this, he took her arm and pulled her to the side door. The cool night air did nothing to lower B.J.'s temperature. "Now." Taylor closed the door behind him and leaned back against the side of the building. He made a small gesture with his hand. "Go right ahead."

"Oh, you make me so mad I could scream!" With this dire threat, B.J. began pacing up and down the porch. "Why do you have to be so…so…"

"Officious?" Taylor offered.

"Yes!" B.J. agreed, wishing passionately that she had thought of the word herself. "Everything's moving along just fine, and then you have to come in and look down your superior nose." For some moments, she paced in silence. The romance of the moonlight filtering through the trees seemed sadly out of place. "People are enjoying themselves in there." She swung her hand toward the open window. A Cole Porter number drifted back to her. "You don't have any right to criticize it. Just because we're not using a live band, or playing top forty numbers, doesn't mean we're not entertaining the guests. I really don't see why you have to..." She broke off abruptly as he grabbed her arm.

"O.K., time's up." As he spun her around, the hair fell over B.J.'s face, and she brushed it back impatiently. "Now, suppose we start this from the beginning."

"You know," she said between her teeth, "I really hate it when you're calm and patient."

"Stick around," he invited. It began to sink into her brain that his voice was dangerously low. "You might see the other end of the scale." Glaring at him did not seem to improve her situation, but B.J. continued to do so. "If you'll think back to the beginning of this remarkable conversation, you'll recall that I asked you a very simple question. And, I believe, a very reasonable one."

"And I told you," she tossed out, then faltered. "At least, I think I did." Frustrated, she threw both hands up in the air. "How am I supposed to remember what you said and what I said? It took you ten minutes to come to the point in the first place." She let out a deep breath as she realized she did not yet have control of her temper. "All right, what was your very simple, very reasonable question?"

"B.J., you would try the patience of a saint." She heard the amused exasperation in his voice and tried not to be charmed. "I would like to know why I stepped into nineteen-thirty-five when I came into the lounge."

"Every Monday night," she began in crisp, practical tones, "the inn offers this sort of entertainment. The Victrola was brought here more than fifty years ago, and it's been used every Monday night since. Guests who've been here before expect it. Of course," she went on, too involved in her story to realize she was being drawn closer into Taylor's arms, "the P.A. system was installed years ago. The other six nights of the week, we switch off between it and a live band, depending on the season. The Monday night gathering is almost as old as the inn itself and an important part of our tradition."

The low, bluesy tones of "Embraceable You" were floating through the open window. B.J. was swaying to its rhythm, as yet unaware that Taylor was leading her in a slow dance. "The guests look forward to it. I've found since I've worked here, that's true no matter how old or how young the clientele is." Her voice had lost its crispness. She found her trend of thought slipping away from her as their bodies swayed to the soft music.

"That was a very reasonable answer." Taylor drew her closer, and she tilted back her head, unwilling to break eye contact. "I'm beginning to see the advantages of the idea myself." Their faces were close, so close she could feel the touch of his breath on her lips. "Cold?" he asked, feeling her tremble. Though she shook her head, he gathered her closer until the warmth of his body crept into hers. Their cheeks brushed as they merged into one gently swaying form.

"I should go back in," she murmured, making no effort to move away. She closed her eyes and let his arms and the music guide her.

"Um-hum." His mouth was against her ear.

Small night sounds added to the lull of the music from the lounge; a whisper of leaves, the quiet call of a bird, the flutter of moth wings against window glass. The air was soft and cool on B.J.'s shoulders. It was touched with the light scent of hyacinth. Moonlight sprinkled through the maples, causing the shadows to tremble. She could feel Taylor's heartbeat, a sure, steady rhythm against her own breast. He trailed his mouth along her temple, brushing it through her hair as his hands roamed along her back.

B.J. felt her will dissolving as her senses grew more and more acute. She could hear the sound of his breathing over the music, feel the texture of his skin beneath his shirt, taste the male essence of him on her tongue. Her surroundings were fading like an old photograph with only Taylor remaining sharp and clear. Untapped desire swelled inside her. Suddenly, she felt herself being swallowed by emotions she was not prepared for, by needs she could not understand.

"No, please." Her bid for freedom was so swift and

unexpected that she broke from Taylor's arms without a struggle. "I don't want this." She clung to the porch rail and faced him.

Closing the distance between them in one easy motion, Taylor circled the back of her neck with his hand. "Yes, you do." His mouth lowered, claiming hers. B.J. felt the porch tilt under her feet.

Longing, painfully sweet, spread through her until she felt she would suffocate. His hands were bringing her closer and closer. With some unexplained instinct, she knew if she were wrapped in his arms again, she would never find the strength to resist him.

"No!" Lifting both hands, she pushed against his chest and freed herself. "I don't!" she cried in passionate denial. Turning, she streaked down the porch steps. "Don't tell me what I want," she flung back at him before she raced around the side of the building.

She paused before she entered the inn to catch her breath and to allow her pounding heart to slow down. Certainly not the usual Monday evening at Lakeside Inn, she thought, smiling wryly to herself. Unconsciously, she hummed a few bars of "Embraceable You," but caught herself with a self-reprimanding frown before she entered the kitchen to remind Dot about the bud vases on the breakfast tables.

5

There are days when nothing goes right. The morning, blue and clear and breezy, looked deceptively promising. Clad in a simple green shirtdress and low heels, B.J. marched down the stairs running the word *businesslike* over and over in her mind. Today, she determined, she would be the manager of the inn conducting business with the owner of the inn. There was no moonlight, no music, and she would not forget her responsibilities again. She strolled into the dining room, prepared to greet Taylor casually, then use the need to oversee breakfast preparations as an excuse not to share the morning meal with him. Taylor, however, was already well into a fluffy mound of scrambled eggs and deep into a conversation with Mr. Leander. Taylor gave B.J. an absent wave as she entered, then returned his full attention to his breakfast companion.

Perversely, B.J. was annoyed that her well-planned excuse was unnecessary. She scowled at the back of Taylor's head before she flounced into the kitchen. Ten minutes later, she was told in no uncertain terms that she was in the way. Banished to her office, she sulked in private.

For the next thirty minutes, B.J. occupied herself with busy work, all the while keeping her ears pricked for Taylor's approach. As the minutes passed, she felt a throbbing tension build at the base of her neck. The stronger the ache became, the deeper became her resentment toward Taylor. She set the reason for her headache and her glum mood at his doorstep, though she could not have answered what he had done to cause either. *He was here,* she decided, then broke the point of her pencil. *That was enough.*

"B.J.!" Eddie swirled into the office as she stood grinding her teeth and sharpening her pencil. "There's trouble."

"You bet there is," she muttered.

"It's the dishwasher." Eddie lowered his eyes as if announcing a death in the family. "It broke down in the middle of breakfast."

B.J. let out her breath in a quick sound of annoyance. "All right, I'll call Max. With any luck it'll be going full swing before lunch."

Luck, B.J. was to find, was a mirage.

An hour later, she stood by as Max the repairman did an exploratory on the dishwasher. She found his continual mutters, tongue cluckings and sighs wearing on her nerves. Time was fleeting, and it seemed to her that Max was working at an impossibly slow pace. Impatient, she leaned over his shoulder and stared at tubes and wires. Bracing one hand on Max's back, she leaned in further and pointed.

"Couldn't you just…"

"B.J." Max sighed and removed another screw. "Go play with the inn and let me do my job."

Straightening, B.J. stuck out her tongue at the back of his head, then flushed scarlet as she spotted Taylor standing inside the doorway.

"Have a problem?" he asked. Though his voice and mouth were sober, his eyes laughed at her. She found his silent mockery infuriating.

"I can handle it," she snapped, wishing her cheeks were cool and her position dignified. "I'm sure you must be very busy." She cursed herself for hinting at his morning involvement. This time he did smile, and she cursed him as well.

"I'm never too busy for you, B.J." Taylor crossed the room, then took her hand and raised it to his lips before she realized his intent. Max cleared his throat.

"Cut that out." She tore her hand away and whipped it behind her back. "There's no need to concern yourself with this," she continued, struggling to assume the businesslike attitude she had vowed to take. "Max is fixing the dishwasher before the lunch rush."

"No, I'm not." Max sat back on his heels and shook his head. In his hand was a small-toothed wheel.

"What do you mean, no you're not?" B.J. demanded, forgetting Taylor in her amazement. "You've got to. I need…"

"What you need is one of these," Max interrupted, holding up the wheel.

"Well, all right." B.J. plucked the part from his hand and scowled at it. "Put one in. I don't see how a silly little thing like this could cause all this trouble."

"When the silly little thing has a broken tooth, it can cause a lot of trouble," Max explained patiently, and glanced at Taylor for masculine understanding. "B.J., I don't carry things like this in stock. You'll have to get it from Burlington."

"Burlington?" Realizing the situation was desperate B.J. used her most pleading look. "Oh, but, Max."

Though well past his fiftieth birthday, Max was not immune to huge gray eyes. He shifted from one foot to the other, sighed and took the part from B.J.'s palm. "All right, all right, I'll drive into Burlington myself. I'll have the machine fixed before dinner, but lunch is out. I'm not a magician."

"Thank you, Max." Rising on her toes, B.J. pecked his cheek. "What would I do without you?" Mumbling, he packed up his tools and started out of the room. "Bring your wife in for dinner tonight, on the house." Pleased with her success, B.J. smiled as the door swung shut. When she remembered Taylor, she cleared her throat and turned to him.

"You should have those eyes registered with the police department," he advised, tilting his head and studying her. "They're a lethal weapon."

"I don't know what you're talking about." She sniffed with pretended indifference while she wished she could have negotiated with Max in private.

"Of course you do." With a laugh, Taylor cupped her chin in his hand. "That look you aimed at him was beautifully timed."

"I'm sure you're mistaken," she replied, wishing his mere touch would not start her heart pounding. "I simply arranged things in the best interest of the inn. That's my job."

"So it is," he agreed, and leaned on the injured dish-washer. "Do you have any suggestions as to what's to be done until this is fixed?"

"Yes." She glanced at the double stainless steel sink. "Roll up your sleeves."

It did not occur to B.J. to be surprised that she and Taylor washed the dozens of breakfast dishes side by side until it was *fait accompli*. The interlude had been odd, B.J. felt, because of the unusual harmony which existed between them. They had enjoyed a companionable banter, an easy partnership without the tension which habitually entered their encounters. When Elsie returned to begin lunch preparations, they scarcely noticed her.

"Not one casualty," Taylor proclaimed as B.J. set the last plate on its shelf.

"That's only because I saved two of yours from crashing on the floor."

"Slander," Taylor stated and swung an arm over her shoulder as he led her from the room. "You'd better be nice to me. What'll you do if Max doesn't fix the dishwasher before dinner? Think of all those lunch dishes."

"I'd rather not. However, I've already given that possibility some consideration." B.J. found the handiest chair in her office and dropped into it. "I know a couple of kids in town that we could recruit in a pinch. But Max won't let me down."

"You have a lot of faith." Taylor sat behind the desk, then lifted his feet to rest on top of it.

"You don't know Max," B.J. countered. "If he said he'd have it fixed before dinner, he will. Otherwise, he'd have said I'll try, or maybe I can, or something of that sort. When Max says I will, he does. That," she added, seeing the opportunity to score a point, "is an advantage of knowing everyone you deal with personally."

Taylor inclined his head in acknowledgement as the phone rang on the desk. Signaling for Taylor not to bother, B.J. rose and answered it.

"Lakeside Inn. Oh, hello, Marilyn. No, I've been tied up this morning." She eased a hip down on the edge of the desk and shuffled through her papers. "Yes, I have your message here. I'm sorry, I just got back into the office. No, you let me know when you have all your acceptances back, then we'll have a better idea of how to plan the food and so on. There's plenty of time. You've got well over a month before the wedding. Trust me; I've handled receptions before. Yes, I know you're nervous. It's all right, prospective brides are meant to be nervous. Call me when you have a definite number. You're welcome, Marilyn. Yes, yes, you're welcome. 'Bye."

B.J. hung up the phone and stretched her back before she realized Taylor was waiting for an explanation. "That was Marilyn," B.J. informed him. "She was grateful."

"Yes, I rather got that impression."

"She's getting married next month." B.J. lifted a hand to rub at the stiffness in the back of her neck. "If she makes it without a nervous breakdown, it'll be a minor miracle. People should elope and not put themselves through all this."

"I'm sure there are countless fathers-of-the-bride who would agree with you after paying the expenses of the wedding." He rose, moving around the desk until he stood in front of her. "Here, let me." Lifting his hands, he massaged her neck and shoulders. B.J.'s protest became a sigh of pleasure. The word *businesslike* floated quietly out of her mind. "Better?" Taylor asked, smiling at her closed eyes.

"Mmm. It might be in an hour or two." She stretched under his hands like a contented kitten. "Ever since Marilyn set the date, she's been on the phone three times a week to check on the reception. It's hard to believe someone could get that excited about getting married."

"Well, not everyone is as cool and collected as you," Taylor remarked as he ran his thumbs along her jawline, stroking his other fingers along the base of her neck. "And, by the way, I wouldn't spread that eloping idea of yours around if I were you. I imagine the inn makes a good profit doing wedding receptions."

"Profit?" B.J. opened her eyes and tried to concentrate on what they had been saying. It was difficult to think with his hands so warm and strong on her skin. "Profit?" she said again and swallowed as her brain cleared. "Oh well…yes." She scooted off the desk and out of his reach. "Yes, usually…that is…sometimes." She wandered the room wishing the interlude in the kitchen had not made her forget who he was. "It depends, you see, on… Oh boy." She ended on a note of disgust and blew out a long breath.

"Perhaps you'd translate all that into English?" Taylor suggested. With a twinge of uneasiness, B.J. watched him seat himself once more behind the desk. *Owner to manager* again, she thought bitterly.

"Well, you see," she began, striving for nonchalance.

"There are occasions when we do wedding receptions or certain parties without charge. That is," she rushed on as his face remained inscrutable, "we charge for the food and supplies, but not for the use of the lounge…"

"Why?" The one word interruption was followed by several seconds of complete silence.

"Why?" B.J. repeated and glanced briefly at the ceiling for assistance. "It depends, of course, and it is the exception rather than the rule." *Why?* she demanded of herself. *Why don't I learn to keep my mouth shut?* "In this case, Marilyn is Dot's cousin. You met Dot, she's one of our waitresses," she continued as Taylor remained unhelpfully silent. "She also works here during the summer season. We decided, as we do on certain occasions, to give Marilyn the reception as a wedding present."

"We?"

"The staff," B.J. explained. "Marilyn is responsible for the food, entertainment, flowers, but we contribute the lounge and our time, and," she added, dropping her voice to a mumble, "the wedding cake."

"I see." Taylor leaned back in the chair and laced his fingers together. "So, the staff donates their time and talent and the inn."

"Just the lounge." B.J. met his accusatory glance with a glare. "It's something we do only a couple of times a year. And if I must justify it from a business standpoint, it's good public relations. Maybe it's even tax deductible. Ask your C.P.A." She began to storm around the office as her temper rose, but Taylor sat calmly. "I don't see why you have to be so picky. The staff works on their own time. We've been doing it for years. It's…"

"Inn policy," Taylor finished for her. "Perhaps I should have you list all the eccentricities of inn policy for me. But I should remind you, B.J., that the inn's policy is not carved in stone."

"You're not going to drop the axe on Marilyn's reception," B.J. stated, prepared for a fight to the finish.

"I've misplaced my black hood, B.J., so I can't play executioner. However," he continued before the look of satisfaction could be fully formed on her face, "you and I will have to have a more detailed discussion on the inn's public relations."

"Yes, sir," she replied in her most wintry voice, and was saved from further argument by the ringing of the phone.

Taylor motioned for her to answer it. "I'll get us some coffee."

B.J. watched him stroll from the room as she lifted the phone to her ear.

When Taylor returned a few moments later, she was seated behind the desk just replacing the receiver. With a sound of annoyance, she supported her chin on her elbows.

"The florist doesn't have my six dozen daffodils."

"I'm sorry to hear that." Taylor placed her coffee on the desk.

"Well, you should be. It's your inn, and they are actually your daffodils."

"It's kind of you to think of me, B.J.," Taylor said amiably. "But don't you think six dozen is a bit extreme?"

"Very funny," she muttered and picked up her coffee cup. "You won't think it's such a joke when there aren't any flowers on the tables."

"So, order something besides daffodils."

"Do I look like a simpleton?" B.J. demanded. "He won't have anything in that quantity until next week. Some trouble at the greenhouse or something. Blast it!" She swallowed her coffee and scowled at the far wall.

"For heaven's sake, B.J., there must be a dozen florists in Burlington. Have them delivered." Taylor dismissed the matter of daffodils with an airy wave.

B.J. gave him an opened mouth look of astonishment. "Delivered from Burlington? Do you have any idea how much those daffodils would cost?" Rising, she paced the room while she considered her options. "I simply can't tolerate artificial flowers," she muttered while Taylor sipped his coffee and watched her. "They're worse than no flowers at all. I hate to do it," she said with a sigh. "It's bad enough having to beg for her jelly, now I'm going to have to beg for her flowers. There's absolutely nothing else I can do. She's got the only garden in town that can handle it." Making a complete circle of the room, B.J. plopped down behind the desk again.

"Are you finished?"

"No," B.J. answered, picking up the phone. "I still have to talk her out of them." Grimly, she set her teeth. "Wish me luck."

Deciding all would be explained in due time, Taylor sat back to watch. "Luck," he said agreeably and finished off his coffee.

When B.J. had completed her conversation, he shook his head in frank admiration. "That," he said as he toasted her with his empty cup, "was the most blatant con job I've ever witnessed."

"Subtlety doesn't work with Betty Jackson." Smug, B.J. answered his toast, then rose. "I'm going to go pick up those flowers before she changes her mind."

"I'll drive you," Taylor offered, taking her arm before she reached the door.

"Oh, you needn't bother." The contact reminded her how slight was her will when he touched her.

"It's no bother," he countered, leading her through the inn's front door. "I feel I must see the woman who, how did you put it? 'Raises flowers with an angel's touch.'"

"Did I say that?" B.J. struggled to prevent a smile.

"That was one of your milder compliments."

"Desperate circumstances call for desperate measures," B.J. claimed and slid into Taylor's Mercedes. "Besides, Miss Jackson does have an extraordinary garden. Her rosebush won a prize last year. Turn left here," she instructed as he came to a fork in the road. "You know, you should be grateful to me instead of making fun. If you'd had your way, we'd be eating up a healthy percentage of the inn's profits in delivery fees."

"My dear Miss Clark," Taylor drawled, "if there's one thing I can't deny, it's that you are a top flight manager. Of course, I'm also aware that a raise is in order."

"When I want a raise, I'll ask for one," B.J. snapped. As she gave her attention to the view out the side window, she missed Taylor's glance of speculation. She had not liked his use of her surname, nor had she liked being reminded again so soon of the status of their positions. He was her employer, and there was no escaping it. Closing her eyes, she chewed on her lower lip. The day had not run smoothly, perhaps that was why she had been so acutely annoyed over such a small thing. *And so rude,* she added to herself. Decidedly, it was her responsibility to offer the olive branch. Turning, she gave Taylor a radiant smile.

"What sort of raise?"

He laughed, and reached over to ruffle her hair. "What an odd one you are, B.J."

"Oh, I know," she agreed, wishing she could understand her own feelings. "I know. There's the house." She gestured as they approached. "Third from the corner."

They alighted from opposite sides of the car, but Taylor took her arm as they swung through Betty Jackson's gate. This visit, B.J. decided, thinking of the silver blue Mercedes and Taylor's elegantly simple silk shirt, should keep Miss Jackson in news for six months. The doorbell was answered before it had stopped ringing.

"Hello, Miss Jackson," B.J. began and prepared to launch into her first thank you speech. She closed her mouth as she noticed Betty's attention was focused well over her head. "Oh, Miss Jackson, this is Taylor Reynolds, the owner of the inn. Taylor, Betty Jackson." B.J. made introductions as Betty simultaneously pulled her apron from her waist and metal clips from her hair.

"Miss Jackson." Taylor took her free hand as Betty held the apron and clips behind her back. "I've heard so much about your talents, I feel we're old friends." Blushing like a teenager, Betty was, for the first time in her sixty odd years, at a loss for words.

"We came by for the flowers," B.J. reminded her, fascinated by Betty's reaction.

"Flowers? Oh, yes, of course. Do come in." She ushered them into the house and into her living room, all the while keeping her hand behind her back.

"Charming," Taylor stated, gazing around at chintz and doilies. Turning, he gave Betty his easy smile. "I must tell you, Miss Jackson, we're very grateful to you for helping us out this way."

"It's nothing, nothing at all," Betty said, fluttering her hand with the words. "Please sit down. I'll fix us a nice pot of tea. Come along, B.J." She scurried from the room, leaving B.J. no choice but to follow. Safely enclosed in the kitchen, Betty began to move at lightning speed. "Why didn't you tell me you were bringing *him?*" she demanded, flourishing a teapot.

"Well, I didn't know until..."

"Goodness, you could have given a person a chance to comb her hair and put her face on." Betty dug out her best china cups and inspected them for chips.

B.J. bit the inside of her lip to keep a grin from forming. "I'm sorry, Betty. I had no idea Mr. Reynolds was coming until I was leaving."

"Never mind, never mind." Betty brushed aside the apology with the back of her hand. "You did bring him after all. I'm positively dying to talk to him. Why don't you run out and get your flowers now before tea?" She produced a pair of scissors. "Just pick whatever you need." She dismissed B.J. with a hasty wave. "Take your time."

After the back door had closed firmly in her face, B.J. stood for a moment, torn between amusement and exasperation before heading towards Betty's early spring blooms.

When she re-entered the kitchen about twenty minutes later, armed with a selection of daffodils and early tulips, she could hear Betty laughing. Carefully placing her bouquet on the kitchen table, she walked into the living room.

Like old friends, Taylor and Betty sat on the sofa, a rose patterned teapot nestled cozily on the low table.

"Oh, Taylor," Betty said, still laughing, "you tell such stories! What's a poor woman to believe?"

B.J. looked on in stunned silence. She was certain Betty Jackson had not flirted this outrageously in thirty years. And, she noted with a shake of her head, Taylor was flirting with equal aplomb. As Betty leaned forward to pour more tea, Taylor glanced over her head and shot B.J. a grin so endearingly boyish it took all her willpower not to cross the room and throw herself into his arms. He was, she thought with a curious catch in her heart, impossible. No female under a hundred and two was safe around him. Unable to do otherwise, B.J. answered his grin.

"Miss Jackson," B.J. said, carefully readjusting her features. "Your garden is lovely as always."

"Thanks, B.J. I really do work hard on it. Did you get all that you wanted?"

"Yes, thank you. I don't know how I would have managed without you."

"Well." Betty sighed as she rose. "I'll just get a box for them."

Some fifteen minutes later, after Betty had exacted a promise from Taylor that he drop by again, B.J. was in the Mercedes beside him. In the back seat were the assortment of flowers and a half a dozen jars of jelly as a gift to Taylor.

"You," B.J. began in the sternest voice she could manage, "should be ashamed."

"I?" Taylor countered, giving her an innocent look. "Whatever for?"

"You know very well what for," B.J. said severely. "You very near had Betty swooning."

"I can't help it if I'm charming and irresistible."

"Oh, yes, you can," she disagreed. "You were deliberately charming and irresistible. If you'd said the word, she'd have ripped up her prize rosebush and planted it at the inn's front door."

"Nonsense," Taylor claimed. "We were simply having an enjoyable conversation."

"Did you enjoy the camomile tea?" B.J. asked sweetly.

"Very refreshing. You didn't get a cup, did you?"

"No." B.J. sniffed and folded her arms across her chest. "I wasn't invited."

"Ah, now I see." Taylor sighed as he pulled in front of the inn. "You're jealous."

"Jealous?" B.J. gave a quick laugh and brushed the dust from her skirt. "Ridiculous."

"Yes, I see it now," he said smugly, repressing a grin. "Silly girl!" With this, he stopped the car, and turning to B.J. lowered his smiling mouth to hers. Imperceptibly, his lips lost their teasing quality, becoming warm and soft on her skin. B.J.'s playful struggles ceased, and she stiffened in his arms.

"Taylor, let me go." She found it was more difficult now to catch her breath than it had been when she had been laughing. A small moan escaped her as his lips trailed to her jawline. "No," she managed, and putting her fingers to his lips, pushed him away. He studied her, his eyes dark and full of knowledge as she fought to control her breathing. "Taylor, I think it's time we established some rules."

"I don't believe in rules between men and women, and I don't follow any." He said this with such blatant arrogance, B.J. was shocked into silence. "I'll let you go now, because I don't think it's wise to make love with you in broad daylight in the front seat of my car. However, the time will come when the circumstances will be more agreeable."

B.J. narrowed her eyes and found her voice. "You seriously don't think I'll agree to that, do you?"

"When the time comes, B.J.," he said with maddening confidence, "you'll be happy to agree."

"Fat chance," she said as she struggled out of the car. "We're never going to agree about anything." Slamming the door gave her some satisfaction.

As she ran up the front steps and into the inn, B.J. decided she never wanted to hear the word *businesslike* again.

6

B.J. was standing on the wide lawn enjoying the warmth of the spring sun. She had decided to avoid Taylor Reynolds as much as possible and concentrate on her own myriad responsibilities. Unfortunately, that had not been as easy as she had hoped: she had been forced to deal with him on a daily business basis.

Though the inn was relatively quiet, B.J. knew that in a month's time, when the summer season began, the pace would pick up. Her gaze traveled the length and height of the inn, admiring the mellowed bricks serene against the dark pines, the windows blinking in the bright spring sun. On the back porch, two guests were engaged in an undemanding game of checkers. From where she was standing, B.J. could barely hear the murmur of their conversation without hearing the words.

All too soon, this peace would be shattered by children shouting to each other as they raced across the lawn, by the purr of motorboats as they sped past the inn. Yet, somehow, the inn never lost its informal air of tranquility. Here, she mused, the shade was for relaxing, the grass invited bare feet, the drifting snow for sleigh rides and snow men. Elegance had its place, B.J. acknowledged, but the Lakeside Inn had a charm of its own. *And Taylor Reynolds was not going to destroy it.*

You've only got ten days left. He leaves in ten days, she reminded herself. She sighed.

The sigh was as much for herself as for the inn's fate. *I wish he'd never come. I wish I'd never laid eyes on him.* Scowling, she headed back towards the inn.

"That face is liable to turn guests away." Startled, B.J. stared at Taylor as he blocked the doorway. "I think it's best for business if I get you away from here for a while." Stepping forward, he took her hand and pulled her across the lawn.

"I have to go in," she protested. "I…I have to phone the linen supplier."

"It'll keep. Your duties as guide come first."

"Guide? Would you please let me go? Where are we going?"

"Yes. No. And we're going to enjoy one of Elsie's famous picnics." Taylor held up the hamper he held in his free hand. "I want to see the lake."

"You don't need me for that. You can't miss it. It's

the huge body of water you come to at the end of the path."

"B.J." He stopped, turning directly to face her. "For two days you've avoided me. Now, I'm well aware we have differences in our outlook on the inn."

"I hardly see…"

"Be quiet," he said pleasantly. "I am willing to give you my word that no major alterations will be started without your being notified. Whatever changes I decide upon will be brought to your attention before any formal plans are drawn up." His tone was brisk and businesslike even while he ignored her attempts to free her hand. "I respect your dedication and loyalty to the inn." His tone was coolly professional.

"But…"

"However," he cut her off easily, "I do own the inn, and you are in my employ. As of now you have a couple hours off. How do you feel about picnics?"

"Well, I…"

"Good. I'm fond of them myself." Smiling easily, he began to move down the well worn path through the woods.

The undergrowth was still soft from winter. Beneath the filtered sunlight wild flowers were a multicolored carpet, bright against their brown background of decaying leaves. Squirrels darted up the trunks of trees where birds had already begun to nest.

"Do you always shanghai your companions?" B.J.

demanded, angry and breathless at keeping pace with Taylor's long strides.

"Only when necessary," he replied curtly.

The path widened, then spread into the grassy banks of the lake. Taylor stopped, surveying the wide expanse of lake with the same absorption that B.J. had observed in him earlier.

The lake was unruffled, reflecting a few clouds above it. The mountains on its opposite edge were gently formed. They were not like the awesome, demanding peaks of the West, but sedate and well behaved. The silence was broken once by the quick call of a chickadee, then lay again like a calming hand on the air.

"Very nice," Taylor said at length, and B.J. listened for but heard no condescension in his tone. "A very lovely view. Do you ever swim here?"

"Only since I was two," B.J. answered, groping for a friendly lightness. She wished he would not continue to hold her hand as if he had done so a thousand times before, wished hers did not fit into his as if molded for the purpose.

"Of course." He turned his head, switching his study from the lake to her face. "I'd forgotten, you were born here, weren't you?"

"I've always lived in Lakeside." Deciding that setting up the picnic things was the most expedient way to break the hand contact, B.J. took the hamper and began spreading Elsie's neatly folded cloth. "My parents moved to New York when I was nineteen, and I lived there for almost a year. I transferred colleges at mid-term and enrolled back here."

"How did you find New York?" Taylor dropped down beside her, and B.J. glimpsed at the bronzed forearms which his casually rolled up sleeves revealed.

"Noisy and confusing," she replied, frowning at a platter of crisp golden chicken. "I don't like to be confused."

"Don't you?" His swift grin appeared at her frown. With one deft motion, he pulled out the ribbon which held her hair neatly behind her back. "It makes you look like my adolescent niece." He tossed it carelessly out of reach as B.J. grabbed for it.

"You are an abominably rude man." Pushing back her newly liberated hair, she glared into his smiling face.

"Often," he agreed and lifted a bottle of wine from the hamper. He drew the cork with the ease of experience while B.J. fumed in silence. "How did you happen to become manager of the Lakeside Inn?"

The question took her off guard. For a moment she watched him pour the inn's best Chablis into Dixie cups. "I sort of gravitated to it." Accepting the offered cup, she met the directness of his gaze and realized he would not be content with the vagueness of her answer. "I worked summers at the inn when I was in high school, sort of filling in here and there at first. By the time I graduated, I was assistant manager. Anyway," she continued, "when I moved back from New York, I just slid back in. Mr. Blakely, the old manager, recommended me when he retired, and I took over." She shrugged and bit into a drumstick.

"Between your education and your dedication to your career, where did you find the time to learn how to swing a bat like Reggie Jackson?"

"I managed to find a few moments to spare. When I was fourteen," she explained, grinning at the memory, "I was madly in love with this older man. He was seventeen." She gave Taylor a sober nod. "Baseball oozed from his pores, so I enthusiastically took up the game. He'd call me shortstop, and my toes would tingle."

Taylor's burst of laughter startled a slumbering blue jay who streaked across the sky with an indignant chatter. "B.J., I don't know anyone like you. What happened to the toe tingler?"

Overcome by the pleasure his laughter had brought her, she fumbled for the thread of the conversation. "Oh…he… uh…he's got two kids and sells used cars."

"His loss," Taylor commented, cutting a thin wedge of cheese.

B.J. broke a fragrant hunk of Elsie's fresh bread and held it out to Taylor for a slice of cheese. "Do you spend much time at your other hotels?" she asked, uncomfortable at the personal tone the conversation seemed to be taking.

"Depends." His eyes roamed over her as she sat crosslegged on the grass, her soft hair tumbling over her shoulders, her lips slightly parted.

"Depends?" she inquired. He stared a moment at her and she fought not to fidget under his encompassing gaze.

"I make certain my managers are competent." He broke the silence with a smile. "If there's a specific problem, I'll deal with it. First, I like to get the feel of a new acquisition, determine if a policy change is warranted."

"But you work out of New York?" The trend of the conversation was much more to her liking. The tension eased from her shoulders.

"Primarily. I've seen fields in Kansas that looked less like wheat than your hair." He captured a generous handful. B.J. swallowed in surprise. "The fog in London isn't nearly as gray or mysterious as your eyes."

B.J. swallowed and moistened her lips. "Your chicken's getting cold."

His grin flashed at her feeble defense but his hand relinquished its possession of her hair. "It's supposed to be cold." Lifting the wine bottle, Taylor refilled his cup. "Oh, by the way, there was a call for you."

B.J. took a sip of Chablis with apparent calm. "Oh, was it important?"

"Mmm." Taylor moved his shoulders under his cream colored tailored shirt. "A Howard Beall. He said you had his number."

"Oh." B.J. frowned, recalling it was about time for her

duty date with Betty Jackson's nephew. Her sigh was automatic.

"My, you simply reek of enthusiasm."

Taylor's dry comment brought on a smile and a shrug. "He's just a man I know."

Taylor contented himself with a slight raising of his brow.

The sky was now an azure arch, without even a puff of cloud to spoil its perfection. Replete and relaxed, B.J. rolled over on her back to enjoy it. The grass was soft and smelled fresh. Overhead, the maple offered a half-shade. Its black branches were touched with young, tender leaves. Through the spreading cluster of trees, dogwoods bloomed white.

"In the winter," she murmured, half to herself, "it's absolutely still here after a snowfall. Everything's white. Snow hangs and drips from the trees and carpets the earth. The lake's like a mirror. The ice is as clear as rain water. You almost forget there's any place else in the world, or that spring will come. Do you ski, Taylor?" She rolled over on her stomach, her elbows supporting her head to smile at him, all animosity forgotten.

"I've been known to." He returned her smile, studying the soft drowsy face, rosy from the sun and the unaccustomed wine.

"The skiing's marvelous here." She tossed back her hair with a quick movement of her shoulders. "Snow skiing's so much more exciting than water skiing, I think. The food at the inn brings the skiing crowd. There's nothing like Elsie's stew after a day on the slopes." Plucking a blade of grass, she twirled it idly.

Taylor moved to lie down beside her. She was too content to be alarmed at his proximity.

"Dumplings?" he inquired, and she grinned down into his face.

"Of course. Hot buttered rum or steaming chocolate."

"I'm beginning to regret I missed the season."

"Well, you're in time for strawberry shortcake," she offered in consolation. "And the fishing's good year round."

"I've always favored more active sports." His finger ran absently up her arm, and B.J. tried hard to ignore the pleasure it gave her.

"Well." Her brow creased as she considered. "There's a good stable about fifteen miles from here, or boats for rent at the marina, or..."

"Those aren't the sports I had in mind." With a swift movement, he dislodged her elbows and brought her toppling onto his chest. "Are they the best you can do?" His arms held her firmly against him, but she was already captured by the fascination of his eyes.

"There's hiking," she murmured, unaware of the strange husky texture of her own voice.

"Hiking," Taylor murmured, before altering their positions in one fluid motion.

"Yes, hiking's very popular." She felt her consciousness drifting as she gazed up at him and struggled to retain some hold on lucidity. "And...and swimming."

"Mmm." Absently, his fingers traced the delicate line of her cheek.

"And there's...uh...there's camping. A lot of people like camping. We have a lot of parks." Her voice faltered as his thumb ran over her lips.

"Parks?" he repeated, prompting her.

"Yes, a number of parks, quite a number. The facilities are excellent for camping." She gave a small moan as his mouth lowered to tease the curve of her neck.

"Hunting?" Taylor asked conversationally as his lips traveled over her jawline to brush the corner of her mouth.

"I, yes. I think...what did you say?" B.J. closed her eyes on a sigh.

"I wondered about hunting," he murmured, kissing closed lids as his fingers slid under her sweater to trace her waist.

"There's bobcat in the mountains to the north."

"Fascinating." He rubbed his mouth gently over hers as his fingers trailed lightly up her flesh to the curve of her breast. "The chamber of commerce would be proud of you." Lazily, his thumb ran over the satin swell. Pleasure became a need as warmth spread from her stomach to tremble in her veins and cloud her brain.

"Taylor." Unable to bring her voice above a whisper, her hand sought the thick mass of his hair. "Kiss me."

"In a minute," he murmured, obviously enjoying the taste of her neck, until with devastating leisure, he moved his mouth to hers.

Trembling with a new, unfamiliar hunger, B.J. pulled him closer until his mouth was no longer teasing but avid on hers. Warmth exploded into fire. His tongue was searching, demanding all of her sweetness, his body as taut as hers was fluid. He took possession of her curves with authority, molding them with firm, strong hands. His mouth no longer roamed from hers but remained to devour what she offered. The heat grew to an almost unbearable intensity, her soul melting in it to flow into his. For a moment, she was lost in the discovery of merging, feeling it with as much clarity as she felt his hands and mouth. Soaring freedom and the chains of need were interchangeable. As time ceased to flow, she plunged deeper and deeper into the all-enveloping present.

His hands took more, all gentleness abandoned. It flashed across the mists in her brain that beneath the control lay a primitive, volatile force from which she had no defense. She struggled weakly. Her protests were feeble murmurs against the demands of his mouth. Feeling her tense, Taylor lifted his head, and she felt the unsteady rhythm of his breathing on her face.

"Please, let me go." Hating the weak timbre of her

own voice, she sank her teeth into the lip still tender from his.

"Why should I do that?" Temper and passion threatened his control. She knew she had neither the strength nor the will to resist him if he chose to take.

"Please."

It seemed an eternity that he studied her, searching the smoky depths of her eyes. She watched the anger fade from his eyes as he took in the fair hair spread across the grass, the vulnerable, soft mouth. Finally, he released her with a brief, muttered oath.

"It appears," he began as she scrambled to sit up, "that pigtails suit you more than I realized." He took out a cigarette and lit it deliberately. "Virginity is a rare commodity in a woman your age."

Color flooded her cheeks as B.J. began to pack up the remains of the picnic. "I hardly see what business that is of yours."

"It doesn't matter," he countered easily and she cursed him for his ability to retain his composure so effortlessly while her entire body still throbbed with need. "It will simply take a bit more time." At her uncomprehending stare, he smiled and folded the cloth. "I told you I always win, B.J. You'd best get used to it."

"You listen to me." Storming, she sprang to her feet. "I am not about to be added to your list. This was…this was…" Her hands spread out to sweep away the incident while her brain searched for the proper words.

"Just the beginning," he supplied. Rising with the hamper, he captured her arm in a firm grip. "We haven't nearly finished yet. I wouldn't argue at the moment, B.J.," he warned as she began to sputter. "I might decide to take what you so recently offered here and now, rather than giving you some time."

"You are the most arrogant—" she began. Her voice sounded hopelessly childish even to her own ears.

"That's enough for now, B.J." Taylor interrupted pleasantly. "There's no point saying anything you might regret." He leaned down and kissed her firmly before helping her to her feet. With an easy swing, he reached for the hamper. B.J. was too dazed to do anything but meekly follow him as he led the way toward the homeward wooded path.

7

Once back at the inn, B.J. wanted nothing more than to disengage her arm from Taylor's grasp and find a dark, quiet hole in which to hide. She knew all too well that she had responded completely to Taylor's demands. Moreover, she knew she had made demands of her own. She was confused by her own reactions. Never before had she had difficulty in avoiding or controlling a romantic interlude, but she was forced to admit that from the moment Taylor had touched her, her mind had ceased to function.

Biology, she concluded, darting Taylor a sidelong glance as they approached the skirting porch. It was simply a matter of basic biology. Any woman would naturally be attracted to a man like Taylor Reynolds. He has a way of looking at you, B.J. mused, that makes

your mind go fuzzy, then blank. He has a way of touching you that makes you feel as though you never had
been touched before. He's nothing like any other man
I've ever known. And *I asked him to kiss me.* Color rose
to her cheeks. *I actually asked him to kiss me.* It must have
been the wine.

Soothed by this excuse, B.J. turned to Taylor as they
entered the side door. "I'll take the basket back to the
kitchen. Do you need me for anything else?"

"That's an intriguing question," he drawled.

B.J. shot him a quelling glance. "I have to get back
to work now," she said briskly. "Now, if you'll excuse
me?"

B.J.'s dignified exit was aborted by a flurry of activity
in the lobby. Curiosity outweighing pride, she allowed
Taylor to lead her toward the source.

A tall, svelte brunette stood by the desk, surrounded
by a clutter of shocking pink luggage. Her pencil-slim
form was draped in a teal blue suit of raw silk. The scent
of gardenias floated toward B.J.

"If you'll see to my luggage, darling, and tell Mr.
Reynolds I'm here, I'd be very grateful." She addressed
these requests in a low, husky voice to Eddie who stood
gaping beside her.

"Hello, Darla. What are you doing here?"

At Taylor's voice, the dark head turned. B.J. noted the
eyes were nearly the same shade as the exquisite suit.

"Taylor." Impossibly graceful on four-inch heels, Darla glided across the lobby to embrace Taylor warmly. "I'm just back from checking on the job in Chicago. I knew you'd want me to look this little place over and give you my ideas."

Disengaging himself, Taylor met Darla's glowing smile with an ironic smile. "How considerate of you. B.J. Clark, Darla Trainor. Darla does the majority of my decorating, B.J. manages the inn."

"How interesting." Darla gave B.J.'s sweater and jeans a brief, despairing glance and patted her own perfectly styled hair. "From what I've seen so far, my work is certainly cut out for me." With a barely perceptible shudder, Darla surveyed the lobby's hand hooked rugs and Tiffany lamps.

"We've had no complaints on our decor." B.J. leaped to the inn's defense.

"Well." She was given a small, pitying smile from deeply colored lips. "It's certainly quaint, isn't it? Rather sweet for Ma and Pa Kettle. You'll have to let me know, Taylor, if you plan to enlarge this room." Transferring her attention, Darla's expression softened and warmed. "But, of course, red's always an eye-catcher. Perhaps red velvet drapes and carpeting."

B.J.'s eyes darkened to flint. "Why don't you take your red velvet drapes and…"

"I believe we'll discuss this later," Taylor said diplomatically, tightening his hold on B.J.'s arm. Struggling to prevent herself from crying with the pain, B.J. found argument impossible.

"I'm sure you'd like to get settled in," she forced out between clenched lips.

"Of course." Darla viewed B.J.'s brief outburst with a fluttering of heavy lashes. "Come up for a drink, Taylor. I assume this place has room service."

"Of course. Have a couple of martinis sent up to Miss Trainor's room," Taylor said to Eddie. "What's your room number, Darla?"

"I don't believe I have one yet." Again using her extensive lashes to advantage, Darla turned to a still dazed Eddie. "There seems to be a small communication problem."

"Give Miss Trainor 314, Eddie, and see to her bags." The sharp command in B.J.'s voice snapped Eddie's daydream, and he scurried to comply. "I hope you find it suitable." B.J. turned her best managerial smile on her new and unwelcome guest. "Please let me know if there's anything you need. I'll see to your drinks."

Taylor's hand held her still another moment. "I'll speak with you later."

"Delighted," B.J. returned, feeling the circulation slowly returning to her arm as he released it. "I'll wait to be summoned at your convenience, Mr. Reynolds. Welcome to the Lakeside Inn, Miss Trainor. Have a nice stay."

★ ★ ★

It was a simple matter to avoid a private meeting with Taylor as he spent the remainder of the day in Darla Trainor's company. They were closeted in 314 for what seemed to B.J. a lifetime. To boost her ego B.J. decided to phone Howard. They arranged a date for the following evening. *Well, at least Howard doesn't closet himself downing martinis with Miss Glamorpuss,* she thought. Somehow this knowledge was not as comforting as it should have been.

The dress B.J. had chosen for dinner was black and sleek. It molded her subtle curves with a lover's intimacy, falling in a midnight pool around her ankles, with a gentle caress for thighs and calves. Small pearl buttons ran from her throat to her waist. The high, puritanical neckline accentuated her firm, small breasts and emphasized her slender neck. She left her hair loose to float in a pale cloud around her shoulders. She touched her scent behind her ears before leaving her room to descend to the dining room.

The candle-lit, corner table where Taylor sat with Darla was intimate and secluded. Glancing in their direction, B.J. could not suppress a scowl. There was no denying that they were a handsome couple. *Made for each other,* she thought bitterly. Darla's vermilion sheath plunged to reveal the creamy swell of her breasts. Taylor's dark suit was impeccably cut. In spite of herself, B.J.'s eyes were drawn to the breadth of his shoulders. She drew in her breath sharply, recalling the feel of his corded muscles now expertly concealed by the fine tailoring, and shivered involuntarily.

Taylor glanced over, his expression indefinable as he made a slow, exacting survey, his eyes lingering on the gentle curves draped in the simplicity of unrelieved black. Though her skin grew warm, B.J. met his eyes levelly. Examination complete, Taylor lifted one brow, whether in approval or disapproval, she could not determine. With a brief gesture of his hand, he ordered B.J. to his table.

Fuming at the casual insolence of the command, she schooled her features into tranquility. She wove her way through the room, deliberately stopping to speak with diners along the route.

"Good evening." B.J. greeted Taylor and his companion with a professional smile. "I hope you're enjoying your meal."

"As always, the food is excellent." Taylor rose and pulled up a chair expectantly. His eyes narrowed in challenge. It was not the moment to cross him, B.J. decided.

"I trust your room pleases you, Miss Trainor," she said pleasantly, as she sat down.

"It's adequate, Miss Clark. Though I must say, I was rather taken aback by the decorating scheme."

"You'll join us for a drink," Taylor stated, motioning

a waitress over without waiting for B.J.'s consent. She glared at him for a moment before she glanced up at Dot.

"My usual," she said, not feeling obliged to explain this was a straight ginger ale. She turned back to Darla, coating her voice with polite interest. "And what is it about the decorating which took you aback, Miss Trainor?"

"Really, Miss Clark," Darla began as though the matter was obvious. "The entire room is *provincial,* don't you agree? There are some rather nice pieces, I admit, if one admires American antiques, but Taylor and I have always preferred a modern approach."

Fighting her annoyance and an all too unwanted spasm of jealousy, B.J. said sarcastically, "I see. Perhaps you'd care to elaborate on the modern approach for this country bumpkin. I so seldom get beyond the local five and dime."

Dot set B.J.'s drink in front of her and scurried away, recognizing storm warnings.

"In the first place," Darla began, immune to her frosty gray eyes, "the lighting is all wrong. Those glass domed lamps with pull chains are archaic. You need wall to wall carpeting. The hand hooked rugs and faded Persians will have to go. And the bathroom… Well, needless to say, the bathroom is hopeless." With a sigh, Darla lifted her champagne cocktail and sipped. "Footed tubs belong in period comedies, not in hotels."

B.J. chewed on a piece of ice to keep her temper from

boiling over. "Our guests have always found a certain charm in the baths."

"Perhaps," Darla acknowledged with a depreciating shrug. "But with the proper changes and improvements, you'll be catering to a different type of clientele." She drew out a slim cigarette, giving Taylor a brief flutter of lashes as he lit it.

"Do you have any objections to footed tubs and pull chains?" B.J. asked him, voice precise, eyes stormy.

"They suit the present atmosphere of the inn." His voice was equally precise, his eyes cool.

"Maybe I've got a few fresh ideas for you, Miss Trainor, if and when you pull out your little book of samples." Setting down her glass, B.J. watched from the corner of her eye as Taylor flicked his lighter at the end of his cigarette. "Mirrors should be good on the ceiling in particular. Just a light touch of decadence. Lots of chrome and glass to give the rooms that spacious, symmetrical look. And white, plenty of white as well, perhaps with fuchsia accents. The bed, of course," she continued with fresh inspiration. "A large circular bed with fuchsia coverings. Do you like fuchsia, Taylor?"

"I don't believe I asked for your advice on decorating tonight, B.J." Taylor drew casually on his cigarette. The smoke traveled in a thin column toward the exposed beam ceiling.

"I'm afraid, Miss Clark," Darla commented, spurred

on by Taylor's mild reproof, "that your taste runs to the vulgar."

"Oh really?" B.J. blinked as if surprised. "I suppose that's what comes from being a country bumpkin."

"I'm sure whatever I ultimately decide will suit you, Taylor." Darla placed a hand with easy familiarity on his as B.J.'s temper rose. "But it will take a bit longer than usual as the alterations will be so drastic."

"Take all the time you need." B.J. gestured with magnanimity as she rose. "In the meantime, keep your hands off my footed tubs."

The dignity of her exit was spoiled by a near collision with Dot who had been discreetly eavesdropping.

"An order of arsenic for table three…on the house," B.J. muttered, skirting around the wide eyed waitress and sweeping from the room.

B.J.'s intention to stalk straight to her room and cool off was undone by a series of small, irritating jobs. It was after ten when the last had been dealt with and she was able to shut the door to her room and give vent to suppressed temper.

"Country bumpkin," she hissed through clenched teeth. Her eyes rested on a William and Mary table. *She'd* probably prefer plastic cubes in black and white checks. Her eyes moved from the dower chest to the schoolmaster's desk and on to the Bostonian rocker and wing chair in softly faded green. Each room of the inn was distinctive, with its own personality, its own treasures. Closing her eyes, B.J. could clearly see the room which Darla now occupied, the delicate pastel of the flowered wallpaper, the fresh gleam of the oak floor, the charm of the narrow, cushioned window seat. The pride of that particular room was an antique highboy in walnut with exquisite teardrop pulls. B.J. could not recall an occasion when a guest who had stayed in that room had done other than praise its comforts, its quiet charm, its timeless grace.

Darla Trainor, B.J. vowed, *is not getting her hands on my inn.* Walking to the mirrored bureau, she stared at her reflection, then let out a long disgusted breath. She's got a face that belongs on a cameo, and mine belongs on a milk commercial, she thought. Picking up her brush, she told herself that these reflections had nothing to do with the problem at hand.

How am I going to convince Taylor that the inn should stay as it is when she's already rattling off changes and giving him intimate smiles? I suppose, B.J. continued, giving her reflection a fierce scowl, *she's not just his decorator.* The kiss she gave him when she arrived wasn't very businesslike. I don't believe for a moment they spent all that time in her room discussing fabrics.

That's no concern of mine, she decided with a strong tug of the brush. But if they think they're going to start steaming off wallpaper without a fight, they're in for a surprise. She put down her brush and turned just as the door swung open to admit Taylor.

Before her astonished eyes, he closed and locked her

door before placing the key in his pocket. As he advanced toward her, she could see that he was obviously angry.

"Being the owner doesn't give you the right to use the master key without cause," she snapped, as she backed against the bureau.

"It appears I haven't made myself clear." Taylor's voice was deceptively gentle. "You have, for the time being, a free hand in the day to day managing of this inn. I have not, nor do I desire to infringe upon your routine. However—" He took a step closer. B.J. discovered her hands were clutching the edge of the bureau in a desperate grip. "All orders, all decisions, all changes in policy come from me, and only me."

"Of all the dictatorial…"

"This isn't a debate," he cut her off sharply. "I won't have you issuing orders over my head. Darla is employed by me. I tell her what to do, and when to do it."

"But surely you don't want her to toss out all these lovely old pieces for gooseneck floor lamps and modular shelving. The server in the dining room is Hepplewhite. There're two Chippendale pieces in your room alone, and…"

The hand which moved from the back of her neck to circle her throat halted B.J.'s furious rush of words. She became uncomfortably aware of the strength of his fingers. No pressure was applied, but the meaning was all too evident.

"Whatever I want Darla to do is my concern, and my concern only." He tightened his grip, bringing her closer. Now B.J. read the extent of his anger in his eyes. Like two dark suns, they burned into hers. "Keep your opinions to yourself until I ask for them. Don't interfere or you'll pay for it. Is that understood?"

"I understand perfectly. Your relationship with Miss Trainor has overruled any opinion of mine."

"That—" his brow lifted "—is none of your business."

"Whatever concerns the inn is my business," B.J. countered. "I offered you my resignation once, and you refused it. If you want to get rid of me now, you'll have to fire me."

"Don't tempt me." He lowered his hand and rested his fingers on the top button of her bodice. "I have my reasons for wanting you around, but don't push it. I agreed to keep you abreast of any alterations I decide on, but if you persist in being rude to others in my employ, you'll be out on your ear."

"I can't see that Darla Trainor needs protection from me," B.J. remarked resentfully.

"Don't you?" His temper appeared to drift toward amusement as he scanned her face. "A couple of centuries ago, you'd have been burned at the stake for looking as you do at this moment. Hell smoke in your eyes, your mouth soft and defiant, all that pale hair tumbling over a black dress." Deftly, his fingers undid the top button and moved down to the next as his eyes kept hers a prisoner. "That dress is just puritanical enough to be seductive. Was it accident or design that you wore it tonight?"

With casual ease, he unloosed half the range of buttons, continuing his progress as his gaze remained fixed on hers.

"I don't know what you mean." Yet her traitorous feet refused to walk away. B.J. found herself powerless to move. "I want…I want you to go."

"Liar," he accused quietly, his hands slipping inside the opened front of her dress. His fingers traced lightly over her skin. "Tell me again you want me to go." His hands rose, his thumbs moving gently under the curve of her breasts. The room began to sway like the deck of a ship.

"I want you to go." Her voice was husky, her lids felt heavy with a tantalizing languor.

"Your body contradicts you, B.J." His hands claimed her breasts briefly before sliding to the smooth skin of her back. He brought her hard against him. "You want me just as much as I want you." His mouth lowered to prove his point.

Surrendering to a force beyond her understanding, B.J. rested in his arms. His demands increased with her submission, his mouth drawing the response she had no strength to withhold. While her mind screamed no, her arms drew him closer. The warnings to run were lost as his lips moved to the vulnerable skin of her throat, teasing the softness with tongue and teeth. She could only cling and fret for more. Mouth returned to mouth. While his hands roamed, arousing fresh pleasure, hers slipped under his jacket.

With a suddenness that gave her no time for defense, no thought of resistance, he fell deep into her heart. He claimed its untouched regions with the deftness of a seasoned explorer. The emotion brought B.J. to a spinning ecstasy which vied with a crushing, hopeless despair. To love him was certain disaster, to need him, undeniable misery, to be in his arms, both the darkness and the light. Trapped in the cage of her own desire, she would never find escape.

Helpless to do other than answer the hunger of his mouth, submit to the caressing journey of his hands, she felt the sting of emptiness behind her closed lids. Her arms pulled him closer to avert the insidious chill of reason.

"Admit it," he demanded, his lips moving again to savage her throat. "Admit you want me. Tell me you want me to stay."

"Yes, I want you." The words trembled on a sob as she buried her face in his shoulder. "Yes, I want you to stay."

She felt him stiffen and burrowed deeper until his hand forced her face to his. Her eyes were luminous, conquering the darkness with the glimmer of unshed tears. Her mouth was soft and tremulous as she fought the need to throw herself into his arms and weep out her newly discovered love. For eternity, he stared, and she watched without comprehension as his features hardened with fresh temper. When he spoke, however, his voice was calm and composed and struck like a fist on the jaw.

"It appears we've gotten away from the purpose of this meeting." Stepping away, his hands retreated to his pockets. "I believe I've made my wishes clear."

She shook her head in confusion. As her hand lifted to her tousled hair, the opening of her dress shifted in innocent suggestion over creamy skin. "Taylor, I..."

"Tomorrow—" she shivered as the coolness of his voice sapped the warmth from her skin "—I expect you to give Miss Trainor your complete cooperation, and your courtesy. Regardless of your disagreement, she is a guest of the inn and shall be treated as such."

"Of course." The hated tears began to flow as pain and rejection washed over her. "Miss Trainor shall be given every consideration." She sniffed, brushed at tears and continued with dignity. "You have my word."

"Your word!" Taylor muttered, taking a step toward her. B.J. streaked to the bath and locked the door.

"Go away!" No longer able to control the sobs, one small fist pounded impotently against the panel. "Go away and leave me alone. I gave you my promise, now I'm off duty."

"B.J., open this door."

She recognized both anger and exasperation in his tone and wept more desperately. "No, go away! Go keep Miss Perfect company and let me alone. Your orders will be carried out to the letter. Just go. I don't have to answer to you until morning."

Taylor's swearing and storming around the room were quite audible, though to B.J. his muttered oaths and comments made little sense. Finally, the bedroom door slammed with dangerous force. In an undignified huddle on the tiled floor, B.J. wept until she thought her heart would break.

8

"Well, you did it again, didn't you?" B.J. stared at her reflection as the morning sun shone in without mercy. *You made a total fool of yourself.* With a weary sigh, she ran a hand through her hair before turning her back on the accusing face in the mirror. *How could I have known I'd fall in love with him?* she argued as she buttoned a pale green cap-sleeved blouse. *I didn't plan it. I didn't want it.*

"Blast," she muttered and pulled on a matching skirt. *How can I control the way he makes me feel? The minute he puts his hands on me, my brain dissolves. To think that I would have let him stay last night knowing all he wanted from me was a quick affair! How could I be so stupid?* And then, she added, shame warring with injured pride, *he didn't want me after all.* I suppose he remembered Darla. Why should he waste his time with me when she's available?

The next ten minutes were spent in fierce self-flagellation as B.J. secured her hair in a roll at the base of her neck. These tasks completed, she squared her shoulders and went out to meet whatever task the day brought.

A casual question to Eddie informed her Taylor was already closeted in the office, and Darla Trainor had not yet risen. B.J. was determined to avoid them both and succeeded throughout the morning.

The lunch hour found her in the lounge, conducting an inventory on the bar stock. The room was quiet, removed from the luncheon clatter. She found the monotony soothing on her nerves.

"So, this is the lounge."

The intrusion of the silky voice jolted B.J.'s calm absorption. She whirled around, knocking bottles of liquor together.

Darla glided into the room looking elegantly businesslike in an oatmeal colored three piece suit, a pad and pencil in perfectly manicured hands. She surveyed the cluster of white clothed tables, the postage stamp dance floor, the vintage upright Steinway. Flicking a finger down the muted glow of knotty pine paneling, she advanced to the ancient oak bar.

"How incredibly drab."

"Thank you," B.J. returned in her most courteous

voice before she turned to replace a bottle on the mirrored shelves.

"Fix me a sweet vermouth," Darla ordered, sliding gracefully onto a stool and dropping her pad on the bar's surface.

B.J.'s mouth opened, furious retorts trembling on her tongue. Recalling her promise to Taylor, she clamped it shut and turned to comply.

"You must remember, Miss Clark," Darla's triumphant smile made B.J.'s hand itch to connect with ivory skin, "I'm merely doing my job. There's nothing personal in my observations."

Attempting to overcome her instinctive dislike, B.J. conceded. "Perhaps that's true. But, I have a very personal feeling about the Lakeside Inn. It's more home than a place of business to me." She set the glass of vermouth at Darla's fingertips before turning back to count bottles.

"Yes, Taylor told me you're quite attached to this little place. He found it amusing."

"Did he?" Feeling her hand tremble, B.J. gripped the shelves until her knuckles whitened. "What a strange sense of humor Taylor must have."

"Well, when one knows Taylor as I do, one knows what to expect." Their eyes met in the mirror. Darla smiled and lifted her glass. "He seems to think you're a valuable employee. What did he say...rather adept at making people comfortable." She smiled again and sipped. "Taylor demands value from his employees as well as obedience. At times, he uses unorthodox methods to keep them satisfied."

"I'm sure you'd know all about that." B.J. turned slowly, deciding wars should be fought face to face.

"Darling, Taylor and I are much more than business associates. And I, of course, understand his...ah...distractions with business."

"How magnanimous of you."

"It would never do to allow emotion to rule a relationship with Taylor Reynolds." Drawing a long, enameled nail over the rim of her glass, Darla gave B.J. a knowledgeable look. "He has no patience with emotional scenes or complications."

The memory of her weeping spell and Taylor's angry swearing played back in B.J.'s mind. "Perhaps we've at last reached a point of agreement."

"The first warning is always friendly, Miss Clark." Abruptly, Darla's voice hardened, throwing B.J. momentarily off balance. "Don't get too close. I don't allow anyone to infringe on my territory for long."

"Are we still talking about Taylor?" B.J. inquired. "Or did I lose part of this conversation?"

"Just take my advice." Leaning over the bar, Darla took B.J.'s arm in a surprisingly strong grip. "If you don't, the next place you manage will be a dog kennel."

"Take your hand off me." B.J.'s tone was soft and ominous, as the well-shaped nails dug into her flesh.

"As long as we understand each other." With a pleasant smile, Darla released B.J.'s arm and finished her drink.

"We understand each other very well." Taking the empty glass, B.J. placed it under the bar. "Bar's closed, Miss Trainor." She turned her back to recount already counted bottles.

"Ladies." B.J. stiffened and watched Taylor's reflection enter the room. "I hadn't expected to find you at the bar at this time of day." His voice was light, but the eyes which met B.J.'s in the glass did not smile.

"I've been wandering around making notes," Darla told him. B.J. watched her hand rub lightly over the back of his. "I'm afraid the only thing this lounge has going for it is its size. It's quite roomy, and you could easily fit in double the tables. But then, you'll have to let me know if you want to go moody, or modern. Actually, it might be an idea to add another lounge and do both, along the lines of your place in San Francisco."

His murmur was absent as he watched B.J. move to the next shelf.

"I thought I'd get a good look at the dining room if the luncheon crowd is gone." Darla's smile was coaxing. "Why don't you come with me, Taylor, and you can give me a clearer picture of what you have in mind?"

"Hmm?" His attention shifted, but the imperceptible frown remained. "No, I haven't decided on anything yet. Go ahead and take a look, I'll get back to you."

Well arched brows rose at the dismissive tone, but

Darla remained cool and composed. "Of course. I'll bring my notes to your office later and we can discuss it."

Her heels echoed faintly on the wooden floor. Her heavy perfume scent lingered in the air after she faded from view.

"Do you want a drink?" B.J. questioned, keeping her back to him and her voice remote.

"No, I want to talk to you."

With great care, B.J. avoided meeting his eyes in the mirror. She lifted a bottle, carefully examining the extent of its contents. "Haven't we covered everything?"

"No, we haven't covered everything. Turn around B.J., I'm not going to talk to your back."

"Very well, you're the boss." As she faced him, she caught a flash of anger in his eyes.

"Do you provoke me purposely, B.J., or is it just an accidental talent?"

"I have no idea. Take your choice." Suddenly, she was struck by inspiration. "Taylor," she said urgently. "I *would* like to talk to you. I'd like to talk to you about buying the inn. It can't be as important to you as it is to me. You could build a resort farther south that would suit you better. I could raise the money if you gave me some time."

"Don't be ridiculous." His abrupt words cooled her enthusiasm. "Where would you come up with the kind of money required to buy a property like this?"

"I don't know." She paced back and forth behind the bar. "Somewhere. I could get a loan for part of it, and you could hold a note for the rest. I've some money saved…"

"No." Standing, he skirted the bar and closed the distance between them. "I have no intention of selling."

"But, Taylor…"

"I said no. Drop it."

"Why are you being so stubborn? You won't even consider changing your mind? I might even be able to come up with a good offer if you gave me time—" Her voice trailed off uncertainly.

"I said I wanted to *talk* to you. At the moment I don't care to discuss the inn or any part of it."

He gripped her arm to spin her around, connecting with the flesh tender from Darla's nails. B.J. gave a cry of pain and jerked away. Taylor loosened his hold immediately, and she fell into the shelves, knocking glasses in a crashing heap on the floor.

"What the devil's got into you?" he demanded as her hand went automatically to nurse her bruised arm. "I barely touched you. Listen, B.J., I'm not tolerating you jumping like a scared rabbit every time I get close. I haven't hurt you. Stop that!" He pulled her hand away, then stared in confusion at the marks on her arm. "Good Lord. I didn't…I'd swear I barely touched you." Astonished, his eyes lifted to hers, darkened with emotions she could not understand. For a moment, she merely stared back, fascinated by seeing his habitual assurance rattled.

"No, I did it before." Dropping her eyes, B.J. busied herself by resecuring the pins in her hair. "It's just a bit sore. You startled me when you grabbed it."

"How did you do that?" He moved to take her arm for a closer examination, but B.J. stepped away quickly.

"I bumped into something. I've got to start looking where I'm going." She began to gather shards of broken glass, fresh resentment causing her head to ache.

"Don't do that," Taylor commanded. "You'll cut yourself."

Like an echo to his words, B.J. jerked as a piece of glass sliced her thumb. Moaning in pain and disgust, she dropped the offending glass back into the heap.

"Let me see." Taylor pulled her to her feet, ignoring her struggles for release. "Ah, B.J." With a sigh of exasperation, he drew a spotless white handkerchief from his pocket, dabbing at the cut. "I'm beginning to think I have to keep you on a very short leash."

"It's nothing," she mumbled, fighting the warmth of his fingers on her wrist. "Let me go, you'll have blood all over you."

"Scourges of war." He brought the wounded thumb briefly to his lips, then wrapped the cloth around it. "You will continue to bind up your hair, won't you?" With his free hand, he dislodged pins, clattering them among broken glass. Studying the flushed face and tumbled hair, his mouth lifted in a smile which brought B.J. new pain. "What is it about you that constantly pulls at my temper? At the moment, you look as harmless as a frazzled kitten."

His fingers combed lightly through her hair, then rested on her shoulders. She felt the sweet, drawing weakness seeping through her limbs. "Do you know how close I came to kicking in that foolish bathroom door last night? You should be careful with tears, B.J., they affect men in strange ways."

"I hate to cry." She lifted her chin, terrified she would do so again. "It was your fault."

"Yes, I suppose it was. I'm sorry."

She stared, stunned by the unexpected apology. In a featherlight caress, he lowered his mouth to brush hers. "It's all right…It doesn't matter." She backed away, frightened by her own need to respond, but found herself trapped against the bar. Taylor made no move toward her, but merely said, "Have dinner with me tonight. Up in my room where we can talk privately."

Her head shook before her lips could form a refusal. He closed the space between them before she could calculate an escape.

"B.J., I'm not going to let you run away. We need to talk somewhere where we won't be interrupted. You know that I want you, and…"

"You should be satisfied with your other acquisitions," she retorted, battling the creeping warmth.

"I beg your pardon?" At her tone, his face hardened. The hand which had lifted to brush through her hair dropped back to his side.

"I'm sure you'll understand if you give it a bit of thought." She lifted her own hand to the sore flesh of her arm as if to keep the memory fresh. His eyes followed her gesture in puzzlement.

"It would be simpler if you elaborated."

"No, I don't think so. Just don't let your ego get out of hand, Taylor. I'm not running from you, I simply have a date tonight."

"A date?" He slipped his hands into his pockets as he rocked back on his heels. His voice was hard.

"That's right. I'm entitled to a personal life. I don't think it's included in my job contract that I have to spend twenty-four hours at your beck and call." Adding salt to her own wound, she continued, "I'm sure Miss Trainor will fill your requirements for the evening very well."

"Undoubtedly," he agreed with a slow nod. Stung by the ease of his answer, B.J.'s ice became fire.

"Well then, that's all decided, isn't it? Have a delightful evening, Taylor. I assure you, I intend to. If you'll excuse me, I've work to do." She brushed by him, only to be brought up short by a hand on her hair.

"Since we're both going to be otherwise engaged this evening, perhaps we can get this out of the way now."

His mouth took hers swiftly, and she could taste his smoldering fury. She made a futile attempt to clamp her lips tightly against his. Ruthlessly, his hand jerked her hair. As she gasped in pained surprise he invaded her mouth, conquering her senses one by one. Just as she had abandoned all semblance of resistance, he drew back, his hands moving with slow insistence from her waist to her shoulders.

"Are you through?" Her voice was husky. Despising the longing to feel his mouth again, she forced herself rigid, keeping her eyes level.

"Oh no, B.J." The tone was confident. "I'm a long way from through. But for now," he continued as she braced herself for another assault, "you'd best tend to that cut."

Too unnerved to answer, B.J. rushed from the lounge. She had left dignity to lay with the scattered pieces of glass.

She felt the kitchen would be the quietest sanctuary at that time of day and entered on the pretext of wanting a cup of coffee.

"What did you do to your hand?" Elsie's question was off-handed as she completed the assembly line production of apple cobblers.

"Just a scratch." Frowning down at Taylor's handkerchief, B.J. shrugged and advanced on the coffee pot.

"Better put some iodine on it."

"Iodine stings."

Tongue clucking, Elsie wiped her hands on her full

apron before foraging in a small cabinet for medical supplies. "Sit down and don't be a baby."

"It's just a scratch. It's not even bleeding now." Helplessly, B.J. dropped into a chair as Elsie flourished a small bottle and a bandage. "It's nothing at all. Ouch! Blast it, Elsie! I told you that wretched stuff stings."

"There." Elsie secured the bandage with a satisfied smile. "Out of sight, out of mind."

"So you say." B.J. rested her chin on her hand and stared into the depth of her coffee cup.

"Miss Snooty tried to get into my kitchen," Elsie announced with an indignant sniff.

"Who? Oh, Miss Trainor." Throbbing thumb momentarily forgotten, B.J. gave her cook her full attention. "What happened?"

"I tossed her out, of course." Elsie flicked flour from her abundant bosom and looked pleased.

"Oh." Leaning back in her chair, B.J. laughed at the picture of Elsie ordering sophisticated Darla out of her kitchen. "Was she furious?"

"Fit to be tied," Elsie returned pleasantly. B.J.'s grin widened before she could prevent it. "Going out with Howard tonight?"

"Yes." Her answer was automatic, not even vaguely surprised that communications had delivered this information to Elsie's ears. "To the movies, I think."

"Don't know why you're wasting your time going off with him when Mr. Reynolds is around."

"Well, it keeps Betty Jackson happy, and…" B.J. stopped and frowned as the complete sentence seeped through. "What does Taylor…Mr. Reynolds have to do with it?"

"I don't see why you're going out with Howard Beall when you're in love with Taylor Reynolds." Elsie's statement was matter-of-factly delivered as she poured herself a cup of coffee.

"I am not in love with Taylor Reynolds," B.J. declared, gulping down coffee and scalding both tongue and throat.

"Yes, you are," Elsie corrected, adding cooling cream to her own cup.

"I am not."

"Are too."

"I am not. I am absolutely not! Just what makes you so smart?" she added nastily.

"Fifty years of living, and twenty-four of knowing you." The reply was smug.

"La de da." B.J. attempted to appear sublimely unconcerned.

"Be real nice if you got married and settled down right here." Ignoring B.J.'s fit of choking, Elsie calmly sipped her coffee. "You could keep right on managing the inn."

"Stick to chicken and dumplings, Elsie," B.J. advised when she had recovered. "As a fortune teller, you're a complete failure. Taylor Reynolds would no more marry me and settle here than he would marry a porcupine and live on the moon. I'm a bit too countrified and inexperienced for his taste."

"Hmph." Elsie sniffed again and shook her head. "Sure does a lot of looking in your direction."

"I'm sure in the vast wisdom you've amassed in your famous fifty years, you know the difference between a physical attraction and the urge to marry and settle down. Even in our sheltered little town, we learn the difference between love and lust."

"My, my, aren't we all grown up and sassy," Elsie observed with the mild tolerance of an adult watching a child's tantrum. "Finish your coffee and scoot, I've got a prime rib that needs tending. And don't worry that bandage off your thumb," she ordered as B.J. swung through the door.

Obviously, B.J. decided as she prepared for her date that evening, I don't project an imposing enough authority figure. She frowned again as she recalled Elsie dismissing her like a bad tempered child. A breeze wafted through her opened window, billowing the curtains and wafting in the smell of freshly mowed grass. B.J. shrugged off her black mood. I'll simply change my image a bit.

She rooted through her closet and pulled out her birthday present from her grandmother. The blouse was pure white silk and plunged deep to cling provocatively to every curve and plane before it tapered to the narrow waist of sleek black pants. The slacks continued a loving embrace over hips and down the length of shapely legs, molding her shape with the accuracy of a second skin.

"I'm not sure I'm ready for a new image," she muttered, turning sideways in front of her mirror. "I'm not sure Howard's ready either." The thought brought an irrepressible giggle as Howard's pleasantly homely face loomed in her mind.

He had the eyes of a faithful puppy, made all the more soulful by the attempt of a moustache which hung apologetically over his top lip. The main problem, B.J. decided, concentrating on his image, is that he lacks a chin. His face seemed to melt into his neck.

But he's a nice man, B.J. reminded herself. A nice, uncomplicated, predictable, undemanding man. Easing her feet into leather slides, she grabbed her bag and scurried from the room.

Her hopes to slip unseen outside to await Howard's arrival were shattered by a panic-stricken Eddie.

"B.J. Hey, B.J.!" He loped across the lobby and cornered her before she could reach the door.

"Eddie, if the place isn't burning down, hold it until tomorrow. I'm just leaving."

"But, B.J.," he continued, grabbing her hand and ignoring her unconscious search of the room for a tall, dark man. "Dot told Maggie that Miss Trainor is going to redecorate the inn, and that Mr. Reynolds plans to

make it into a resort with saunas in every room and an
illegal casino in the back." Horrified, his hand clung to
hers for reassurance, his eyes pleading behind the thickness of his glasses.

"In the first place," B.J. began patiently, "Mr. Reynolds
has no intention of running an illegal casino."

"He has one in Las Vegas," Eddie whispered in confidence.

"Gambling is a prerequisite in Las Vegas, it's not
illegal."

"But, B.J., Maggie said the lounge is going to be
done in red and gold plush with nude paintings on the
walls."

"Nonsense." She patted his hand in amusement as
color rose to his cheeks. "Mr. Reynolds hasn't decided
anything yet. When he does, I'm sure it won't run to red
and gold plush, and nudes!"

"Thank you," Taylor said at her back. B.J. jumped.
"Eddie, I believe the Bodwin sisters are looking for you,"
he added.

"Oh, yes, sir." Face flaming, Eddie shot off, leaving
B.J. in the very position she had sought to avoid.

"Well, well." Taylor surveyed her, an encompassing,
thoroughly male examination, lingering on the point
where her blouse joined above her breasts. "I trust your
date has a high boiling point."

She started to snap that Howard had no boiling point
at all, but changed her mind. "Do you really like it?"

Tossing clouds of hair over her shoulder, B.J. gave Taylor the benefit of a melting, sultry smile.

"Let's say I might find it appealing under different circumstances," he said dryly.

Pleased to observe he was annoyed, B.J. recklessly gave his cheek a brief pat and glided to the door. "Good night, Taylor. Don't wait up now." Triumphant, she stepped out into the pink-clouded evening.

Howard's reaction to her appearance caused her ego to soar yet higher. He swallowed, eyes blinking rapidly, and stammered in small, incoherent sentences the entire distance to town. Finding this a pleasant change from self-assured amusement, B.J. basked in his admiration as she watched the hazy sun sink beyond the hills through the car window.

In town, the streets were already quiet with the mid-week, mid-evening hush which isolates small towns from the outside world. A few windows glowed like cats' eyes in the dark, but most of the houses had bedded down for the night like so many contented domestic pets.

At the far end of town where the theater was, there were more signs of activity. Howard pulled into the parking lot with his usual, plodding precision. The neon sign glowed somewhat ludicrously against the quiet sky. The *L* in PLAZA had been retired for the past six months.

"I wonder," B.J. mused as she alighted from Howard's sensible Buick, "if Mr. Jarvis will ever get that sign fixed or if each of the letters will die a quiet death." Howard's

answer was muffled by the car door slam. She was faintly
surprised as he took her arm with a possessive air and led
her into the theater.

An hour through the feature, B.J decided Howard was
not at all himself. He did not consume his popcorn with
his usual voracity, nor did he shift throughout the film
on the undeniably uncomfortable seats the Plaza offered.
Rather, he sat in a glazed-eyed state that seemed almost
catatonic.

"Howard." Keeping her voice low, B.J. placed her
hand on his. To her surprise he jumped as though she
had pinched him. "Howard, are you all right?"

Her astonishment changed to stunned disbelief when
he grabbed her, scattering popcorn, and pressed a passionate if fumbling kiss to her mouth. At first, B.J. sat
stunned. All other advances by Howard had consisted
of a brotherly embrace at the door of the inn. Then,
hearing a few snickers from the back of the theater, she
wiggled from his arms and pushed against his stocky
chest.

"Howard, behave yourself!" She gave an exasperated
sigh and straightened in her seat.

Abruptly, Howard gripped her arm and pulled her
to her feet, dragging her up the aisle and out of the
theater.

"Howard, have you lost your mind?"

"I couldn't sit in there any more," he muttered, bun-
dling her into his car. "It's too crowded."

"Crowded?" She blew an errant curl from her eyes. "Howard, there couldn't have been more than twenty people in there. I think you should see a doctor." She patted his shoulder then tested his brow for signs of fever. "You're a bit warm and not at all yourself. I can get a ride back, you'd better just go home."

"No!" There was no mistaking the vehemence of his tone.

B.J. gave Howard a long, searching stare before settling back uneasily into her seat. Though it was too dark to tell much, he appeared to be concentrating on his driving. He drove rapidly over the winding country road. Soon B.J. was able to distinguish the blinking lights of the hotel.

Suddenly, Howard pulled off the road and seized her. In the beginning, B.J. was more surprised than angry. "Stop it! Stop this, Howard! What in the world has gotten into you?"

"B.J." His mouth searched for hers, and this time his kiss was neither fumbling nor brotherly. "You're so beautiful." His groping hand reached for her blouse.

"Howard Beall, I'm ashamed of you!" B.J. remonstrated, pushing Howard firmly away and sliding toward the car door. "You get home right now and take a cold shower and go to bed!"

"But, B.J.—"

"I mean it." She wrenched open the car door and jumped out. Standing by the road, she tossed back her hair and adjusted her clothes. "I'm walking right back to the inn before you grow fangs again. Consider yourself lucky if I don't say something to your aunt about your temporary bout of insanity." Turning, she began the half-mile hike to the hotel.

Ten minutes later, shoes in hand and muttering disjointed imprecations toward the entire male sex, B.J. panted up the steep hill. The shadowy trees sighed softly in the moonlight. A lone owl hooted above her. But B.J. was in no mood for the beauties of the evening. "You be quiet," she commanded, glaring up at the bundle of feathers.

"I haven't said anything yet," a deep voice answered.

On the verge of screaming, B.J. found a hand over her mouth. Struggling to escape, she found a hard arm gripping her around the waist. "What the—?"

"Out for a stroll?" Taylor inquired mildly, releasing her. "It does seem an odd place to take a walk," he commented.

"Very funny." She managed two outraged steps before he caught her wrist.

"What's the matter? Your friend run out of gas?"

"Listen, I don't need this right now." Realizing she had dropped her shoes in her fright, B.J. searched the ground. "I've just walked a hundred miles after wrestling with a crazy man."

"Did he hurt you?" The grip on her wrist increased, as Taylor examined her more closely.

"Of course not." Tossing back her hair, B.J. let out a sigh of exasperation. "Howard wouldn't hurt a fly. I don't know what came over him. He's never acted like that before."

"Are you really that artless, or am I watching the second feature?" At her baffled expression, Taylor took her shoulders and administered a brief shake. "Grow up, B.J.! Look at yourself, the poor guy didn't have a chance."

"Don't be ridiculous." She shrugged out of his hold. "Howard's known me forever. He's never behaved like this before. He's just been reading too many romances or something. Good grief, I used to go skinny dipping with him when I was ten years old."

"Has anyone bothered to point out that you're no longer ten years old?"

Something in his voice made her raise her eyes to his.

"Stand still, B.J." He spoke in quiet command, and she felt her knees tremble. "I feel like a mountain lion stalking a house kitten."

For a moment, they stood apart, the stars glimmering above their heads, the moon a pale white guardian. Somewhere, a nightbird called to its mate, a plaintive sound. It echoed into silence as she melted in his arms.

She rose on her toes to offer him the gift of her mouth,

her sigh of surrender merging with the wind's murmur. Her breasts crushed against his chest as his hands molded her hips closer. For this moment, she was his. Her heart sought no past or future but only the warmth and knowledge of now—the eternity of the present. She moaned with pleasure as his mouth sought the curve of her neck. Her fingers tangled with his dark hair as his mouth met hers again and she opened her lips to his kiss.

Locked together, they were oblivious to the sounds of night; the sigh of wind, the mellow call of an owl and the chirp of crickets. With a harsh suddenness, the inn door opened, pooling them in artificial light.

"Oh, Taylor, I've been waiting for you."

B.J. pulled away in humiliation as Darla leaned against the doorway, draped in a flowing black negligee. Her ivory skin gleamed against the lace. Her smooth, raven hair fell loose and full down her back.

"What for?" Taylor's question was abrupt.

Darla pouted and moved lace clad shoulders. "Taylor, darling, don't be a bear."

Devastated that he should have used her so blatantly while he had another woman waiting, B.J. stooped to retrieve her shoes.

"Where do you think you're going?" Taylor captured her wrist and aborted her quick escape.

"To my room," B.J. informed him with her last vestige of calm. "It appears you have a previous engagement."

"Just a minute."

"Please, let me go. I've done my quota of wrestling for one evening."

His fingers tightened on her flesh. "I'm tempted to wring your neck." Taylor tossed her wrist away as though the small contact was abhorrent.

Turning on bare heels, B.J. rushed up the steps and past a sweetly smiling Darla.

9

B.J. moved her files to her room. There, she determined, she could work in peace without Taylor's disturbing presence. She immersed herself in paperwork and tried to block all else from her mind. The gray, drizzling rain which hissed at her windows set the stage for her mood. Thick, low hanging clouds allowed no breath of sun. Still, her eyes were drawn to the misty curtain, her mind floating with the clear rivulets which ran down the glass. Shaking her head to bring herself to order, B.J. concentrated on her linen supply.

Her door swung open, and she turned from the slant top desk. With sinking heart, she watched Taylor enter.

"Hiding out?"

It was apparent from the set of his mouth that his

mood had not mellowed since her departure the previous evening.

"No." The lifting of her chin was instinctive. "It's simply more convenient for me to work out of my room while you need the office."

"I see." He towered menacingly over her desk, making her feel small and insignificant. "Darla tells me you two had quite a session yesterday in the lounge."

B.J.'s mouth opened in surprise. She could not believe Darla would have disclosed her own behavior so readily.

"I warned you, B.J., that as long as Darla is a guest at the inn, you're to treat her with the same courtesy you show all other guests."

B.J. was astonished. "I'm sorry, Taylor, perhaps I'm dim. Would you mind explaining that?"

"She told me you were inexcusably rude, that you made some comments on her relationship with me, refused to serve her a drink, made yourself generally unpleasant, and told the staff not to cooperate with her."

"She said that, did she?" B.J.'s eyes darkened with rage. She set her pen down carefully and rose despite Taylor's proximity. "Isn't it odd how two people can view the same scene from entirely different perspectives! Well." She stuck her hand in her pockets and planted her feet firmly. "I have news for you—"

"If you've another version," Taylor returned evenly, "I'd like to hear it."

"Oh!" Unable to prevent herself, she lifted her fist to give his chest a small, inadequate punch. His eyes dropped to it in amused indulgence. "How generous of you. The condemned man is given a fair trial." Whirling, she paced the room in a swirl of agitation, debating whether to give him a verbatim account of her meeting with Darla. Finally, her pride won over her desire to clear herself in Taylor's eyes. "No thanks, your honor. I'll just take the fifth."

"B.J." Taylor took her shoulders and spun her to face him. "Must you constantly provoke me?"

"Must you constantly pick on me?" she countered.

"I wouldn't have said I was doing that." His tone had changed from anger to consideration.

"That's your opinion. I'm the one who's constantly in the position of justifying myself. I'm tired of having to explain my every move, of trying to cope with your moods. I never know from one minute to the next if you're going to kiss me or sit me in the corner with a dunce hat. I'm tired of feeling inadequate, naive and stupid. I never felt like any of those things before, and I don't like it."

Her words tumbled out in a furious rush while Taylor merely looked on, politely attentive.

"And I'm sick of your precious Darla altogether. Sick of her criticizing every aspect of the inn, sick of her looking at me as though I were some straw-chewing hick from Dogpatch. And, I resent her running to you with fabricated stories, and, I detest your using me to boost your over-inflated ego while she's floating around half naked waiting to warm your bed. And… Oh, blast!"

Her torrent of complaints was interrupted by the shrill ringing of the phone. Ripping the receiver from its cradle, B.J. snapped into it.

"What is it? No, nothing's wrong. What is it, Eddie?" Pausing, she listened, her hand lifting to soothe the back of her neck where tension lodged. "Yes, he's here." She turned back to Taylor and held out the phone. "It's for you, a Mr. Paul Bailey."

He took the receiver in silence, his eyes still on her face. As she turned to leave the room, his hand caught her wrist. "Stay here." Waiting for her nod of agreement, he released her. B.J. moved to the far side of the room and stared out at the insistent rain.

Taylor's conversation consisted of monosyllabic replies which B.J. blocked from her mind. Frustrated by the inability to complete her outburst, she now felt the impetus fading. Just as well, she admitted with a sigh of weary resignation. I've already said enough to insure the job at that dog kennel Darla mentioned. Blast! She rested her forehead on the cool glass. Why did I have to fall in love with an impossible man?

"B.J." She started at the sound of her name, then twisted her head to watch Taylor cradle the phone. "Pack," he said simply and moved to the door.

Closing her eyes, she tried to tell herself it was better

that she leave, better not to be connected with him even as an employee. Nodding mutely, she turned back to the window.

"Enough for three days," he added in afterthought as his hand closed over the knob.

"What?" Thrown into confusion, she turned, staring with a mixture of grief and bewilderment.

"We'll be gone for three days. Be ready in fifteen minutes." Halting, Taylor's features softened suddenly at her clouded expression. "B.J., I'm not firing you. Give me credit for a bit more class than that."

She shook her head, washed with relief and the knowledge of the inevitable. He started to cross the room, then paused and merely leaned against the closed door.

"That was a call from the manager of one of my resorts. There's a bit of a problem, and I've got to see to it. You're coming with me."

"Coming with you?" Her fingers lifted to her temple as if she could smooth in understanding. "What on earth for?"

"In the first place, because I say so." He folded his arms across his chest and became the complete employer. "And secondly, because I like my managers well rounded. No pun intended," he added, smiling as her color rose. "This is a good opportunity for you to see how my other hotels are run."

"But I can't just leave at a moment's notice," she objected, as her mind struggled to cope with the new development. "Who'll take care of things here?"

"Eddie will. It's about time he had a bit more responsibility. You let him lean on you too much. You let all of them lean on you too much."

"But we have five new reservations over the weekend, and…"

"You're down to ten minutes, B.J.," he informed her with a glance at his watch. "If you don't stop arguing, you'll only have the clothes on your back to take with you."

Seeing all of her objections would be overruled, she tried not to think of what going away with Taylor would do to her nervous system. *Business,* she reminded herself. *Just business.*

Somewhat annoyed that he was already walking through the door, having taken it for granted that she was going with him, she called after him, "I can't simply pack because you say to."

He turned back, his temper fraying. "B.J."

"You never said where," she reminded him. "I don't know if I need mukluks or bikinis."

A ghost of a smile played on his lips before he answered. "Bikinis. We're going to Palm Beach."

B.J. was to find her surprises were not yet over for the morning. First, her last minute flurry of instructions was cut off by Taylor's order as she was bundled out of the dripping rain and into his car. On the drive to the airport, she mentally reviewed every possible disaster which could occur during her absence. She opened her mouth to enlighten Taylor only to be given a quelling look which had her suffering in silence.

At the airport, she found herself confronted not with a commercial jet, but with Taylor's private one, already primed for take-off. B.J. stood motionless staring at the small trim plane as he retrieved their luggage.

"B.J., don't stand in the rain. Go on up."

"Taylor." Unmindful of the rain which pelted her, B.J. turned to him. "I think there's something you should know. I'm not very good at flying."

"That's all right." He secured cases under his arm and grabbed her hand. "The plane does most of the work."

"Taylor, I'm serious," she objected, as he dragged her inside the plane.

"Do you get air sick? You can take a pill."

"No." She swallowed and lifted her shoulders. "I get paralyzed. Stewardesses have been known to stow me in the baggage compartment so I don't panic the other passengers."

He rubbed his hands briskly through her hair, scattering rain drops. "So, I've found your weakness. What are you afraid of?"

"Mostly of crashing."

"It's all in your head," he said easily as he helped her off with her jacket. "There's a term for it."

"Dying," she supplied, causing him to laugh again. Miffed by his amusement, she turned away to examine the plush luxury of the cabin. "This looks more like an apartment than a plane." She ran a hand over the soft maroon of a chair. "Everyone's entitled to a phobia," she muttered.

"You're absolutely right." His voice trembled on the edge of laughter. B.J. turned to snap at him but found his smile too appealing.

"You won't think it's so funny when I'm lying in a moaning heap on your shag carpet."

"Possibly not." He moved toward her and she stiffened in defense. Brooding down at her a moment, he searched her wary gray eyes. "B.J.," he began, "shall we call a moratorium on our disagreements? At least for the duration of the trip?"

"Well, I…" His voice was soft and persuasive, and she lowered her eyes to study the buttons of his shirt.

"An armed truce?" he suggested, capturing her chin between his thumb and forefinger and lifting her face. "With negotiations to follow?" He was smiling, his charming, utterly disarming smile. She knew resistance was hopeless.

"All right, Taylor." Unable to prevent her own smile from blossoming, she remained still as his finger lifted to trace it.

"Sit down and fasten your seat belt." He kissed her brow with an easy friendliness which left her weak.

B.J. found that the easy flow of his conversation from the moment of take off eased her tension. Incredibly, she felt no fear as the plane soared into the air.

"It's so flat and so warm!" B.J. exclaimed as she stepped off the plane steps and looked around her.

Taylor chuckled as he led the way to a sleek black Porsche. He exchanged a few words with a waiting attendant, accepted the keys, unlocked the door, and motioned B.J. inside.

"Where is your hotel?" she asked.

"In Palm Beach. This is West Palm Beach. We have to cross Lake Worth to get to the island."

"Oh!" Enchanted by roadside palms, she lapsed into silence.

The white, sandy soil and splashes of brilliant blossoms were so far removed from the scenery of her native New England, she felt as though she had entered another world. The waters of Lake Worth, separating Palm Beach from the mainland, sparkled blue and white under the afternoon sun. The oceanside was lined with resort hotels. B.J. recognized the elaborate initials *T.R.* atop a sleek white building which rose twelve stories over the Atlantic. Hundreds of windows winked back at her. Taylor pulled into the semi-circular macadam drive and stopped the car. B.J. narrowed her eyes against the streaming rays of the sun. The archway which formed the entrance was guarded by palms and semi-tropical plants, their tangle of color obviously well planned and scrupulously tended. The lawn spread, perfectly level and unbelievably green.

"Come," said Taylor, coming around to open the door for her. He helped her out of the car and led her inside.

To B.J. the lobby was a tropical paradise. The floor was flagstoned, the walls a half-circle of windows at the front. A center fountain played over a rocky garden, dotted with lush plants and ferns. B.J. saw that the interior was round, an open circle spiraling to the ceiling where a mural emulating the sky had been painted. The effect was one of limitless space. *How different from the cozy familiarity of the Lakeside Inn!* she thought.

"Ah, Mr. Reynolds." Her meditation was interrupted by the appearance of a slender, well dressed man with a shock of steel gray hair and a lean, bronzed face. "So good to see you."

"Paul." Taylor accepted the proffered hand and returned the smile of greeting. "B.J., this is Paul Bailey, the manager. Paul, B.J. Clark."

"A pleasure, Miss Clark." B.J.'s hand was engulfed by a smooth, warm grasp. His eyes surveyed her fresh, slender beauty with approval. She found herself smiling back.

"See to our bags and I'll take Miss Clark up. After we've settled in a bit, I'll get back to you."

"Of course. Everything's quite ready." With another flash of teeth, he led the way to the registration desk and secured a key. "Your bags will be right up, Mr. Reynolds. Is there anything else you'd like?"

"Not at the moment. B.J.?"

"What?" B.J. was still admiring the luxurious lobby.

"Would you like anything?" Taylor smiled at her and brushed a curl from her cheek.

"Oh…no, nothing. Thank you."

With a final nod for Bailey, Taylor secured her hand in his and led her to one of the three elevators. They glided up in a cage of octagon glass high above the cluster of greenery.

When they reached the top floor, Taylor moved along the thick carpeting to unlock the door. B.J. entered and crossing the silent plush of ivory carpet, stared down from the dizzying height at the white beach which jutted out into an azure span of sea. In the distance, she could see the churning whitecaps and the flowing grace of gulls as they circled and dove.

"What an incredible view. I'm tempted to dive straight off the balcony." Turning, she caught Taylor watching her from the center of the room. She could not decipher the expression in his eyes. "This is lovely," she said to break the long silence.

She ran a finger over the smooth surface of an ebony bar and wondered if Darla had decorated the room. Grudgingly, she admitted to herself if this were the case, Darla had done a good job.

"Would you like a drink?" Taylor pushed a button

cunningly concealed in the mirror tiles on the wall behind the bar. A panel slid open to reveal a fully stocked bar.

"Very clever," B.J. smiled. "Some club soda would be nice," she said, leaning elbows on the bar.

"Nothing stronger?" he asked as he poured the soda over crackling ice. "Come in," he responded to the quiet knock on the door.

"Your luggage, Mr. Reynolds." A red-and-black-uniformed bellboy carried in the cases. B.J. was conscious of his curious gaze and blushed self-consciously.

"Fine, just leave them there." He accepted the tip from Taylor and vanished, closing the door with quiet respect.

B.J. eyed the cases. Taylor's elegant gray sat neatly beside her practical brown. "Why did he bring it all in here?" Setting down her glass, she lifted her eyes. "Shouldn't he have just taken mine to my room?"

"He did." Taylor secured another bottle and poured himself a portion of Scotch.

"But, I thought this was your suite." B.J. glanced around the luxurious room again.

"It is."

"But you just said…" She faltered, as her color rose. "Surely you don't think I'm going to—to…"

"What did you have in mind?" Taylor inquired with infuriating amusement.

"You said you wanted me to see how one of your

other hotels was run, you never said anything about... about..."

"You really must learn to complete a sentence, B.J."

"I'm not sleeping with you," she stated very positively, her eyes like two summer storm clouds.

"I don't believe I asked you to," he said lazily before he took an easy sip of Scotch. "There are two very adequate bedrooms in this suite. I'm sure you'll find yours comfortable."

Embarrassment flooded her cheeks. "I'm not staying in here with you. Everyone will think that I'm...that we're..."

"I've never known you to be quite so coherent." His mockery increased her wrath, and her eyes narrowed to dangerous slits. "In any case," he continued unperturbed, "the purity of your reputation is already in question. As you're traveling with me, it will naturally be assumed that we're lovers. As we know differently," he went on as her mouth dropped open, "that hardly matters. Of course, if you'd like to make rumor fact, I might be persuaded."

"Oh, you insufferable, egotistical, conceited..."

"Name calling can hardly be considered persuasion," Taylor admonished, patting her head in an infuriating manner. "I assume, therefore, you'll want your own bedroom?"

"As this is off season," B.J. began, gaining a tenuous

grip on her temper, "I'm sure there are a surplus of available rooms."

Smiling, he ran a finger down her arm. "Afraid you won't be able to resist temptation, B.J.?"

"Of course not," she said though her senses tingled at his touch.

"Then that's settled," he said, finishing off his drink. "If you're harboring the notion that I'll be overcome by lust, there's a perfectly sturdy lock on your bedroom door. I'm going down to see Bailey; why don't you change and grab some time at the beach? Your room's the second door on your left down the hall." He pointed as he moved to the door and slipped through before she had time to frame a response.

Before lifting her case and beginning to unpack, B.J. thought of at least a half a dozen withering remarks she should have made. However, she soon regained her sense of proportion.

After all, it wasn't every day that she had the opportunity to indulge in such luxury. She might as well enjoy it. Besides, the suite was certainly large enough for both of them.

Slipping into brief tan shorts and a lime green halter, B.J. decided to finish her unpacking later and head for the beach.

Taylor had certainly made the most of nature's gift, offering a luxury playground with an ocean and sky backdrop. B.J. had seen the huge mosaic tiled pool for those who preferred its filtered water to the sea. On her way to the beach, she glimpsed at the expanse of tennis courts with palms and flowering shrubs skirting about the entrance gate. She had seen enough of the hotel's interior to be certain that Taylor left his guests wanting for nothing.

From the beach B.J. shaded her eyes and studied again the perfection of the imposing resort. It was, she admitted with a sigh, elegantly appealing. As far out of her realm as its owner. *Egg noodles and caviar,* she thought ruefully, reflecting both on the comparison between inn and resort and Taylor and herself. They simply don't belong on the same plate.

"Hello."

Startled, B.J. turned, blinked against the brilliant sun and stared at an even white smile in a bronzed face.

"Hello." Returning the smile with a bit more caution, B.J. studied the attractive face surrounded by thick masses of light, sun bleached hair.

"Aren't you going to give the ocean a try?"

"Not today."

"That's very unusual." He fell into step beside her as she began to cross the sand. "Usually everyone spends their first day roasting and splashing."

"How did you know it was my first day?" B.J. asked.

"Because I haven't noticed you here before, and I would have." He gave her an encompassing and intensely male survey. "And because you're still peaches and cream instead of parboiled."

"Hardly the time of year," B.J. commented, admiring the deep, even tan as he shrugged on his shirt. "I'd say you've been here for some time."

"Two years," he returned, with an appealing grin. "I'm the tennis pro, Chad Hardy."

"B.J. Clark." She paused on the tiled walkway which led to the hotel's beach entrance. "How come you're on the beach instead of the courts?"

"My day off," he explained and surprised her by winding the tips of her hair around his finger. "But if you'd like a private lesson, it could be arranged."

"No, thanks," she declined lightly and turned again toward the door.

"How about dinner?" Chad captured her hand, gently but insistently bringing her back to face him.

"I don't think so."

"A drink?"

She smiled at his persistence. "No, sorry, it's a bit early."

"I'll wait."

Laughing, she shook her head and disengaged her hand. "No, but I appreciate the offer. Goodbye, Mr. Hardy."

"Chad." He moved with her through the archway into the hotel's coolness. "What about tomorrow? Breakfast, lunch, a weekend in Vegas?"

B.J. laughed; such ingenuous charm was hard to resist. "I don't think you'll have any trouble finding a companion."

"I'm having a great deal of trouble securing the one I want," he countered. "If you had any compassion, you'd take pity on me."

With a rueful smile, B.J. surrendered. "All right, I wouldn't mind an orange juice."

In short order, B.J. found herself seated at an umbrella table beside the pool.

"It's not really that early," Chad objected when she adhered to her choice of fruit juice. "Most of the crowd is straggling in to wash off the sand and change for dinner."

"This hits the spot." She sipped from the frosted glass. Then, gesturing with one slender hand, she glanced around at green fan palms and scarlet blooms. "You must find it easy to work here."

"It suits me," Chad agreed, swirling his own drink. "I like the work, the sun." He lifted his glass and smiled with the half toast. "And the benefits." His smile widened. Before she had the opportunity to draw them away, his hand captured her fingers. "How long will you be here?"

"A couple of days." She let her hand lie limp, feeling a struggle would make her appear foolish. "This was actually a spur-of-the-moment trip rather than a vacation."

"Then I'll drink to spur-of-the-moment trip," said Chad.

The friendly, polished charm was potent, and B.J. could not resist beaming him a smile. "Is that your best serve?"

"Just a warm-up." Returning the smile, his grip on her hand tightened slightly. "Watch out for my ace."

"B.J."

Twisting her head, she stared up at Taylor, frowning above her. "Hello, Taylor. Are you finished with Mr. Bailey?"

"For the moment." His glance shifted to Chad, drifted over their joined hands and returned to her face. "I've been looking for you."

"Oh?" Feeling unaccountably guilty, B.J. nibbled her lip in a tell-tale sign of agitation. "I'm sorry, this is Chad Hardy," she began.

"Yes, I know. Hello, Hardy."

"Mr. Reynolds," Chad returned with a polite nod. "I didn't know you were in the hotel."

"For a day or two. When you've finished," he continued, giving B.J. the full benefit of a cold disapproving stare, "I suggest you come up and change for dinner. I don't think that outfit's suitable for the dining room." With a curt nod, he turned on his heel and stalked away.

"Well, well." Releasing her hand, Chad leaned back in his chair and studied B.J. with new interest. "You might have told me you were the big man's lady. I'm rather fond of my job here."

Her mouth opened and closed twice. "I am not Taylor's lady," B.J. spurted on her third try.

Chad's lips twisted in a wry grin. "You'd better tell him that. A pity." He sighed with exaggerated regret. "I was working on some interesting fantasies, but I steer clear of treading on dangerous ground."

Standing, he lifted her chin and gave her a rather wistful smile. "If you find yourself down here again without complications, look me up."

10

The emphatic slamming of the suite's door gave B.J. small satisfaction. Advancing with purpose on Taylor's bedroom, she pounded on his door.

"Looking for me?" The voice was dry.

She whirled around. For a moment, she could only gape at the sight of Taylor leaning against the bathroom door, clad only in a dark green towel tied low over lean hips. His hair fell in tendrils over the lean planes of his face.

"Yes, I…" She faltered and swallowed. "Yes," she repeated with more firmness as she recalled Chad's comments. "That was an uncalled for exhibition out there. You deliberately left Chad with the impression that I was your…" She hesitated, eyes darkening with outraged impotence, as she searched for the right word.

"Mistress?" Taylor suggested amiably.

B.J.'s pupils dilated with fury. "He at least used the term lady." Forgetting the corded arms and dark mat of hair covering his chest, she stalked forward until she stood toe to toe. "You did it on purpose, and I won't tolerate it."

"Oh, really?" Had she not been so involved venting her own anger, B.J. might have recognized the dangerous pitch of his voice. "It appears by the speed with which Hardy lured you into his corner, you're remarkably easy prey. I feel it's my obligation to look out for you."

"Find someone else to protect," she retorted. "I'm not putting up with it."

"Just what do you intend to do about it?" The simple arrogance of the question was accompanied by a like smile which robbed B.J. of all coherency. "If giving Hardy and others of his type the impression that you're my property keeps you from making a fool of yourself, that's precisely what I'll do. Actually," he continued, "you should be grateful."

"*Grateful?*" B.J. repeated, her voice rising. "Your property? *A fool of myself?* Of all the arrogant, unspeakable gall!"

Her arm pulled back with the intention of connecting her fist with his midsection, but she found it twisted behind her back with astonishing speed. Her body was crushed against the hard undraped lines of his.

"I wouldn't try that again." The warning was soft. "You wouldn't like the consequences." His free hand lowered to her hip, bringing her closer as she tried to back away. "Don't do that," he ordered, holding her still and trapped against him. "You'll just hurt yourself. It seems we've broken our truce." His words were light, though she saw the signs of lingering temper in his eyes.

"You started it." Her declaration was half-defiant, half-defensive. She kept her eyes level with sheer determination.

"Did I?" he murmured before he took her mouth.

She was washed by the familiar flood of need. Offering no struggle, she went willingly into the uncharted world where only the senses ruled. His hand released her arm in order to roam over the bareness of her back, and she circled his neck, wanting only to remain in the drifting heat and velvet darkness.

Abruptly, he set her free. She stumbled back against the wall, thrown off balance by the swiftness of her liberation.

"Go change." He turned and gripped the knob of his door.

B.J. reached out to touch his arm.

"Taylor…"

"Go change!" he shouted. She stumbled back again, eyes round and wide at the swift flare of violence. He slammed the door behind him.

B.J. retreated to her room to sort out her feelings. Was it injured pride? Or was it rage? She could not for the life of her tell.

★ ★ ★

The early sky lightened slowly from black to misty blue. The stars faded, then died as the sun still lay hidden beneath the horizon. B.J. rose, grateful the restless night was behind her.

She had shared an uncomfortably polite dinner with Taylor, the elegance of the dining room only adding to the sensation that she had stood aside and watched two strangers go through the motions of dining. Taylor's solicitous and unfamiliar formality had disturbed her more than his sudden seething fury. Her own responses had been stilted and cool. Immediately after dinner she pleaded fatigue and crept off unescorted to pass the evening hours alone and miserably awake in her room.

It had been late when she had heard Taylor's key in the lock, his footsteps striding down the hall to pause outside her room. She had held her breath as if he might sense her wakefulness through the panel. Not until she had heard the muffled sound of his door closing had she let it out again.

B.J. felt no better the next morning. The events of the day before had left her with a lingering sense of loss and sorrow. Though she knew that there was little hope, she had finally acknowledged to herself that she was in love with Taylor. But there was no point thinking about it.

She slipped on her bikini, grabbed a terry robe, and tiptoed from her room.

The view from the wide window in the living room drew her. With a sigh of pleasure, she moved closer to watch the birth of day. The sun had tinted the edge of sea and sky with rose-gold streaks. Pinks and mauves shot through the dawning sky.

"Quite a view."

With a gasp, B.J. spun around, nearly colliding with Taylor whose footsteps had been hidden by the thickness of carpet. "Yes," she returned as their hands lifted simultaneously to brush back the fall of her hair which tumbled to her cheek. "There's nothing so beautiful as a sunrise." Disturbed by his closeness, she found her own words silly.

He was clad only in short denim cut-offs, frayed at the cuffs.

"How did you sleep?" His voice was politely concerned.

She shrugged off his question, evading a direct lie. "I thought I'd take an early swim before the beach gets crowded."

Deliberately, he turned her to face him, while he searched her face with habitual thoroughness. "Your eyes are shadowed." His finger traced the mauve smudges as a frown deepened the angles of his face. "I don't believe I've ever seen you look tired before. You seem to have some inner vitality that continually feeds itself. You look pale and fragile, quite unlike the pigtailed brat I watched sliding into home plate."

His touch was radiating the weakness through her so she stepped back in defense. "I…It's just the first night in a strange bed."

"Is it?" His brow lifted. "You're a generous creature, B.J. You don't even expect an apology, do you?"

Charmed by his smile, her weariness evaporated. "Taylor, I want…I'd like it if we could be friends." She finished in an impulsive rush.

"Friends?" he repeated as the sudden boyish grin split his face. "Oh, B.J., you're sweet, if a bit slow." Taking both hands in his, he lifted them to his lips before speaking again. "All right, friend, let's go for a swim."

But for gulls, the beach was deserted, a stretch of white pure and welcoming. The air already glowed with the promise of heat and light. B.J. stopped and gazed around, pleased with the quiet and the solitude.

"It's like everyone went away."

"You're not much for crowds, are you, B.J.?"

"No, I suppose not." She turned to him with a lift of bare shoulders. "I enjoy people, but more on a one to one level. When I'm around people, I like to know who they are, what they need. I'm good with small problems. I can shore up a brick here, hammer a nail there. I don't think I'm equipped to construct an entire building the way you are."

"One can't keep a building standing without someone shoring up bricks and hammering nails."

She smiled, so obviously pleased and surprised by his observation that he laughed and tousled her hair. "I'll race you to the water."

Giving him a considering look, B.J. shook her head in reluctance. "You're a lot taller than I am. You have an advantage."

"You forget, I've seen you run. And—" His eyes dropped to the length of shapely legs. "For a small woman, you have amazingly long legs."

"Well." She drew the word out, lips pursed. "O.K." Without waiting for his assent, she streaked across the sand and plunged into the sea, striking out with long strokes.

She was brought up short by hands on her waist. Laughing, she struggled away, only to be caught and submerged in the ensuing tussle.

"Taylor, you're going to drown me," she protested as her legs tangled with his.

"That is not my intention," he informed her as he drew her closer. "Hold still a minute or you'll take yourself under again."

Relaxing in his hold, B.J. allowed him to keep them both afloat. She permitted herself a few moments of ecstasy cradled in his arms as the water pooled around them like a cool satin blanket. The change began like a gradual drizzle as she became more aware of his shoulder beneath her cheek, the possessive hold of the arm which banded her bare waist. Powerless to resist, she floated with him

as his lips descended to the sleek cap of her hair, then
wandered to tease the lobe of her ear with tongue and
teeth before moving to the curve of her neck. His fingers
traced the low line of the bikini snug at her hips as his
mouth roamed her cheek in its journey to hers.

Her lips parted before he requested it, but his kiss remained gentle, the passion simmering just below the surface. His hand touched and fondled, slipping easily under
the barrier of her brief top to trail over the curve of her
breast. The water sighed gently as flesh met flesh.

What with gentle caresses, the drifting buoyancy of
the sea, and the growing heat of the ascending sun B.J.
fell into a trancelike state. Perhaps, she thought, mind
and limbs lethargic, she was meant to float forever in his
arms. She shivered with pleasure.

"You're getting cold," Taylor murmured, drawing
her away to study her face. "Come on." He released
her, leaving her without support in the sighing sea. The
magic shattered. "We'll sit in the sun."

B.J. started for the shore with Taylor swimming easily
beside her.

On the beach, she fanned her hair in the sun while
Taylor stretched negligently beside her. She tried not to
look at the strong planes of his face, his bronzed, glisten-
ing skin.

He told me how it would be, she reminded herself.
Right from the beginning. I don't seem to be able to do
anything about it and if I don't, I'll end up being just

another Darla in his life. Bringing her knees to her chest, she rested her chin on them and stared at the distant horizon. *He's attracted to me for some reason, perhaps because I'm different from other women in his life. I haven't their sophistication or experience and I suppose he finds that appealing and amusing. I don't know how to fight both loving him and wanting him. If it were just physical, I could avoid being hurt. If it were only an attraction, I could resist him.*

She recalled suddenly his quick violence of the previous day and realized he was a man capable of employing whatever means necessary to gain an objective. At the moment, she knew he was playing her like a patient fisherman casting his line into calm waters. But ultimately, they both knew she would be captured in his net. Though it might be silk, it would still lead to eventual disaster.

"You're very far away." Sitting up, Taylor tangled his fingers in her damp hair and turned her to face him.

Silently, she studied every plane and angle of his face, engraving them on both heart and mind. *There is too much strength there,* she thought, rocked by a surge of love. Too much virility, too much knowledge. She scrambled to her feet, needing to postpone the inevitable.

"I'm starving," she claimed. "Are you going to spring for breakfast? After all, I did win the race."

"Did you?" He rose as she pulled the short robe over the briefness of her bikini.

"Yes," she said, "positively." Picking up Taylor's light blue pullover, she held it out. "I was the undisputed winner." She watched as he dragged the snug, crew necked shirt over his head then bent to retrieve the towels.

"Then you should buy my breakfast." Smiling, he held out his hand. After a brief hesitation, she accepted.

"How do you feel about corn flakes?"

"Unenthusiastic."

"Well." Her shoulders moved in regret. "I'm afraid my funds are rather limited as I was hauled to Florida without ceremony."

"Your credit's good." He released her hand and swung a friendly arm around her shoulders. They moved away from the sea.

By mid afternoon, B.J. felt euphoric. There was a new, charming friendliness about Taylor that made her realize she liked him every bit as much as she loved him.

She was given a thorough if belated tour of the hotel, allowed to wander through the silver and cobalt lounge, linger in the two elegantly stocked boutiques and examine the enormous expanse of the steel and white kitchen. In the game room, she was provided with an endless supply of change as Taylor watched her reckless enthusiasm with tolerance.

Leaning against a machine, he looked on as she steered her computer car to another horrendous wreck. "You know," he commented as she held her hand for another quarter, "by the time you've finished, you'll have spent every bit as much as that dress in the boutique cost. Why is it, you'll take the money for these noisy machines, but you refuse to let me buy you that very appealing dress?"

"This is different," she said vaguely, maneuvering the car around obstructions.

"How?" He grimaced as she narrowly missed an unwary pedestrian and skidded around a corner.

"You never said if you worked out the problem," B.J. murmured as she twisted the wheel to avoid a slow moving vehicle.

"Problem?"

"Yes, the one you came down here to see to."

"Oh, yes." He smiled and brushed an insistent wisp from her cheek. "It's working out nicely."

"Oh, blast!" B.J. frowned as her car careened into a telephone pole, flipped through the air and landed with an impressive show of computer color and sound.

"Come on." Taylor grabbed her hand as she looked up hopefully. "Let's have some lunch before I go bankrupt."

On the sundeck above the pool, they enjoyed quiche Lorraine and Chablis. A handful of people splashed and romped in the pale blue water. Toying with the remains of her meal, B.J. stared down at the swimmers and sun bathers. Her gaze swept to include the curve of beach before returning to Taylor. He was watching her, a small secret smile on his lips and in his eyes. She blinked in confused embarrassment.

"Is something wrong?" Battling the urge to wipe her cheek to see if it was smudged, she lifted her glass and sipped the cool wine.

"No, I just enjoy looking at you. Your eyes are constantly changing hues. One minute they're like peat smoke, and the next clear as a lake. You'll never be able to keep secrets; they say too much." His smile spread as her color rose. Her eyes shifted to the golden lights in her glass. "You're an incredibly beautiful creature, B.J."

She lifted her head, her eyes wide in surprise.

With a light chuckle, he captured her hand and brought it to his lips. "I don't suppose I should tell you that too often. You'll begin to see how true it is and lose that appealing air of innocence."

Rising, he maintained possession of her hand, pulling her to her feet. "I'm going to take you to the Health Club. You can get a first hand impression of how this place works."

"All right, but..."

"I'm leaving instructions that you're to have the complete routine," he interrupted. "And when I meet you at seven for dinner, I don't want to see any shadows under your eyes."

Transferred from Taylor's authority to a perfectly shaped brunette, B.J. was whirlpooled, saunaed, pummeled and massaged. For three hours, she was alternately steamed and sprayed, plied with iced fruit juice and submerged in churning water. Her first instinct was to retrieve her clothes and quietly slip out. After finding they had been conveniently cached out of sight, she submitted, and soon found tensions she had been unaware of possessing seeping out of her.

Stomach down on a high table, she sighed under the magic hands of the masseuse and allowed her mind to float in the twilight world of half sleep. Dimly, the conversation of two women enjoying the same wonder drifted across to her.

"I happened to be staying here two years ago...so incredibly handsome...what a marvelous catch...All that lovely money as well...The Reynolds empire."

At Taylor's name, B.J.'s eyes opened and her inadvertent eavesdropping became deliberate.

"It's a wonder some smart woman hasn't snagged him yet." An auburn haired woman tucked a bright strand behind her ear and folded her arms under her chin.

"Darling, you can be sure scores have tried." Her brunette companion stifled a yawn and smiled with wry humor. "I don't imagine he's averse to the chase. A man like that thrives on feminine adulation."

"He's got mine."

"Did you see his companion? I caught a glimpse last night and again today by the pool."

"Mmm, I saw them when they arrived, but I was too

busy looking at him to take much notice. A blonde, wasn't she?"

"Um-hum, though I don't think that pale wheat shade was a gift of nature."

B.J.'s first surge of outrage was almost immediately replaced by amusement. So, she decided, if I'm to be Taylor's temporary, if fictional mistress, I might as well hear the opinion of the masses.

"Do you think this one will get her hooks in? Who is she anyway?"

"That's precisely what I attempted to find out." The brunette grimaced and mirrored her companion's position of chin on arms. "It cost me twenty dollars to learn her name is B.J. Clark of all things. Beyond that, not even dear Paul Bailey knows anything. She just popped up out of the blue. She's never been here before. As for getting her hooks in." Elegantly tanned shoulders shrugged. "I wouldn't bet either way. His eyes simply devour her; it's enough to make you drool with envy."

B.J. raised a skeptical eyebrow.

"I suppose," the brunette went on, "huge gray eyes and masses of blond hair are appealing. And she is rather attractive in a wholesome, peaches and cream sort of way."

B.J. rose on her elbows and smiled across the room. "Thank you," she said simply, then lowered her head and grinned into the ensuing silence.

11

Refreshed and pleased with herself, B.J. entered Taylor's suite, carrying a dress box under her arm. Though she had lost the minor tussle with the sales clerk in the boutique, she remained in high spirits. After her session in the spa, she had returned to the shop. Pointing to the gown of silver silk which Taylor had admired, she was prepared to surrender a large hunk of her bank account only to be told Mr. Reynolds had left instructions that any purchases she made were to be billed to him.

Annoyed by his arrogance, however generous, B.J. had argued with the implacable salesgirl. Ultimately, she had left the shop with the dress in hand vowing to see to the monetary details later.

If, she decided, pouring a substantial stream of bath salts under the rushing water of the tub, she was to portray the image of the mysterious lady from nowhere she was going to dress the part. She lowered herself into hot, frothy water and had just begun to relax when the door swung open.

"So, you're back," Taylor said easily, leaning against the door, "Did you enjoy yourself?"

"Taylor!" B.J. slid down in the tub, attempting to cover herself with the blanket of bubbles. "I'm having a bath!"

"Yes. I can see that, and little else. There's no need to drown yourself. Would you like a drink?" The question was pleasant and impersonal.

Recalling the overheard conversation in the spa, B.J.'s pride rallied. It's time, she decided, to give him back a bit of his own.

"That would be lovely." Fluttering her lashes, she hoped her expression was unconcerned. "Some sherry would be nice, if it's no bother."

Watching his brow lift in surprise, B.J. felt decidedly smug. "It's no trouble," he said as he retreated, leaving the door ajar. She prayed fervently the bubbles would not burst until she had a chance to leave the tub and slip into her robe.

"Here you are." Reentering, Taylor handed her a small glass shimmering with golden liquid.

B.J. gave him a smile and sipped. "Thanks. I'll be finished soon if you want the bath."

"Don't rush," he returned, delighted to see her coolness had somewhat rattled him, "I'll use the other."

"Suit yourself," she said agreeably, making sure her
shrug was mild and did little to disturb her peaceful
waters. Relieved that the door closed behind him, B.J.
expelled a long breath and set the remains of her drink on
the edge of the tub.

For a full five minutes, B.J. stared at her reflection in
the full-length mirror. Silver silk draped crossways over
the curve of each breast, narrowing to thin straps over
her shoulders before continuing down her sides to leave
her back bare to the waist. The skirt fell straight over her
slender hips and legs, one side slit to mid-thigh. She had
piled her hair in a loose knot on top of her head, allowing a few curling tendrils to escape and frame her face.

B.J. found the stranger in the mirror intimidating.
With a flash of intuition, she knew B.J. Clark could not
live up to the promises hinted at by the woman in the
glass.

"Almost ready?" Taylor's knock and question jolted
her out of her reverie.

"Yes, just coming." Shaking her head, she gave the
reflection a reassuring smile. "It's just a dress," she reminded both B.J. Clarks and turned from the mirror.

Taylor's hand paused midway in the action of pouring pre-dinner drinks. He lifted his cigarette to his lips,

inhaling slowly as he surveyed B.J.'s entrance. "Well," he said as she hesitated, "I see you bought it after all."

"Yes." With a surge of confidence, she crossed the room to join him. "As a woman of ill fame I felt my wardrobe inadequate."

"Care to elaborate?" He handed B.J. a delicate glass.

She accepted automatically. "Just a conversation I overheard in the spa." Her eyes lit with amusement, she set her glass on the bar. "Oh, Taylor, it was funny. I'm sure you have no idea how ardently your...ah...affairs are monitored." Describing her afternoon at the spa, she was unable to suppress her giggles.

"I can't tell you how it boosts the ego to be envied and touted as a woman of mystery! I certainly hope it's not discovered that I'm a hotel manager from Lakeside, Vermont. It would spoil it."

"No one would believe it anyway." He did not appear to be amused by her story as, frowning, he sipped at his drink.

Confused by his expression, B.J. asked, "Don't you like the dress after all?"

"I like it." He took her hand, the smile at last taking command of his mouth. "Obviously, we'll have to have champagne. You look much too elegant for anything else."

They began their meal with oysters Rockefeller and champagne. Their table sat high in the double level dining room, in front of a wide wall aquarium. As the London broil was served, B.J. sipped her wine and glanced around the room.

"This is a lovely place, Taylor." She gestured with a fine-boned hand to encompass the entire resort.

"It does the job." He spoke with the smooth confidence of one who knew the worth of his possessions.

"Yes, it certainly does. It runs beautifully. The staff is efficient and discreet, almost to the point of being invisible. You hardly know they're there, yet everything's perfect. I suppose it's elbow to elbow in here during the winter."

With a movement of his shoulders, he followed her gaze. "I try to avoid hitting the resorts during the heavy season."

"Our summer season will begin in a few weeks," she began, only to find her hand captured and her glass replenished with champagne.

"I've managed to keep you from bringing up the inn all day; let's see if we can finish the evening without it. When we get back tomorrow, we can talk about vacancies and cancellations. I don't discuss business when I'm having dinner with a beautiful woman."

B.J. smiled and surrendered. If only one evening remained of the interlude, she wanted to savor each moment.

"What do you discuss over dinner with a beautiful woman?" she countered, buoyed by the wine.

"More personal matters." His finger traced the back

of her hand. "The way her voice flows like an easy river, the way her smile touches her eyes before it moves her mouth, the way her skin warms under my hand." With a low laugh, he lifted her hand, lips brushing the inside of her wrist.

Glancing up warily, B.J. asked, "Taylor, are you making fun of me?"

"No." His voice was gentle. "I have no intention of making fun of you, B.J."

Satisfied with his answer, she smiled and allowed him to lead the conversation into a lighter vein.

Flickering candles, the muted chink of crystal and silver, the low murmur of voices, Taylor's eyes meeting hers—it was an evening B.J. knew she would always remember.

"Let's go for a walk." Taylor rose and pulled back her chair. "Before you fall asleep in your champagne." Hand in hand they walked to the beach.

They walked in silence, enjoying each other and the night. Merging with the aroma of the sea and the night was the tenuous scent of orange blossoms. B.J. knew the fragrance would be forever melded with her memory of the man whose hand lay warm and firm over hers. Would she ever look at the moon again without thinking of him? Ever walk beneath the stars without remembering? Ever draw a breath without longing for him?

Tomorrow, she reflected, it would be business as usual, and a handful of days after, he would be gone. Only a name on a letterhead. Still, she would have the inn, she reminded herself. He'd said no more about changes. She'd have her home and her work and her memories, and that was much more than some ever had.

"Cold?" Taylor asked, and she shivered, afraid he had read her mind. "You're trembling." His arm slipped around her shoulders, bringing aching warmth. "We'd better go back."

Mutely, she nodded and forced tomorrows out of her mind. Relaxing, she felt the remnants of champagne mist pleasurably in her head.

"Oh, Taylor," she whispered as they crossed the lobby. "That's one of the women from the spa this afternoon." She inclined her head toward the brunette watching them with avid interest.

"Hmm." Taylor pushed the button for the glass enclosed elevator.

"Do you think I should wave?" B.J. asked before Taylor pulled her inside.

"No, I've a better idea."

Before she realized his intent, he had her gathered into his arms, silencing her protest with a mind-spinning kiss. Releasing her, he grinned down at the openly staring brunette.

B.J. turned to Taylor as the door of the suite shut behind him. "Really, Taylor, it's a crime I haven't a lurid past she could dig up."

"It's perfectly all right, she'll invent one for you. Want a brandy?" He moved to the bar and released the concealing panel.

"No, my nose is already numb."

"I see; is that a congenial condition?"

"It is," she stated, sliding onto a bar stool, "my gauge for the cautious consumption of liquor. When my nose gets numb, I've already had one more than my limit."

"I see." Turning, he poured amber liquid into a solitary snifter. "Obviously, my plans to ply you with liquor is doomed to fail."

"I'm afraid so."

"What's your weakness, B.J.?" The question was so unexpected she was caught unaware. *You,* she almost answered but caught herself in time. "I'm a pushover for soft lights and quiet music."

"Is that so?"

Magically, the lights lowered and music whispered through the room.

"How did you do that?"

He rounded the bar and stood in front of her. "There's a panel in back of the bar."

"The wonders of technology." Nerves prickling, she tensed like a cornered cat when his hand took her arm.

"I want to dance with you." He drew her to her feet. "Take the pins out of your hair. It smells like wildflowers; I want to feel it in my hands."

"Taylor, I…"

"Ssh." Slowly, he took out the pins until her hair tumbled free over her shoulders. Then, his fingers combed through the length of it before he gathered her close in his arms.

He moved gently to the music, keeping her molded against him. Her tension flowed away, replaced by a sleepy excitement. Her cheek rested naturally in the curve of his shoulder, as if they had danced countless times before, would dance countless times again.

"Are you going to tell me what B.J. stands for?" he murmured against her ear.

"No one knows," she responded hazily as his fingers followed the tingling delight along her bare skin. "Even the F.B.I. is baffled."

"I suppose I'll have to get it from your mother."

"She doesn't remember." She sighed and snuggled closer.

"How do you sign official papers?" His hand caressed the small of her back.

"Just B.J., I always use B.J."

"On a passport?"

She shrugged, her lips unconsciously brushing his neck, her cheek nuzzling the masculine roughness of his chin. "I haven't got one. I've never needed one."

"You need one to fly to Rome."

"Yes, I'll make sure I have one the next time I do. But I'd sign it Bea Jay." She grinned, knowing he would not realize she had just answered his question. She lifted her face to smile at him and found her lips captured in a gentle, teasing kiss.

"B.J.," he murmured and drew her away before her lips were satisfied. "I want…"

"Kiss me again, Taylor." Sweet and heavy, love lay on her. "Really kiss me," she whispered, shutting out the voice of reason. Her eyes fluttered closed as she urged his mouth back to hers.

He said her name again, the words soft on the lips which clung to his in silent request. With a low groan, he crushed her against him.

He swept her feet off the floor as his mouth took hers with unbridled hunger. In dizzying circles, the room whirled as she felt herself lowered to the thick plush of carpet. Unrestrained, his mouth savaged the yielding softness of hers, tongue claiming the sweet moistness. His hand pushed aside the thin silk of her bodice, seeking and finding the smooth promise for more, his mouth and hands roaming over her, finding heat beneath the cool silk, fingers trailing up the slit of her skirt until they captured the firm flesh of her thigh.

Tossed on the turbulent waves of love and need, B.J. responded with a burst of fire. His possession of her mouth and flesh was desperate. She answered by instinct, moving with a woman's hidden knowledge as he took with insatiable appetite the fruits she offered. Her own hands, no longer shy, found their way under his jacket to explore the hard ripple of muscles of his back and shoul-

ders, half-terrified, half-delighting in their strength.
From the swell and valley of her breasts, his mouth traveled, burning, tantalizing, to burrow against her neck.
Her own lips sought to discover his taste and texture, to assuage her new and throbbing hunger.

His loving had lost all gentleness, his mouth and hands now bringing painful excitement. Her fragile innocence began to dissolve with the ancient cravings of womanhood. B.J. began to tremble with fear and anticipation.

Taylor's mouth lifted from the curve of her neck, and he stared into the eyes cloudy with desire and uncertainty. Abruptly he rose and pulled her to her feet. "Go to bed," he commanded shortly. Turning to the bar, he poured himself another brandy.

Dazed by the abruptness of the rejection, B.J. stood frozen.

"Didn't you hear me? I said go to bed." Downing half his brandy, Taylor pulled out a cigarette.

"Taylor, I don't understand. I thought…" A hand lifted to push at her hair, her eyes liquid and pleading. "I thought you wanted me."

"I do." He drew deep on his cigarette. "Now, go to bed."

"Taylor." The fury in his eyes caused her to flinch.

"Just get out of here before I forget all the rules."

B.J. straightened her shoulders and swallowed her tears. "You're the boss." She ignored the swift flame of temper in his eyes and plunged on. "But I want you to know, what I offered you tonight was a one-time deal. I'll never willingly go into your arms again. From now on, the only thing between you and me is the Lakeside Inn."

"We'll leave it at that for now," he said in curt agreement as he turned away and poured another drink. "Just go to bed."

B.J. ran from the room and turned the lock on her door with an audible click.

12

B.J. threw herself into the inn's routine like a bruised child returning to a mother's arms. She and Taylor had flown from Florida to Vermont in almost total silence, he working on his papers while she had buried herself in a magazine. Avoiding Taylor for the next two days was easy. He made no effort to see her. Annoyance made hurt more tolerable. B.J. worked with dedication to construct a wall of resentment to shield the emptiness she would experience when he left both the inn and her.

Furthering her resentment was the stubborn presence of Darla Trainor. Although B.J. observed Taylor was not often in her company, her mere existence rubbed the sore of wounded pride. Seeing Darla was a constant reminder of B.J.'s uncomfortable and confusing relationship with Taylor.

B.J. knew she could not have mistaken the desire he had felt for her the last night in Florida. She concluded, watching Darla's sensuous elegance, that he had ultimately been disappointed in her lack of experience in the physical demands of love.

Wanting to avoid any unnecessary contact with Taylor, B.J. established her office in her room for the duration of his stay. Buried to her elbows in paperwork one afternoon, she jumped and scattered receipts as the quiet afternoon was shattered by screams and scrambling feet above her head. Racing to the third floor, B.J. followed the sounds into 314. For a moment she could only stand in the doorway and gape at the tableau. In the center of the braid rug, Darla Trainor was engaged in a major battle with one of the housemaids. A helpless Eddie was caught in the middle, his pleas for peace ignored.

"Ladies, ladies, please." Taking her life in her hands, B.J. plunged into the thick of battle and attempted to restore order. Hands and mixed accusations flew. "Louise, Miss Trainor is a guest! What's gotten into you?" She tugged, without success, on the housemaid's arm, then switched her attention to Darla. "Please, stop shouting, I can't understand." Frustrated because she was shouting herself, B.J. lowered her voice and tried to pull Darla away. "Please, Miss Trainor, she's half your size and twice your age. You'll hurt her."

"Take your hands off me!" Darla flung out an arm, and by accident or design, her fist connected, sending

B.J. sprawling against the bedpost. The light shattered into fragments, then smothered with darkness as she slid gently to the floor.

"B.J." A voice called from down a long tunnel. B.J. responded with a moan and allowed her eyes to open into slits. "Lie still," Taylor ordered. Gingerly, she permitted her eyes to open further and focused on his lean features. He was leaning over her, his face lined with concern while he stroked the hair away from her forehead.

"What happened?" She ignored his command and attempted to sit up. Taylor pushed her back against the pillow.

"That's precisely what I want to know." As he glanced around, B.J. followed his gaze. Eddie sat on a small settee with his arm around a sniffling Louise. Darla stood by the window, her profile etched in indignation.

"Oh." Memory clearing, B.J. let out a long breath and shut her eyes. Unconsciousness, she decided, had its advantages. "The three of them were wrestling in the middle of the room. I'm afraid I got in the path of Miss Trainor's left hook."

The hand stroking her cheek stopped as Taylor's fingers tensed against her skin. "She hit you?"

"It was an accident, Taylor." Darla interrupted B.J.'s response, her eyes shining with regret and persecution. "I was simply trying to take these tacky curtains down when this…this maid " she gestured regally toward Louise "—this maid comes in and begins shouting and pulling on me. Then he's shouting—" She fluttered a hand toward Eddie before passing it across her eyes. "Then Miss Clark appears from nowhere, and she begins pulling and shouting. It was a dreadful experience." With a long, shuddering sigh, Darla appeared to collect herself. "I only tried to push her away. She had no business coming into my room in the first place. None of these people belong in my room."

"She had no business trying to take down those curtains," Louise chimed in, wringing Eddie's handkerchief. She waved the soggy linen until all eyes shifted to the window in question. The white chintz hung drunkenly against the frame. "She said they were out-of-date and impractical like everything else in this place. I washed those curtains myself two weeks ago." Louise placed a hand on her trembling bosom. "I was not going to have her soiling them. I asked her very nicely to stop."

"Nicely?" Darla exploded. "You attacked me."

"I only attacked her," Louise countered with dignity, "when she wouldn't come down. B.J., she was standing on the Bentwood chair. Standing on it!" Louise buried her face in Eddie's shoulder, unable to go on.

"Taylor." Tucking an errant lock behind her ear, Darla moved toward him, blinking moist eyes. "You aren't going to allow her to speak to me that way, are you? I want her fired. She might have injured me. She's unstable." Darla placed a hand on his arm as the first tear trembled on her lashes.

Infuriated by the display of helpless femininity, B.J. rose. She ignored both Taylor's restraining hand and the throbbing in her head. "Mr. Reynolds, am I still manager of this inn?"

"Yes, Miss Clark."

B.J. heard the annoyance in his voice and added it to her list of things to ignore. "Very well. Miss Trainor, it falls under my jurisdiction as manager of the inn to over-see all hirings and firings. If you wish to lodge a formal complaint, please do so in writing to my attention. In the meantime, I should warn you that you will be held re-sponsible for any damages done to the furnishings of your room. You should know, as well, that the inn will stand behind Louise in this matter."

"Taylor." Nearly sputtering with anger, Darla turned back to him. "You're not going to allow this?"

"Mr. Reynolds," B.J. interrupted, wishing for a bottle of aspirin and oblivion. "Perhaps you'll take Miss Trainor to the lounge for a drink, and we can discuss this matter later."

After a brief study, Taylor nodded. "All right, we'll talk later. Rest in your room for the remainder of the day. I'll see you're not disturbed."

B.J. accepted the display of gratitude and sympathy by both Eddie and Louise before trudging down to her room. Stepping over scattered papers, she secured much needed aspirin then curled up on the quilt of her bed. Dimly, she heard the door open and felt a hand brush through her hair. The grip of sleep was too strong, and she could not tell if the elusive kiss on her mouth was dream or reality.

When she woke up the throbbing had decreased to a negligible ache. Sitting up, B.J. stared at the neat stack of papers on her desk. Maybe it was a dream, she mused, confused by the lack of disorder on her floor. She touched the back of her head and winced as her fingers contacted with a small lump. Maybe I picked them up and don't remember. It's always the mediator who gets clobbered, she thought in disgust, and prepared to go downstairs to confront Taylor. In the lobby, she came upon Eddie, Maggie and Louise in a heated, low-voiced debate. With a sigh, she moved toward them to restore order.

"Oh, B.J." Maggie started with comical guilt. "Mr. Reynolds said you weren't to be disturbed. How are you feeling? Louise said that Miss Trainor gave you a nasty lump."

"It's nothing." She glanced from one solemn face to the next. She moved her shoulders in resignation. "All right, what's the problem?"

The question produced a jumble of words from three different tongues. Pampering her still aching head, B.J. held up a hand for silence. "Eddie," she decided, choosing at random.

"It's about the architect," he began, and she raised her brows in puzzlement.

"What architect?"

"The one who was here when you were in Florida. Only we didn't know he was an architect. Dot thought he was an artist because he was always walking around with a pad and pencil and making drawings."

Resigning herself to a partially coherent story, B.J. prompted, "Drawings of what?"

"Of the inn," Eddie announced with a flourish. "But he wasn't an artist."

"He was an architect," Maggie interrupted, unable to maintain her silence. Eddie shot her a narrow-eyed frown.

"And how do you know he was an architect?" After asking, B.J. wondered why it mattered. Her wandering attention was soon drawn back with a jolt.

"Because Louise heard Mr. Reynolds talking to him on the phone."

B.J.'s gaze shifted to the housemaid as a hollow feeling grew in the pit of her stomach. "How did you hear, Louise?"

"I wasn't eavesdropping," she claimed with dignity, then amended as B.J. raised her brows. "Well, not really, until I heard him talking about the inn. I was going to dust the office, and since Mr. Reynolds was on the phone, I waited outside. When I heard him say something about a new building, and he said the man's name, Fletcher, I remembered Dot talking about this man named Fletcher making sketches of the inn." She gave the group a small smile in self-reward for her memory. "Anyway, they talked awhile, technical sort of things about dimensions and timber. Then Mr. Reynolds said how he appreciated the Fletcher person not letting on he was an architect until he had everything settled."

"B.J.," Eddie began urgently, grabbing her arm. "Do you think he's going to remodel the inn after all? Do you think he's going to let us all go?"

"No." Feeling her head increase its throbbing, B.J. repeated more emphatically, "No, it's just some mix up, I'll see about it. Now, you all go back to work and don't spread this around anymore."

"It's no mix up." Darla glided over to the group.

"I told you three to go back to work," B.J. ordered in a voice which they recognized as indisputable. They dispersed, waiting until a safe distance before murmuring among themselves. "If you'll pardon me, Miss Trainor, I'm busy."

"Yes, Taylor's quite anxious to see you."

Cursing herself, B.J. nibbled at the bait. "Is he?"

"Oh, yes. He's ready to tell you about his plans for this little place. It's quite a challenge." She surveyed the lobby with the air of one planning a siege.

"What exactly do you know of his plans?" B.J. demanded.

"You didn't really think he intended to leave this place in this condition simply because you want him to?" With a light laugh, Darla brushed away a fictional speck of dust from her vivid blue blouse. "Taylor is much too practical for grand gestures. Though, he might keep you on in some minor capacity once the alterations are complete. You're hardly qualified to manage one of his resorts, but he does seem to think you have some ability. Of course, if I were you, I'd pack up and bow out now to spare myself the humiliation."

"Are you saying," B.J. began, spacing words with great care, "that Taylor has made definite plans to convert the inn into a resort?"

"Well, of course." Darla smiled indulgently. "He'd hardly need me and an architect otherwise, would he? I wouldn't worry. I'm sure he'll keep the bulk of your staff on, at least temporarily."

With a final smile, Darla turned and left B.J. staring at her retreating back.

After the first flow of despair, fury bubbled. She took the steps two at a time and slammed into her room. Minutes later, she sped out again, taking stairs in a headlong flight and stomping into the office unannounced.

"B.J." Rising from the desk, Taylor studied her furious face. "What are you doing out of bed?"

For an answer, she slammed the paper on his desk. He lifted it, scanning her resignation. "It seems we've been through this before."

"You gave me your word." Her voice trembled at the breach of trust but she lifted her chin. "You can tear that

one up too, but it won't change anything. Find yourself
a new patsy, Mr. Reynolds. I quit!"

Streaking from the room, she collided bodily with
Eddie, brushed him aside and rushed up the stairs. In her
room, she pulled out her cases and began to toss articles
in them at random. Clothing, cosmetics, knick-knacks,
whatever was close at hand was dumped, until the first
case overflowed.

She stopped her frantic activities to whirl around at
the metallic click of the lock. The door opened to admit
Taylor.

"Get out!" she commanded, wishing fleetingly she
was big enough to toss him out. "This is my room until
I leave."

"You're making one beautiful mess," he observed
calmly. "You might as well stop that, you're not going
anywhere."

"Yes, I am." She caught herself before she tossed her
asparagus fern among her lingerie. "I'm leaving just as
fast as I can pack. Not only is working for you intol-
erable, but being under the same roof is more than I can
stand. You promised!" She spun to face him, cursing the
mist which clouded her eyes. "I believed you. I trusted
you. How could I have been so stupid! There's no way
I could have prevented you once you'd made your decision, and I would have adjusted somehow. You could
have been honest with me."

Tears were spilling over with more speed than she

could blink them away, and impatiently she brushed at them with the back of her hand. "Oh!" She spun away to pull pictures from the wall. "I wish I were a man!"

"If you were a man, we'd have had no problem to begin with. If you don't stop tearing up the room, I'll have to stop you. I think you've been battered enough for one day."

She heard it in his voice, the calm control, the half-amused exasperation. Despair for her abiding love merged with fury at his betrayal.

"Just leave me alone!"

"Lie down, B.J., and we'll talk later."

"No, don't you touch me," she ordered as he made to take her arm. "I mean it, Taylor, don't touch me!"

At the desperation in her voice, he dropped his hand to his side. "All right then." The first warning signals of anger touched his face. In the cool precision of his voice, she could hear the danger. "Suppose you tell me what exactly it is I've done?"

"You know very well."

"Spell it out for me," he interrupted, moving away and lighting a cigarette.

"That architect you brought here while we were in Florida."

"Fletcher?" Taylor cut her off again, but this time he gave her his full attention. "What about him?"

"What about him?" B.J. repeated incredulously. "You brought him here behind my back, making all his little drawings and plans. You probably took me to Florida just to get me out of the way while he was here."

"That was a consideration."

His easy admission left her speechless. A wave of pain washed over her, reflecting in her eyes.

"B.J." Taylor's expression became more curious than angry. "Suppose you tell me precisely what you know."

"Darla was only too happy to enlighten me." Turning away, she assuaged the hurt with more furious packing. "Go talk to her."

"She's gone by now. I told her to leave, B.J., did you think I'd let her stay after she hit you?" The soft texture of his voice caused her hands to falter a moment. Quickly, she forced them to move again. "What did she say to you?"

"She told me everything. How you'd brought in the architect to draw up plans for turning the inn into a resort. That you're going to bring in someone to manage it, how…" Her voice broke. "It's bad enough you've been lying to me, Taylor, bad enough you broke your word, but that's personal. What is more important is that you're going to change the whole structure of this community, alter dozens of lives for a few more dollars you don't even need. Your resort in Palm Beach is beautiful and perfect for where and what it is, but the inn…"

"Be quiet, B.J." He crushed out his cigarette then thrust his hands in his pockets. "I told you before, I make my own decisions. I called Fletcher in for two reasons." A swift gesture of his hand haltered her furious retort. "One, to design a house for a piece of property my agent picked up for me last week. It's about ten miles outside of town, five acres on a hill overlooking the lake. You probably know it."

"Why do you need…"

"The second purpose," he continued, ignoring her, "was to design an addition to the inn, adhering to its present architecture. The office space is just too limited. Since I plan to move my base from New York to the inn after we're married, I require larger accommodations."

"I don't see…" Her words stumbled to a halt, as she stared into calm brown eyes. A medley of emotions played through her, eradicating the ache in her head. "I never agreed to marry you," she managed at length.

"But you will," he countered and leaned against her desk. "In the meantime, you can ease the various minds downstairs that the inn will remain as is, and you'll remain in the position of manager with some adjust-ments."

"Adjustments?" She could only parrot his last word and sink into a chair.

"I have no problem basing my business in Vermont, but I won't base my marriage in a hotel. Therefore, we'll live in the house when it's completed, and Eddie can take over some of your duties. You'll also have to be free to travel from time to time. We leave for Rome in three weeks."

"Rome?" she echoed him again, dimly remembering his speaking of Rome and passports.

"Yes, your mother's sending your birth certificate so you can see to getting a passport."

"My mother?" Unable to sit, B.J. rose and paced to the window, trying to clear the fog which covered her brain. "You seem to have everything worked out very neatly." She struggled for control. "I don't suppose it occurred to you to ask my feelings on the matter?"

"I know your feelings." His hands descended to her shoulders, and she stiffened. "I told you once, you can't keep secrets with those eyes."

"I guess it's very convenient for you that I happen to be in love with you." She swallowed, focusing on the gleam of the sun as it filtered through the pines on the hillside.

"It makes things less complicated." His fingers worked at the tension in her shoulders but she held herself rigid.

"Why do you want to marry me, Taylor?"

"Why do you think?" She felt his lips in her hair and squeezed her eyes shut.

"You don't have to marry me for that, and we both know it." Taking a deep breath, she gripped the windowsill tighter. "That first night you came to my room, you'd already won."

"It wasn't enough." His arms circled her waist and brought her back against him. She struggled to keep her mind clear. "The minute you swaggered into the office with invisible six guns at your hips, I made up my mind to marry you. I knew I could make you want me, I'd felt that the first time I held you, but the night in your room, you looked up at me, and I knew making you want me wasn't enough. I wanted you to love me."

"So——" she moved her shoulders as if it was of little consequence "——you comforted yourself with Darla in the meantime."

She was spun around so quickly, her hair flew out to fall over her face, obscuring vision. "I never touched Darla or anyone from the first minute I saw you. That little charade in the nightgown was strictly for your benefit, and you were stupid enough to fall for it. Do you think I could touch another woman when I had you on my mind?"

Without giving her time to answer, his mouth closed over hers, commanding and possessive. His arms banded her waist, dragging her against him. "You've been driving me crazy for nearly two weeks." Allowing her time to draw a quick breath, his mouth crushed hers again. Slowly, the kiss altered in texture, softening, sweetening, his hand moving with a tender lightness which drugged her reason.

"B.J.," he murmured, resting his chin on her hair. "It would be less intimidating if you owned a few more pounds and inches. I've had a devil of a time fighting my natural instincts. I don't want to hurt you, and you're too small and much too innocent." Lifting her chin, he framed her face with his hands. "Have I told you yet that I love you?"

Her eyes grew wide, her mouth opening, but powerless to form sound. She shook her head briskly and swallowed the obstruction in her throat.

"I didn't think I had. Actually, I think I was hit the minute you stood up from home plate, turned those eyes on me and claimed you were absolutely safe." He bent down and brushed her lips.

She threw her arms around his neck as though he might vanish in a puff of smoke. "Taylor, why have you waited so long?"

Drawing her away, he lifted a brow in amusement, reminding her of the brevity of their relationship.

"It's been years," she claimed, burying her face in his shoulder as joy washed over her. "Decades, centuries."

"And during the millennium," he replied, stroking fingers through her hair, "you've been more exasperating than receptive. The day I came into the lounge and found you ticking off bourbon bottles, I had hoped to start things along a smooth road, but you turned on the ice very effectively. The next day in your room, when you switched to fire, it was very illuminating. The things you said made a great deal of sense, so I decided a change of setting and attitude were in order. Providentially, Bailey called from Florida."

"You said you had to go to Palm Beach to help him with a problem."

"I lied," he said simply, then laughed with great enjoyment at her astonishment. "I had planned," he began, dropping into a chair and pulling her into his lap, "to get you away from the inn for a couple of days. More important to have you to myself. I wanted you relaxed and perhaps a bit off guard." He laughed again and nuzzled her ear. "Of course, then I had to see you sitting with Hardy and looking like a fresh peach ripe for picking."

"You were jealous." Indescribably pleased, she sighed and burrowed closer.

"That's a mild word for it."

They spent the next few minutes in mutually agreeable silence. Taylor lingered over the taste of her mouth, his hand sliding beneath the barrier of her shirt. "I was quite determined to do things properly, hence the dinner and wine and soft music. I had fully intended to tell you I loved you and ask you to marry me that last night in Florida."

"Why didn't you?"

"You distracted me." His lips trailed along her cheek, reminding her of the power of their last night together. "I had no intention of allowing things to progress the way they did, but you have a habit of stretching my willpower. That night it snapped. Then, I felt you trembling, and your eyes were so young." He sighed and rested his cheek on her hair. "I was furious with myself for losing control of the situation."

"I thought you were furious with me."

"It was better that you did. If I had told you then how I felt about you, nothing would have stopped me from taking you. I was in no frame of mind to introduce you gently to the ways of love. I've never needed anyone so much in my life as I needed you that night."

Round and liquid with love, her eyes lifted to his. "Do you need me, Taylor?"

His hand lifted to brush back her hair. The arm cradling her shifted her closer. "You look like a child," he murmured, tracing her lips with his finger. "A child's mouth, and I can't seem to do without the taste of it. Yes, B.J., I need you."

His mouth lowered, featherlight, but her arm circled his neck and demanded more. The pressure increased, and the door opened to the world of heat and passion. She felt his hand on her breast, never aware that the buttons of her shirt had been loosened. Her fingers tightened in his hair, willing him to prolong the ecstasy.

His mouth moved to her brow, then rested on her hair, his fingers tracing lightly over her bare skin. "You can see why I've been keeping away from you the last day or so."

With a soft sound of agreement, she buried her face against his shoulder.

"I wanted to get everything set up before I got near

you again. I could have done with one more day; we still need a marriage license."

"I'll talk to Judge Walker," she murmured, "if you want one quickly. He's Eddie's uncle."

"Small towns are the backbone of America," Taylor decided. He pulled her close to cover her mouth again when a frantic knock sounded on the door.

"B.J." Eddie's voice drifted through the panel. "Mrs. Frank wants to feed Julius, and I can't find his dinner. And the Bodwin sisters are out of sunflower seeds for Horatio."

"Who's Horatio?" Taylor demanded.

"The Bodwins' parakeet."

"Tell him to feed Horatio to Julius," he suggested, giving the door a scowl.

"It's a thought." Lingering on it briefly, B.J. cast it aside. "Julius's dinner is on the third shelf right hand side of the fridge," she called out. "Send someone into town for a package of sunflower seeds. Now, go away, Eddie, I'm very busy. Mr. Reynolds and I are in conference." With a smile, she circled Taylor's neck again. "Now, Mr. Reynolds, perhaps you'd like my views on the construction of this house you're planning as well as my educated opinion on the structure of your office space."

"Be quiet, B.J."

"You're the boss," she agreed the moment before their lips met.

★ ★ ★ ★ ★

Her Mother's Keeper

1

The taxi zipped through the airport traffic. Gwen let out a long sigh as the Louisiana heat throbbed around her. She shifted as the thin material of her ivory lawn blouse dampened against her back. The relief was brief. Squinting out of the window, she decided the July sun hadn't changed in the two years she had been away. The cab veered away from downtown New Orleans and cruised south. Gwen reflected that very little else here had changed in the past two years but herself. Spanish moss still draped the roadside trees, giving even the sun-drenched afternoon a dreamlike effect. The warm, thick scent of flowers still wafted through the air. The atmosphere was touched with an easygoing indolence she nearly had forgotten during the two years she'd spent in Manhattan. Yes, she mused, craning her neck to catch a glimpse of a sheltered bayou, I'm the one who's changed. I've grown up.

When she had left Louisiana, she'd been twenty-one and a starry-eyed innocent. Now, at twenty-three, she felt mature and experienced. As an assistant to the fashion editor of *Style* magazine, Gwen had learned how to cope with deadlines, soothe ruffled models, and squeeze in a personal life around her professional one. More, she had learned how to cope alone, without the comfort of familiar people and places. The gnawing ache of homesickness she had experienced during her first months in New York was forgotten, the torture of insecurity and outright fear of being alone were banished from her memory. Gwen Lacrosse had not merely survived the transplant from magnolias to concrete, she felt she had triumphed. This is one small-town southern girl who can take care of herself, she reflected with a flash of defiance. Gwen had come home not merely for a visit, a summer sabbatical. She had come on a mission. She folded her arms across her chest in an unconscious gesture of determination.

In the rearview mirror, the taxi driver caught a glimpse of a long, oval face surrounded by a shoulder-length mass of caramel curls. The bone structure of his passenger's face was elegant, but the rather sharp features were set in grim lines. Her huge brown eyes were focused on some middle distance, and her full, wide mouth was unsmiling. In spite of her severe expression, the cabbie decided, the face was a winner. Unaware of the scrutiny, Gwen continued to frown, absorbed by her thoughts. The land-scape blurred, then disappeared from her vision.

How, she wondered, could a forty-seven-year-old woman be so utterly naive? What a fool she must be making of herself. Mama's always been dreamy and im-practical, but this! It's all *his* fault, she thought resentfully. Her eyes narrowed as she felt a fresh surge of temper, and color rose to warm the ivory tone of her skin. *Luke Powers*—Gwen gritted her teeth on the name—success-ful novelist and screenwriter, sought-after bachelor and globe-trotter. *And rat,* Gwen added, unconsciously twist-ing her leather clutch bag in a movement suspiciously akin to that of wringing a neck. A thirty-five-year-old rat. Well, Mr. Powers, Gwen's thoughts continued, your little romance with my mother is through. I've come all these miles to send you packing. And by hook or crook, fair means or foul, that's what I'm going to do.

Gwen sat back, blew the fringe of curls from her eyes and contemplated the pleasure of ousting Luke Powers from her mother's life. Researching a new book, she sniffed. He'll have to research his book without research-ing my mother. She frowned, remembering the corre-spondence from her mother over the past three months. Luke Powers had been mentioned on almost every page of the violet-scented paper; helping her mother garden, taking her to the theater, hammering nails, making him-self generally indispensable.

At first Gwen had paid little attention to the constant

references to Luke. She was accustomed to her mother's enthusiasm for people, her flowery, sentimental outlook. And, to be honest, Gwen reflected with a sigh, I've been preoccupied with my own life, my own problems. Her thoughts flitted back to Michael Palmer—practical, brilliant, selfish, dependable Michael. A small cloud of depression threatened to descend on her as she remembered how miserably she had failed in their relationship. He deserved more than I could give him, she reflected sadly. Her eyes became troubled as she thought of her inability to share herself as Michael had wanted. Body and mind, she had held back both, unwilling or unable to make the commitment. Quickly shaking off the encroaching mood, Gwen reminded herself that while she had failed with Michael, she was succeeding in her career.

In the eyes of most people, the fashion world was glamorous, elegant, full of beautiful people moving gaily from one party to the next. Gwen almost laughed out loud at the absurdity of the illusion. What it really was, as she had since learned, was crazy, frantic, grueling work filled with temperamental artists, high-strung models and impossible deadlines. And I'm good at handling all of them, she mused, automatically straightening her shoulders. Gwen Lacrosse was not afraid of hard work any more than she was afraid of a challenge.

Her thoughts made a quick U-turn back to Luke Powers. There was too much affection in her mother's words when she wrote of him, and his name cropped up too often for comfort. Over the past three months, Gwen's concern had deepened to worry, until she felt she had to do something about the situation and had arranged for a leave of absence. It was, she had decided, up to her to protect her mother from a womanizer like Luke Powers.

She was not intimidated by his reputation with words or his reputation with women. He might be said to be an expert with both, she mused, but I know how to take care of myself and my mother. Mama's trouble is that she's too trusting. She sees only what she wants to see. She doesn't like to see faults. Gwen's mouth softened into a smile, and her face was suddenly, unexpectedly breathtaking. I'll take care of her, she thought confidently, I always have.

The lane leading to Gwen's childhood home was lined with fragile magnolia trees. As the taxi turned in and drove through patches of fragrant shade, Gwen felt the first stirrings of genuine pleasure. The scent of wisteria reached her before her first glimpse of the house. It had three graceful stories and was made of white-washed brick with high French windows and iron balconies like lacework. A veranda flowed across the entire front of the house, where the wisteria was free to climb on trellises at each end. It was not as old or as elaborate as many other antebellum houses in Louisiana, but it had the charm and grace so typical of that period. Gwen felt that the house suited her mother to perfection. They were both fragile, impractical and appealing.

She glanced up at the third story as the taxi neared the end of the drive. The top floor contained four small suites that had been remodeled for "visitors," as her mother called them, or as Gwen more accurately termed them, boarders. The visitors, with their monetary contributions, made it possible to keep the house in the family and in repair. Gwen had grown up with these visitors, accepting them as one accepts a small itch. Now, however, she scowled up at the third-floor windows. One of the suites housed Luke Powers. Not for long, she vowed, as she slipped out of the cab with her chin thrust forward.

As she paid her fare, Gwen glanced absently toward the sound of a low, monotonous thudding. In the side yard, just past a flourishing camellia, a man was in the process of chopping down a long-dead oak. He was stripped to the waist, and his jeans were snug over narrow hips and worn low enough to show a hint of tan line. His back and arms were bronzed and muscled and gleaming with sweat. His hair was a rich brown, touched with lighter streaks that showed a preference for sun. It curled damply at his neck and over his brow.

There was something confident and efficient in his stance. His legs were planted firmly, his swing effortless. Though she could not see his face, she knew he was enjoying his task: the heat, the sweat, the challenge. She stood in the drive as the cab drove off and admired his raw, basic masculinity, the arrogant efficiency of his movements. The ax swung into the heart of the tree with a violent grace. It occurred to her suddenly that for months she had not seen a man do anything more physical than jog in Central Park. Her lips curved in approval and admiration as she watched the rise and fall of the ax, the tensing and flow of muscle. The ax, tree and man were a perfect whole, elemental and beautiful. Gwen had forgotten how beautiful simplicity could be.

The tree shuddered and moaned, then hesitated briefly before it swayed and toppled to the ground. There was a quick whoosh and thump. Gwen felt a ridiculous urge to applaud.

"You didn't say timber," she called out.

He had lifted a forearm to wipe the sweat from his brow, and at her call, he turned. The sun streamed behind his back. Squinting against it, Gwen could not see his face clearly. There was an aura of light around him, etching the tall, lean body and thickly curling hair. He looks like a god, she thought, like some primitive god of virility. As she watched, he leaned the ax against the stump of the tree and walked toward her. He moved like a man more used to walking on sand or grass than on concrete. Ridiculously, Gwen felt as though she were being stalked. She attributed the strange thrill she felt to the fact that she could not yet make out his features. He was a faceless man, therefore somehow the embodiment

of man, exciting and strong. In defense against the glare
of the sun, she shaded her eyes with her hand.

"You did that very well." Gwen smiled, attracted by
his uncomplicated masculinity. She had not realized how
bored she had become with three-piece suits and smooth
hands. "I hope you don't mind an audience."

"No. Not everyone appreciates a well-cut tree." His
voice was not indolent with vowels. There was nothing
of Louisiana in his tone. As his face at last came into
focus, Gwen was struck with its power. It was narrow
and chiseled, long-boned and with the faintest of clefts in
the chin. He had not shaved, but the shadow of beard in-
tensified the masculinity of the face. His eyes were a clear
blue-gray. They were calm, almost startlingly intelligent
under rough brows. It was a calm that suggested power,
a calm that captivated the onlooker. Immediately, Gwen
knew he was a man who understood himself. Though
intrigued, she felt discomfort under the directness of his
gaze. She was almost sure he could see beyond her words
and into her thoughts.

"I'd say you have definite talent," she told him. There
was an aloofness about him, she decided, but it was not
the cold aloofness of disinterest. He has warmth, she
thought, but he's careful about who receives it. "I'm sure
I've never seen a tree toppled with such finesse." She gave
him a generous smile. "It's a hot day for ax swinging."

"You've got too many clothes on," he returned simply.
His eyes swept down her blouse and skirt and trim, stock-

inged legs, then up again to her face. It was neither an insolent assessment nor an admiring one; it was simply a statement. Gwen kept her eyes level with his and prayed she would not do anything as foolish as blushing.

"More suitable for plane travelling than tree chopping I suppose," she replied. The annoyance in her voice brought a smile to the corners of his mouth. Gwen reached for her bags, but her hand met his on the handle. She jerked away and stepped back as a new source of heat shot through her. It seemed to dart up her fingers, then explode. Stunned by her own reaction, she stared into his calm eyes. Confusion flitted across her face and creased her brow before she smoothed it away. Silly, she told herself as she struggled to steady her pulse. Absolutely silly. He watched the shock, confusion and annoyance move across her face. Like a mirror, her eyes reflected each emotion.

"Thank you," Gwen said, regaining her poise. "I don't want to take you away from your work."

"No hurry." He hoisted her heavy bags easily. As he moved up the flagstone walk, she fell into step beside him. Even in heels, she barely reached his shoulder. Gwen glanced up to see the sun play on the blond highlights in his hair.

"Have you been here long?" she asked as they mounted the steps to the veranda.

"Few months." He set down her bags and placed his hand on the knob. Pausing, he studied her face with exacting care. Gwen felt her lips curve for no reason at all. "You're much lovelier than your picture, Gwenivere," he said unexpectedly. "Much warmer, much more vulnerable." With a quick twist, he opened the door, then again picked up her bags.

Breaking out of her trance, Gwen followed him inside, reaching for his arm. "How do you know my name?" she demanded. His words left her puzzled and defenseless. He saw too much too quickly.

"Your mother talks of you constantly," he explained as he set her bags down in the cool, white-walled hallway. "She's very proud of you." When he lifted her chin with his fingers, Gwen was too surprised to protest. "Your beauty is very different from hers. Hers is softer, less demanding, more comfortable. I doubt very much that you inspire comfort in a man." His eyes were on her face again, and fascinated, Gwen stood still. She could nearly feel the heat flowing from his body into hers. "She worries about you being alone in New York."

"One can't be alone in New York, it's a contradiction in terms." A frown shadowed her eyes and touched her mouth with a pout. "She's never told me she worried."

"Of course not, then you'd worry about her worrying." He grinned.

Resolutely Gwen ignored the tingle of pleasure his touch gave her. "You seem to know my mother quite well." Her frown deepened and spread. The grin reminded her of someone. It was charming and almost irresistible. Recognition struck like a thunderbolt. *"You're Luke Powers,"* she accused.

"Yes." His brows lifted at the tone of her voice, and his head tilted slightly, as if to gain a new perspective. "Didn't you like my last book?"

"It's your current one I object to," Gwen snapped. She jerked her chin from his hold.

"Oh?" There was both amusement and curiosity in the word.

"To the fact that you're writing it here, in this house," Gwen elaborated.

"Have you a moral objection to my book, Gwenivere?"

"I doubt you know anything about morals," Gwen tossed back as her eyes grew stormy. "And don't call me that, no one but my mother calls me that."

"Pity, such a romantic name," he said casually. "Or do you object to romance, as well?"

"When it's between my mother and a Hollywood Casanova a dozen years younger than she, I have a different name for it." Gwen's face flushed with the passion of her words. She stood rigid. The humor faded from Luke's face. Slowly, he tucked his hands in his pockets.

"I see. Would you care to tell me what you'd call it?"

"I won't glorify your conduct with a title," Gwen retorted. "It should be sufficient that you understand I won't tolerate it any longer." She turned, intending to walk away from him.

"Won't you?" There was something dangerously cold in his tone. "And your mother has no voice in the matter?"

"My mother," Gwen countered furiously, "is too gentle, too trusting and too naive." Whirling, she faced him again. "I won't let you make a fool of her."

"My dear Gwenivere," he said smoothly. "You do so well making one of yourself."

Before Gwen could retort, there was the sharp click of heels on wood. Struggling to steady her breathing, Gwen moved down the hall to greet her mother.

"Mama." She embraced a soft bundle of curves smelling of lilac.

"Gwenivere!" Her mother's voice was low and as sweet as the scent she habitually wore. "Why, darling, what are you doing here?"

"Mama," Gwen repeated and pulled away far enough to study the rosy loveliness of her mother's face. Her mother's skin was creamy and almost perfectly smooth, her eyes round and china blue, her nose tilted, her mouth pink and soft. There were two tiny dimples in her cheeks. Looking at her sweet prettiness, Gwen felt their roles should have been reversed. "Didn't you get my letter?" She tucked a stray wisp of pale blond hair behind her mother's ear.

"Of course, you said you'd be here Friday."

Gwen smiled and kissed a dimpled cheek. "This is Friday, Mama."

"Well, yes, it's *this* Friday, but I assumed you meant *next* Friday, and... Oh, dear, what does it matter?" Anabelle brushed away confusion with the back of her hand. "Let me look at you," she requested and, stepping back, subjected Gwen to a critical study. She saw a tall, striking beauty who brought misty memories of her young husband. Widowed for more than two decades, Anabelle rarely thought of her late husband unless reminded by her daughter. "So thin," she clucked, and sighed. "Don't you eat up there?"

"Now and again." Pausing, Gwen made her own survey of her mother's soft, round curves. How could this woman be approaching fifty? she wondered with a surge of pride and awe. "You look wonderful," Gwen murmured, "but then, you always look wonderful."

Anabelle laughed her young, gay laugh. "It's the climate," she claimed as she patted Gwen's cheek. "None of that dreadful smog or awful snow you have up there." New York, Gwen noted, would always be "up there." "Oh, Luke!" Anabelle caught sight of him as he stood watching the reunion. A smile lit up her face. "Have you met my Gwenivere?"

Luke shifted his gaze until his eyes met Gwen's. His brow tilted slightly in acknowledgement. "Yes." Gwen thought his smile was as much a challenge as a glove slapped across her cheek. "Gwen and I are practically old friends."

"That's right." Gwen let her smile answer his. "Already we know each other quite well."

"Marvelous." Anabelle beamed. "I do want you two to get along." She gave Gwen's hand a happy squeeze. "Would you like to freshen up, darling, or would you like a cup of coffee first?"

Gwen struggled to keep her voice from trembling with rage as Luke continued to smile at her. "Coffee sounds perfect," she answered.

"I'll take your bags up," Luke offered as he lifted them again.

"Thank you, dear." Anabelle spoke before Gwen could refuse. "Try to avoid Miss Wilkins until you have a shirt on. The sight of all those muscles will certainly give her the vapors. Miss Wilkins is one of my visitors," Anabelle explained as she led Gwen down the hall. "A sweet, timid little soul who paints in watercolors."

"Hmm," Gwen answered noncommittally as she glanced back over her shoulder. Luke stood watching them with sunlight tumbling over his hair and bronzed skin. "Hmm," Gwen said again, and turned away.

The kitchen was exactly as Gwen remembered: big, sunny and spotlessly clean. Tillie, the tall, waspishly thin cook stood by the stove. "Hello, Miss Gwen," she said without turning around. "Coffee's on."

"Hello, Tillie." Gwen walked over to the stove and sniffed at the fragrant steam. "Smells good."

"Cajun jambalaya."

"My favorite," Gwen murmured, glancing up at the appealingly ugly face. "I thought I wasn't expected until next Friday."

"You weren't," Tillie agreed, with a sniff. Lowering her thick brows, she continued to stir the roux.

Gwen smiled and leaned over to peck Tillie's tough cheek. "How are things, Tillie?"

"Comme ci, comme ça," she muttered, but pleasure touched her cheeks with color. Turning, she gave Gwen a quick study. "Skinny" was her quick, uncomplimentary conclusion.

"So I'm told." Gwen shrugged. Tillie never flattered anyone. "You have a month to fatten me up."

"Isn't that marvellous, Tillie?" Anabelle carefully put a blue delft sugar and creamer set on the kitchen table. "Gwen is staying for an entire month. Perhaps we should have a party! We have three visitors at the moment. Luke, of course, and Miss Wilkins and Mr. Stapleton. He's an artist, too, but he works in oils. Quite a talented young man."

Gwen seized the small opening. "Luke Powers is considered a gifted young man, too." She sat across from her mother as Anabelle poured the coffee.

"Luke *is* frightfully talented," Anabelle agreed with a proud sigh. "Surely you've read some of his books, seen some of his movies? Overwhelming. His characters are so real, so vital. His romantic scenes have a beauty and intensity that just leave me weak."

"He had a naked woman in one of his movies," Tillie stated in an indignant mutter. "Stark naked."

Anabelle laughed. Her eyes smiled at Gwen's over the rim of her cup. "Tillie feels Luke is singlehandedly responsible for the moral decline in the theater," Anabelle continued.

"Not a stitch on," Tillie added, setting her chin.

Though Gwen was certain Luke Powers had no morals whatsoever, she made no reference to them. Her voice remained casual as instead she commented, "He certainly has accomplished quite a bit for a man of his age. A string of best-sellers, a clutch of popular movies…and he's only thirty-five."

"I suppose that shows how unimportant age really is," Anabelle said serenely. Gwen barely suppressed a wince. "And success hasn't spoiled him one little bit," she went on. "He's the kindest, sweetest man I've ever known. He's so generous with his time, with himself." Her eyes shone with emotion. "I can't tell you how good he's been for me. I feel like a new woman." Gwen choked on her coffee. Anabelle clucked in sympathy as Tillie gave Gwen a sturdy thump on the back. "Are you all right, honey?"

"Yes, yes, I'm fine." Gwen took three deep breaths to steady her voice. Looking into her mother's guileless blue eyes, she opted for a temporary retreat. "I think I'll go upstairs and unpack."

"I'll help you," Anabelle volunteered, and started to rise.

"No, no, don't bother." Gwen placed a gentle hand on her shoulder. "It won't take long. I'll shower and change and be down in an hour." In an hour, Gwen hoped to have her thoughts more in order. She looked down at her mother's smooth, lovely face and felt a hundred years old. "I love you, Mama," she sighed, and kissed Anabelle's brow before she left her.

As Gwen moved down the hall, she realigned her strategy. Obviously, there was little she could say to her mother that would discourage her relationship with Luke Powers. It was going to be necessary, she decided, to go straight to the source. While climbing the stairs, she searched her imagination for an appropriate name for him. She could find nothing vile enough.

𝒬

A shaft of sunlight poured over the floor in Gwen's room. The walls were covered in delicate floral paper. Eggshell-tinted sheer curtains were draped at the windows, matching the coverlet on the four-poster bed. As she always did when she entered the room, Gwen crossed to the French windows and threw them open. Scents from Anabelle's flower garden swam up to meet her. Across the lawn was a spreading cypress, older than the house it guarded, festooned with gray-green moss. The sun filtered through it, making spiderweb patterns on the ground. Birdsong melded with the drone of bees. She could barely glimpse the mystery of the bayou through a thick curtain of oaks. New York's busy streets seemed nonexistent. Gwen had chosen that world for its challenges, but she discovered that coming home was like a sweet dessert after a full meal. She had missed its taste. Feeling unaccountably more lighthearted, she turned back into her room. She plucked up her white terry-cloth robe and headed for the shower.

Mama's romanticizing again, Gwen mused as the water washed away her travel weariness. She simply doesn't understand men at all. *And you do?* her conscience asked as she thought uncomfortably of Michael. Yes, I do understand them, she answered defiantly as she held her face up to the spray. I understand them perfectly. I won't let Luke hurt my mother, she vowed. I won't let him make a fool of her. I suppose he's used to getting his own way because he's successful and attractive. Well, I deal with successful, attractive people every day, and I know precisely how to handle them. Refreshed and ready for battle, Gwen stepped from the shower. With her confidence restored, she hummed lightly as she towel-dried her hair. Curls sprang to life on her forehead. Slipping on her robe, she tied the belt at her waist and strolled back into the bedroom.

"You!" Gwen jerked the knot tight as she spied Luke Powers standing beside her dresser. "What are you doing in my room?"

Calmly, his eyes traveled over her. The frayed robe was short, revealing slender legs well above the knee. Its simplicity outlined her nearly boyish slenderness. Without makeup, her eyes were huge and dark and curiously sweet.

Luke watched her damp curls bounce with the outraged toss of her head.

"Anabelle thought you'd like these," he said as he indicated a vase of fresh yellow roses on the dresser. His hand made the gesture, but his eyes remained on Gwen. Gwen frowned.

"You should have knocked," she said ungraciously.

"I did," he said easily. "You didn't answer." To her amazement, he crossed the distance between them and lifted a hand to her cheek. "You have incredibly beautiful skin. Like rose petals washed in rainwater."

"Don't!" Knocking his hand away, Gwen stepped back. "Don't touch me." She pushed her hair away from her face.

Luke's eyes narrowed fractionally at her tone, but his voice was calm. "I always touch what I admire."

"I don't want you to admire me."

Humor lit his face and added to its appeal. "I didn't say I admired you, Gwen, I said I admired your skin."

"Just keep your hands off my skin," she snapped, wishing the warmth of his fingers would evaporate and leave her cheek as it had been before his touch. "And keep your hands off my mother."

"What gives you the notion I've had my hands on your mother?" Luke inquired, lifting a bottle of Gwen's scent and examining it.

"Her letters were clear enough." Gwen snatched the bottle from him and slammed it back on the dresser.

"They've been full of nothing but you for months. How you went to the theater or shopping, how you fixed her car or sprayed the peach trees. Especially how you've given her life fresh meaning." Agitated, Gwen picked up her comb, then put it down again. His direct, unruffled stare tripped her nerves.

"And from that," Luke said into the silence, "you've concluded that Anabelle and I are having an affair."

"Well, of course." His tone confused her for a moment. Was he amused? she wondered. His mouth was beautiful, a smile lurking on it. Furious with herself, Gwen tilted her chin. "Do you deny it?"

Luke slipped his hands into his pockets and wandered about the room. Pausing, he studied the view from the open French windows. "No, I don't believe I will. I believe I'll simply tell you it's none of your business."

"None of my..." Gwen sputtered, then swallowed in a torrent of fury. "None of my business? She's my mother!"

"She's also a person," Luke cut in. When he turned back to face her, there was curiosity on his face. "Or don't you ever see her that way?"

"I don't feel it's—"

"No, you probably don't," he interrupted. "It's certainly time you did, though. I doubt you feel Anabelle should approve of every man you have a relationship with."

Color flared in Gwen's cheeks. "That's entirely different," she fumed, then stalked over to stand in front of him. "I don't need you to tell me about my mother. You can flaunt your affairs with actresses and socialites all you want, but—"

"Thank you," Luke replied evenly. "It's nice to have your approval."

"I won't have you flaunting your affair with my mother," Gwen finished between her teeth. "You should be ashamed," she added with a toss of her head, "seducing a woman a dozen years older than you."

"Of course, it would be perfectly acceptable if I were a dozen years older than she," he countered smoothly.

"I didn't *say* that," Gwen began. Her brow creased with annoyance.

"You look too intelligent to hold such views, Gwen. You surprise me." His mild voice was infuriating.

"I don't!" she denied hotly. Because the thought made her uncomfortable, her mouth moved into a pout. Luke's eyes dropped to her lips and lingered.

"A very provocative expression," he said softly. "I thought so the first time I saw it, and it continues to intrigue me." In one swift motion, he gathered her into his arms. At her gasp of surprised protest, he merely smiled. "I told you I always touch what I admire." Gwen squirmed, but she was pinned tight against him, helpless as his face lowered toward her.

His lips feathered lightly along her jawline. Gwen was caught off guard by the gentleness. Though his chest was solid and strong against her yielding breasts, his mouth was soft and sweet. Disarmed, she stood still in the circle of his arms as his mouth roamed her face. Through the slight barrier of the robe, she could feel every line of his body. They merged together as if destined to do so. Heat began to rise in her, a sudden, unexpected heat as irresistible as his mouth. Her lips throbbed for the touch of his. She moaned softly as he continued to trace light, teasing kisses over her skin. Her hands slipped up from his chest to find their way into his hair, urging him to fulfill a silent promise. At last his lips brushed hers. They touched, then clung, then devoured.

Lost in pleasure, riding on sensations delirious and new, Gwen answered his demands with fervor. She rose on her toes to meet them. The kiss grew deeper. The roughness of his beard scratched her skin and tripled her heartbeat. A tenuous breeze fanned the curtains at the open windows, but Gwen felt no lessening of heat. Luke moved his hands down her spine, firmly caressing her curves before he took her hips and drew her away.

Gwen stared up at him with dark, cloudy eyes. Never had a kiss moved her more, never had she been so filled with fire and need. Her soft mouth trembled with desire for his. The knowledge of what could be hers lay just beyond her comprehension. Luke lifted his hand to her damp curls, tilting back her head for one last, brief kiss. "You taste every bit as good as you look."

Abruptly Gwen remembered who and where she was.

The fires of passion were extinguished by fury. "Oh!"
She gave Luke's chest a fierce push and succeeded in putting an entire inch between them. "How could you?"

"It wasn't hard," he assured her.

Gwen shook her head. Tiny droplets of water danced
in the sunlight. "You're despicable!"

"Why?" Luke's smile broadened. "Because I made you
forget yourself for a moment? You made me forget myself
for a moment too." He seemed to enjoy the confession.
"Does that make you despicable?"

"I didn't… It was you…I just…" Her words stumbled
to a halt, and she made ineffectual noises in her throat.

"At least try to be coherent," Luke said.

"Just let me go," Gwen demanded. She began a violent
and fruitless struggle. "Just let me go!"

"Certainly," Luke said obligingly. He brushed back
her disheveled hair with a friendly hand. "You know,
one day you might just be the woman your mother is."

"Oh!" Gwen paled in fury. "You're disgusting."

Luke laughed with pure masculine enjoyment.
"Gwenivere, I wasn't speaking of your rather excep-
tional physical virtues." He sobered, then shook his head.
"Anabelle is the only person I know who looks for the
good in everyone and finds it. It's her most attractive
asset." His eyes were calm again and thoughtful. "Perhaps
you should take time to get to know your mother while
you're here. You might be surprised."

Gwen retreated behind a film of ice. "I told you, I don't need you to tell me about my mother."

"No?" Luke smiled, shrugged, and moved to the door. "Perhaps I'll spend my time teaching you about yourself, then. See you at dinner." He closed the door on her furious retort.

The front parlor had both the color and the scent of roses. It was furnished in Anabelle's delicate and feminine style. The chairs were small and elegant, with dusky pink cushions; the lamps, china and terrifyingly fragile; the rugs, faded and French. Even when she was not there, Anabelle's presence could be felt.

Gwen pushed aside a pale pink curtain and watched the sun go down while Anabelle chattered happily. The sky gradually took on the hues of sunset, until it glowed with defiant gold and fiery reds. Its passion suited Gwen much more than the soft comfort of the room at her back. She lifted her palm to the glass of the window, as if to touch that explosion of nature. She still felt the aftershocks of the explosion that had burst inside her only a few hours before in the arms of a stranger.

It meant nothing, she assured herself for the hundredth time. I was off guard, tired, confused. I'm sure most of what I felt was pure imagination. I'm on edge, that's all, everything's exaggerated. She ran the tip of her tongue experimentally along her lips, but found no remnants of the heady flavor she remembered. Exaggerated, she told herself again.

"A month's quite a long time for you to be away from your job," Anabelle said conversationally as she sorted through a basket of embroidery thread.

Gwen shrugged and made a small sound of agreement. "I haven't taken more than a long weekend in nearly two years."

"Yes, darling, I know. You work too hard."

The cerulean blue dress suited Gwen well, but as Anabelle glanced up at her, she again thought how thin her daughter looked. She was slim and straight as a wand. Gwen's hair caught some of the last flames of the sun, and the mass of curls became a flood of rose-gold light. *How did she get to be twenty-three?* Anabelle wondered. She went back to sorting her thread. "You always were an overachiever. You must get that from your father's side. His mother had two sets of twins, you know. That's overachievement."

With a laugh, Gwen rested her forehead against the glass of the window. It was as refreshing as her mother. "Oh, Mama, I do love you."

"I love you, too, dear," she answered absently as she scrutinized two tones of green. "You haven't mentioned that young man you were seeing, the attorney. Michael, wasn't it?"

"It was," Gwen returned dryly. Dusk began to fall as she watched. With the mellowing of light came an odd, almost reverent hush. She sighed. Dusk, she thought, was the most precious time, and the most fleeting. The sound of the first cricket brought her out of her reverie. "I'm not seeing Michael anymore."

"Oh, dear." Anabelle looked up, distressed. "Did you have a disagreement?"

"A series of them. I'm afraid I don't make the ideal companion for a corporate attorney." Gwen made a face in the glass and watched it reflect. "I have too many deep-rooted plebeian values. Mostly, I like to see the little guy get a break."

"Well, I hope you parted friends."

Gwen closed her eyes and stifled a sardonic laugh as she recalled the volatile parting scene. "I'm sure we'll exchange Christmas cards for years to come."

"That's nice," Anabelle murmured comfortably as she threaded her needle. "Old friends are the most precious."

With a brilliant smile, Gwen turned toward her mother. The smile faded instantly as she spotted Luke in the doorway. As her eyes locked with his, she felt herself trembling. He had changed into tan slacks and a rust-colored shirt. The effect was casual and expensive. But somehow there seemed little difference between the clean-shaven, conventionally clad man Gwen now saw and the rugged woodsman she had met that morning. Clothes and a razor could not alter the essence of his virility.

"It's a fortunate man who has two exquisite women to himself."

"Luke!" Anabelle's head lifted. Instantly, her face was touched with pleasure. "How lovely it is to be flattered! Don't you agree, Gwen?"

"Lovely," Gwen assented, as she sent him her most frigid smile.

With easy assurance, Luke crossed the room. From Gwen's grandmother's Hepplewhite server, he lifted a crystal decanter. "Sherry?"

"Thank you, darling." Anabelle turned her smile from him to Gwen. "Luke bought the most delightful sherry. I'm afraid he's been spoiling me."

I'll just bet he has, Gwen muttered silently. Temper flared in her eyes. Had she seen it, Anabelle would have recognized the look. Luke both saw it and recognized it. To Gwen's further fury, he grinned.

"We shouldn't dawdle long," Anabelle said, unconscious of the war being waged over her head. "Tillie has a special supper planned for Gwen. She dotes on her, you know, though she wouldn't admit it for the world. I believe she's missed Gwen every bit as much as I have these past two years."

"She's missed having someone to scold," Gwen smiled ruefully. "I still carry the stigma of being skinny and unladylike that I acquired when I was ten."

"You'll always be ten to Tillie, darling." Anabelle

sighed and shook her head. "I have a difficult time realizing you're more than twice that myself."

Gwen turned toward Luke as he offered her a glass of sherry. "Thank you," she said in her most graciously insulting voice. She sipped, faintly disappointed to find that it was excellent. "And will you be spoiling me, as well, Mr. Powers?"

"Oh, I doubt that, Gwenivere." He took her hand, although she stiffened and tried to pull it away. His eyes laughed over their joined fingers. "I doubt that very much."

3

Over dinner Gwen met Anabelle's two other visitors. Though both were artists, they could not have been more different from each other. Monica Wilkins was a small, pale woman with indifferent brown hair. She spoke in a quiet, breathy voice and avoided eye contact at all costs. She had a supply of large, shapeless smocks, which she wore invariably and without flair. Her art was, for the most part, confined to illustrating textbooks on botany. With a touch of pity, Gwen noticed that her tiny, bird-like eyes often darted glances at Luke, then shifted away quickly and self-consciously.

Bradley Stapleton was tall and lanky, casually dressed in an ill-fitting sweater, baggy slacks and battered sneakers. He had a cheerful, easily forgettable face and a surprisingly beautiful voice. He studied his fellow humans with unquenchable curiosity and painted for the love of it. He yearned to be famous but had settled for regular meals.

Gwen thoroughly enjoyed dinner, not only because of Tillie's excellent jambalaya but for the oddly interesting company of the two artists. Separately, she thought each might be a bore, but somehow together, the faults of one enhanced the virtues of the other.

"So, you work for *Style*," Bradley stated as he scooped up a second, generous helping of Tillie's jambalaya. "Why don't you model?"

Gwen thought of the frantic, nervous models, with their fabulous faces. She shook her head. "No, I'm not at all suitable. I'm much better at stroking."

"Stroking?" Bradley repeated, intrigued.

"That's what I do, basically." Gwen smiled at him. It was better, she decided, that her mother had seated her next to Luke rather than across from him. She would have found it uncomfortable to face him throughout an entire meal. "Soothe, stroke, bully. Someone has to keep the models from using their elegant nails on each other and remind them of the practical side of life."

"Gwen's so good at being practical," Anabelle interjected. "I'm sure I don't understand why. I've never been. Strange," she said, and smiled at her daughter. "She grew up long before I did."

"Practicality wouldn't suit you, Anabelle," Luke told her with an affectionate smile.

Anabelle dimpled with pleasure. "I told you he was spoiling me," she said to Gwen.

"So you did." Gwen lifted her water glass and sipped carefully.

"You must sit for me, Gwen," Bradley said, as he buttered a biscuit.

"Must I?" Knowing the only way she could get through a civilized meal was to ignore Luke, Gwen gave Bradley all her attention.

"Absolutely." Bradley held both the biscuit and knife suspended while he narrowed his eyes and stared at her. "Fabulous, don't you agree, Monica? A marvelous subject," he went on without waiting for her answer. "In some lights the hair would be the color Titian immortalized, in others, it would be quieter, more subtle. But it's the eyes, isn't it, Monica? It's definitely the eyes. So large, so meltingly brown. Of course, the bone structure's perfect, and the skin's wonderful, but I'm taken with the eyes. The lashes are real, too, aren't they, Monica?"

"Yes, quite real," she answered as her gaze flew swiftly to Gwen's face and then back to her plate. "Quite real."

"She gets them from her father," Anabelle explained as she added a sprinkle of salt to her jambalaya. "Such a handsome boy. Gwen favors him remarkably. His eyes were exactly the same. I believe they're why I first fell in love with him."

"They're very alluring," Bradley commented with a nod to Anabelle. "The size, the color, the shape. Very alluring." He faced Gwen again. "You will sit for me, won't you, Gwen?"

Gwen gave Bradley a guileless smile. "Perhaps."

The meal drifted to a close, and the evening waned. The artists retreated to their rooms, and Luke wandered off to his. At Gwen's casual question, Anabelle told her that Luke "worked all the time." It was odd, Gwen mused to herself, that a woman as romantic as her mother wasn't concerned that the man in her life was not spending his evening with her.

Anabelle chattered absently while working tiny decorative stitches into a pillowcase. Watching her, Gwen was struck with a sudden thought. Did Anabelle seem happier? Did she seem more vital? If Luke Powers was responsible, should she, Gwen, curse him or thank him? She watched Anabelle delicately stifle a yawn and was swept by a fierce protective surge. She needs me to look out for her, she decided, and that's what I plan to do.

Once in her bedroom, however, Gwen could not get to sleep. The book she had brought with her to pass the time did not hold her attention. It grew late, but her mind would not allow her body to rest. A breeze blew softly in through the windows, lifting the curtains. It beckoned. Rising, Gwen threw on a thin robe and went outside to meet it.

The night was warm and lit by a large summer moon. The air was filled with the scent of wisteria and roses.

She could hear the continual hum of the crickets. Now and then, there was the lonely, eerie call of an owl. Leaves rustled with the movements of night birds and small animals. Fireflies blinked and soared.

As Gwen breathed in the moist, fragrant air, an unexpected peace settled over her. Tranquility was something just remembered, like a childhood friend. Tentatively Gwen reached out for it. For two years, her career had been her highest priority. Independence and success were the goals she had sought. She had worked hard for them. And I've got them, she thought as she plucked a baby coral rose from its bush. Why aren't I happy? I am happy, she corrected as she lifted the bloom and inhaled its fragile scent, but I'm not as happy as I should be. Frowning, she twisted the stem between her fingers. *Complete*. The word came from nowhere. I don't feel complete. With a sigh, she tilted her head and studied the star-studded sky. Laughter bubbled up in her throat suddenly and sounded sweet in the silence.

"Catch!" she cried as she tossed the bloom in the air. She gasped in surprise as a hand plucked the rose on its downward journey. Luke had appeared as if from nowhere and was standing a few feet away from her twirling the flower under his nose. "Thanks," he said softly. "No one has ever tossed me a rose."

"I wasn't tossing it to you." Automatically, Gwen clutched her robe together where it crossed her breasts.

"No?" Luke smiled at her and at the gesture. "Who then?"

Feeling foolish, Gwen shrugged and turned away. "I thought you were working."

"I was. The muse took a break so I called it a night. Gardens are at their best in the moonlight." He paused, and there was an intimacy in his voice. Stepping closer, he added, "I've always thought the same held true for women."

Gwen felt her skin grow warm. She struggled to keep her tone casual as she turned to face him.

Luke tucked the small flower into her curls and lifted her chin. "They are fabulous eyes, you know. Bradley's quite right."

Her skin began to tingle where his fingers touched it. Defensively, she stepped back. "I wish you wouldn't keep doing that." Her voice trembled, and she despised herself for it.

Luke gave her an odd, amused smile. "You're a strange one, Gwenivere. I haven't got you labeled quite yet. I'm intrigued by the innocence."

Gwen stiffened and tossed back her hair. "I don't know what you're talking about."

Luke's smile broadened. The moonlight seemed trapped in his eyes. "Your New York veneer doesn't cover it. It's in the eyes. Bradley doesn't know why they're appealing, and I won't tell him. It's the innocence and the promise." Gwen frowned, but her shoulders relaxed.

Luke went on, "There's an unspoiled innocence in that marvelous face, and a warmth that promises passion. It's a tenuous balance."

His words made Gwen uncomfortable. A warmth was spreading through her that she seemed powerless to control. Tranquility had vanished. An excitement, volatile and hot, throbbed through the air. Suddenly she was afraid. "I don't want you to say these things to me," she whispered, and took another step in retreat.

"No?" The amusement in his voice told her that a full retreat would be impossible. "Didn't Michael ever use words to seduce you? Perhaps that's why he failed."

"Michael? What do you know about…?" Abruptly she recalled the conversation with her mother before dinner. "You were listening!" she began, outraged. "You had no right to listen to a private conversation! No gentleman listens to a private conversation!"

"Nonsense," Luke said calmly. "Everyone does, if he has the chance."

"Do you enjoy intruding on other people's privacy?"

"People interest me, emotions interest me. I don't apologize for my interests."

Gwen was torn between fury at his arrogance and admiration for his confidence. "What *do* you apologize for, Luke Powers?"

"Very little."

Unable to do otherwise, Gwen smiled. Really, she thought, he's outrageous.

"Now that was worth waiting for," Luke murmured, as his eyes roamed her face. "I wonder if Bradley can do it justice? Be careful," he warned, "you'll have him falling in love with you."

"Is that how you won Monica?"

"She's terrified of me," Luke corrected as he reached up to better secure the rose in her hair.

"Some terrific observer of humanity you are." Gwen sniffed, fiddling with the rose herself and managing to dislodge it. As it tumbled to the ground, both she and Luke stooped to retrieve it. Her hair brushed his cheek before she lifted her eyes to his. As if singed, she jolted back, but before she could escape, he took her arm. Slowly, he rose, bringing her with him. Involuntarily, she shivered as he brought her closer until their bodies touched. Just a look from him, just the touch of him, incited her to a passion that she had not known she possessed. His hands slid up her arms and under the full sleeves of her robe to caress her shoulders. She felt her mantle of control slip away as she swayed forward and touched her lips to his.

His mouth was avid so quickly, her breath caught in her throat. Then all was lost in pleasure. Lights fractured and exploded behind her closed lids as her lips sought to give and to take with an instinct as old as time. Beneath her palms she felt the hard, taut muscles of his back. She shuddered with the knowledge of his strength and the sudden realization of her own frailty. But even her weakness had a power she had never tapped, never experienced.

His hands roamed over her, lighting fires, learning secrets, teaching and taking. Gwen was pliant and willing. He was like a drug flowing into her system, clouding her brain. Only the smallest grain of denial struggled for survival, fighting against the growing need to surrender. Reason surfaced slowly, almost reluctantly. Suddenly, appalled by her own behavior, she began to struggle. But when she broke away, she felt a quick stab of loneliness.

"No." Gwen lifted her hands to her burning cheeks. "No," she faltered.

Luke watched in silence as she turned and fled to the house.

4

The morning was hazy and heavy. So were Gwen's thoughts. As dawn broke with a gray, uncertain light, she stood by her window.

How could I? she demanded of herself yet again. Closing her eyes and groaning, Gwen sank down onto the window seat. I kissed him. *I* kissed *him.* Inherent honesty kept her from shifting what she considered blame. I can't say I was caught off guard this time. I knew what was going to happen, and worse yet, I *enjoyed* it. She brought her knees up to her chin. I enjoyed the first time he kissed me too. The silent admission caused her to shut her eyes again. *How could I?* As she wrestled with this question, she rose and paced the room. I came thousands of miles to get Luke Powers out of Mama's life, and I end up kissing him in the garden in the middle of the night. And liking it, she added wretchedly. What kind of a person am I? What kind of a daughter am I? I never thought of Mama once in that garden last night. Well, I'll think of her today, she asserted, and pulled a pair of olive-drab shorts from her drawer. I've got a month to move Luke Powers out, and that's just what I'm going to do.

As she buttoned up a short-sleeved khaki blouse, Gwen nodded confidently at herself in the mirror. No more moonlit gardens. I won't take the chance of having midsummer madness creep over me again. That's what it was, wasn't it? she asked the slender woman in the glass. She ran a nervous hand through her hair. Another answer seemed just beyond her reach. Refusing any attempt to pursue it, Gwen finished dressing and left the room.

Not even Tillie was in the kitchen at such an early hour. There was a certain enjoyment in being up alone in the softly lit room. She made the first pot of coffee in the gray dawn. She sipped at a cupful while watching dark clouds gather. Rain, she thought, not displeased. The sky promised it, the air smelled of it. It gave an excitement to the quiet, yawning morning. There would be thunder and lightning and cooling wind. The thought inexplicably lifted Gwen's spirits. Humming a cheerful tune, she began searching the cupboards. The restless night was forgotten.

"What are you up to?" Tillie demanded,

sweeping into the room. Hands on her bony hips, she watched Gwen.

"Good morning, Tillie." Used to the cook's abrasiveness, Gwen answered good-naturedly.

"What do you want in my kitchen?" she asked suspiciously. "You made coffee."

"Yes, it's not too bad." Gwen's tone was apologetic, but her eyes danced with mischief.

"I make the coffee," Tillie reminded her. "I always make the coffee."

"I've certainly missed it over the past couple of years. No matter how I try, mine never tastes quite like yours." Gwen poured a fresh cup. "Have some," she offered. "Maybe you can tell me what I do wrong."

Tillie accepted the cup and scowled. "You let it brew too long," she complained. Lifting her hand, she brushed curls back from Gwen's forehead. "Will you never keep your hair out of your eyes? Do you want to wear glasses?"

"No, Tillie," Gwen answered humbly. It was an old gesture and an old question. She recognized the tenderness behind the brisk words and quick fingers. Her lips curved into a smile. "I made Mama's breakfast." Turning, Gwen began to arrange cups and plates on a tray. "I'm going to take it up to her, she always liked it when I surprised her that way."

"You shouldn't bother your *maman* so early in the morning," Tillie began.

"Oh, it's not so early," Gwen said airily as she lifted the tray. "I didn't leave much of a mess," she added with the carelessness of youth. "I'll clean it up when I come back." She whisked through the door before Tillie could comment.

Gwen moved quickly up the stairs and down the corridor. Balancing the tray in one hand, she twisted the knob on her mother's door with the other. She was totally stunned to find it locked. Automatically, she jiggled the knob in disbelief. Never, as far back as her childhood memories stretched, did Gwen remember the door of Anabelle's room being locked.

"Mama?" There was a question in her voice as she knocked. "Mama, are you up?"

"What?" Anabelle's voice was clear but distracted. "Oh, Gwen, just a minute, darling."

Gwen stood outside the door listening to small, shuffling sounds she could not identify. "Mama," she said again, "are you all right?"

"Yes, yes, dear, one moment." The creaks and shuffles stopped just before the door opened. "Good morning, Gwen." Anabelle smiled. Though she wore a gown and robe and her hair was mussed by sleep, her eyes were awake and alert. "What have you got there?"

Blankly, Gwen looked down at the tray she carried. "Oh, chocolate and *beignets*. I know how you like them. Mama, what were you…?"

"Darling, how sweet!" Anabelle interrupted, and drew

Gwen into the room. "Did you really make them yourself? What a treat. Come, let's sit on the balcony. I hope
you slept well."

Gwen evaded a lie. "I woke early and decided to test
my memory with the *beignet* recipe. Mama, I don't remember you ever locking your door."

"No?" Anabelle smiled as she settled herself in a
white, wrought-iron chair. "It must be a new habit,
then. Oh, dear, it looks like rain. Well, my roses will be
thankful."

The locked door left Gwen feeling slighted. It reminded her forcibly that Anabelle Lacrosse was a person,
as well as her mother. Perhaps she would do well to remember it, Gwen silently resolved. She set the tray on
a round, glass-topped table and bent to kiss Anabelle's
cheek. "I've really missed you. I don't think I've told you
that yet."

"Gwenivere." Anabelle smiled and patted her daughter's fine-boned hand. "It's so good to have you home.
You've always been such a pleasure to me."

"Even when I'd track mud on the carpet or lose frogs
in the parlor?" Grinning, Gwen sat and poured the
chocolate.

"Darling." Anabelle sighed and shook her head. "Some
things are best forgotten. I never understood how I could
have raised such a hooligan. But even as I despaired of
you ever being a lady, I couldn't help admiring your
freedom of spirit. Hot-tempered you might have been,"

Anabelle added as she tasted her chocolate, "but never malicious and never dishonest. No matter what dreadful thing you did, you never did it out of spite, and you always confessed."

Gwen laughed. Her curls danced as she tossed back her head. "Poor Mama, I must have done so many dreadful things."

"Well, perhaps a bit more than your share," Anabelle suggested kindly. "But now you're all grown up, so difficult for a mother to accept. Your job, Gwen, you do enjoy it?"

Gwen's automatic agreement faltered on her lips. Enjoy, she thought. I wonder if I do. "Strange," she said aloud, "I'm not at all certain." She gave her mother a puzzled smile. "But I need it, not just for the money, I need the responsibility it imposes, I need to be involved."

"Yes, you always did... My, the *beignets* look marvelous."

"They are," Gwen assured her mother as she rested her elbows on the table and her chin on her open palms. "I felt obligated to try one before I offered them to you."

"See, I've always told you you were sensible," Anabelle said with a smile before she tasted one of the oddly shaped doughnuts. "Delicious," she proclaimed. "Tillie doesn't make them any better, though that had best be our secret."

Gwen allowed time to pass with easy conversation until she poured the second cup of chocolate. "Mama," she began cautiously, "how long does Luke Powers plan to stay here?"

The lifting of Anabelle's delicate brows indicated her surprise. "Stay?" she repeated as she dusted powdered sugar from her fingers. "Why, I don't know precisely, Gwen. It depends, I should say, on the stage of his book. I know he plans to finish the first draft before he goes back to California."

"I suppose," Gwen said casually as she stirred her chocolate, "he'll have no reason to come back here after that."

"Oh, I imagine he'll be back." Anabelle smiled into her daughter's eyes. "Luke is very fond of this part of the country. I wish I could tell you what his coming here has meant to me." Dreamily, she stared out into the hazy sky. Gwen felt a stab of alarm. "He's given me so much. I'd like you to spend some time with him, dear, and get to know him."

Gwen's teeth dug into the tender inside of her lip. For the moment, she felt completely at a loss. She raged in silence while Anabelle smiled secretly at rain clouds. Despicable man. How can he do this to her? Gwen glanced down into the dregs of her cup and felt a weight descend on her heart. And what is he doing to me? No matter how she tried to ignore it, Gwen could still feel the warmth of his lips on hers. The feeling clung, taunting and enticing. She was teased by a feeling totally foreign to her, a longing she could neither identify nor understand. Briskly, she shook her head to clear her thoughts. Luke Powers was only a problem while he was in Louisiana. The aim was to get him back to the West Coast and to discourage him from coming back.

"Gwen?"

"Hmm? Oh, yes, Mama." Blinking away the confused images and thoughts of Luke, Gwen met Anabelle's curious look.

"I said blueberry pie would be nice with supper. Luke's very fond of it. I thought perhaps you'd like to pick some berries for Tillie."

Gwen pondered briefly on the attractive prospect of sprinkling arsenic over Luke's portion, then rejected the idea. "I'd love to," she murmured.

The air was thick with moisture when, armed with a large bucket, Gwen went in search of blueberries. With a quick glance and shrug at the cloudy sky, she opted to risk the chance of rain. She would use her berry picking time to devise a plan to send Luke Powers westward. Swinging the bucket, she moved across the trim lawn and into the dim, sheltering trees that formed a border between her home and the bayou. Here was a different world from her mother's gentle, tidy, well-kept home. This was a primitive world with ageless secrets and endless demands. It had been Gwen's refuge as a child, her personal island. Although she remembered each detail perfectly, she stood and drank in its beauty anew.

There was a mist over the sluggish stream. Dull and brown, cattails peeked through the surface in search of the hidden sun. Here and there, cypress stumps rose above the surface. The stream itself moved in a narrow path, then curved out of sight. Gwen remembered how it twisted and snaked and widened. Over the straight, slender path, trees arched tunnellike, garnished with moss. The water was silent, but Gwen could hear the birds and an occasional plop of a frog. She knew the serenity was a surface thing. Beneath the calm was a passion and violence and wild, surging life. It called to her as it always had.

With confidence, she moved along the riverbank and searched out the plump wild berries. Silence and the simplicity of her task were soothing. Years slipped away, and she was a teenager again, a girl whose most precious fantasy was to be a part of a big city. She had dreamed in the sheltered bayou of the excitement, the mysteries of city life, the challenges of carving out her own path. Hard work, determination and a quick mind had hurried her along that path. She had earned a responsible job, established an interesting circle of friends and acquired just lately a nagging sense of dissatisfaction.

Overwork, Gwen self-diagnosed, and popped a berry into her mouth. Its juice was sweet and full of memories. And, of course, there's Michael. With a frown, Gwen dropped a handful of berries into the bucket. Even though it was my idea to end things between us, I could be suffering from the backlash of a terminated romance. And those things he said… Her frown deepened, and unconsciously she began to nibble on berries. That I was cold and unresponsive and immature…I must not have loved him. Sighing, Gwen picked more berries and ate them, one by one. If I had loved him, I'd have wanted him to make love to me.

I'm not cold, she thought. I'm not unresponsive. Look at the way I responded to Luke! She froze with a berry halfway to her mouth. Her cheeks filled with color. That was different, she assured herself quickly. Entirely different. She popped the berry into her mouth. That was simply physical, it had nothing to do with emotion. Chemistry, that's all. Why, it's practically scientific.

She speculated on the possibility of seducing Luke. She could flirt and tease and drive him to the point of distraction, make him fall in love with her and then cast him off when all danger to Anabelle was past. It can't be too difficult, she decided. I've seen lots of the models twist men around their fingers. She looked down at her own and noted they were stained with berry juice.

"Looks as though you've just been booked by the FBI."

Whirling, Gwen stared at Luke as he leaned back comfortably against a thick cypress. Again he wore jeans and a T-shirt, both faded and well worn. His eyes seemed to take their color from the sky and were more gray now than blue. Gwen's heart hammered at the base of her throat.

"Must you continually sneak up on me?" she snapped. Annoyed with the immediate response of her body to his presence, she spoke heatedly. "You have the most annoying habit of being where you're not wanted."

"Did you know you become more the Southern belle when you're in a temper?" Luke asked with an easy, unperturbed smile. "Your vowels flow quite beautifully."

Gwen's breath came out in a frustrated huff. "What do you want?" she demanded.

"To help you pick berries. Though it seems you're doing more eating than picking."

It trembled on her tongue to tell him that she didn't need or want his help. Abruptly, she remembered her resolve to wind him around her berry-stained finger. Carefully she smoothed the frown from between her brows and coaxed her mouth into a charming smile. "How sweet of you."

Luke raised a quizzical eyebrow at her change of tone. "I'm notoriously sweet," he said dryly. "Didn't you know?"

"We don't know each other well, do we?" Gwen smiled and held out the bucket. "At least, not yet."

Slowly, Luke straightened from his stance and moved to join her. He accepted the bucket while keeping his eyes fastened on hers. Determinedly, Gwen kept her own level and unconcerned. She found it difficult to breathe with him so close. "How is your book going?" she asked, hoping to divert him while she regained control of her respiratory system.

"Well enough." He watched as she began to tug berries off the bush again.

"I'm sure it must be fascinating." Gwen slid her eyes up to his in a manner she hoped was provocative and exciting. "I hope you won't think me a bore if I confess I'm quite a fan of yours. I have all your books." This part was easier because it was true.

"It's never a bore to know one's work is appreciated."

Emboldened, Gwen laid her hand on his on the handle of the bucket. Something flashed in his eyes, and her courage fled. Quickly slipping the bucket from his hold, she began to pick berries with renewed interest while cursing her lack of bravery.

"How do you like living in New York?" Luke asked as he began to add to the gradually filling bucket.

"New York?" Gwen cleared her head with a quick mental shake. Resolutely, she picked up the strings of her plan again. "It's very exciting—such a sensual city, don't you think?" Gwen lifted a berry to Luke's lips. She hoped her smile was invitingly alluring, and wished she had thought to practice in a mirror.

Luke opened his mouth to accept her offering. His tongue whispered along the tips of her fingers. Gwen felt them tremble. It took every ounce of willpower not to snatch her hand away. "Do you—do you like New

York?" Her voice was curiously husky as she began to pull berries again. The tone was uncontrived and by far the most enticing of her tactics.

"Sometimes," Luke answered, then brushed the hair away from her neck.

Moistening her lips, Gwen inched away. "I suppose you live in Louisiana."

"No, I have a place near Carmel, at the beach. What marvellously soft hair you have," he murmured, running his hand through it.

"The beach," Gwen repeated, swallowing. "It must be wonderful. I've—I've never seen the Pacific."

"It can be very wild, very dangerous," Luke said softly before his lips brushed the curve of Gwen's neck.

There was a small, strangled sound from Gwen's throat. She moved farther away and fought to keep up a casual front. "I've seen pictures, of course, and movies, but I expect it's quite different to actually see it. I'm sure it's a wonderful place to write."

"Among other things." From behind, Luke dropped his hands to her hips as he caught the lobe of her ear between his teeth. For a moment, Gwen could only lean back against him. Abruptly she stiffened, straightened, and put a few precious inches between them.

"You know," she began, completely abandoning her plans to seduce him, "I believe we have enough." As she turned around, her breasts brushed against his chest. She began to back up, stammering. "Tillie won't want to make more than two—two pies, and there's plenty here for that." Her eyes were wide and terrified.

Luke moved forward. "Then we won't have to waste any more time picking berries, will we?" The insinuation was clear.

"No, well..." Her eyes clung helplessly to his as she continued to back up. "Well, I'll just take these in to Tillie. She'll be waiting."

He was still advancing, slowly. Just as Gwen decided to abandon her dignity and run, she stepped backward into empty space. With a sharp cry, she made a desperate grab for Luke's hand. He plucked the bucket from her as she tumbled into the stream.

"Wouldn't want to lose the berries," he explained as Gwen surfaced, coughing and sputtering. "How's the water?"

"Oh!" After beating the surface of the water violently with her fists, Gwen struggled to her feet. "You did that on purpose!" Her hair was plastered to her face, and impatiently she pushed it out of her eyes.

"Did what?" Luke grinned, appreciating the way her clothes clung to her curves.

"Pushed me in." She took two sloshing steps toward the bank.

"My dear Gwenivere," Luke said in a reasonable tone. "I never laid a hand on you."

"Exactly." She kicked at the water in fury. "It's precisely the same thing."

"I suppose it might be from your point of view," he agreed. "But then, you were getting in over your head in any case. Consider the dunking the lesser of two evils. By the way, you have a lily pad on your…" His pause for the sake of delicacy was belied by the gleam in his eyes.

Flushing with embarrassment and fury, Gwen swiped a hand across her bottom. "As I said before, you are no gentleman."

Luke roared with laughter. "Why, Miss Gwenivere, ma'am, your opinion devastates me." His drawl was mocking, his bow low.

"At least," she began with a regal sniff, "you could help me out of this mess."

"Of course." With a show of gallantry, Luke set down the bucket and reached for Gwen's hand. Her wet shoes slid on the slippery bank. To help balance her, he offered his other hand. Just as she reached the top edge, Gwen threw all her weight backward, tumbling them both into the water. This time, Gwen surfaced convulsed with laughter.

As she stood, she watched him rise from the water and free his eyes of wet hair with a jerk of his head. Laughter blocked her speech. In silence, Luke watched as the sounds of her uninhibited mirth filled the air.

"How's the water?" she managed to get out before dissolving into fresh peals of laughter. Though she covered her mouth with both hands, it continued to escape and dance on the air. A quick hoot of laughter emerged as she saw his eyes narrow. He took a step toward her, and she began a strategic retreat. She moved with more speed than grace through the water, kicking it high. Giggles caused her to stumble twice. She scrambled up the slope but before she could rise to her feet, Luke caught her ankle. Pulling himself up onto the grass, he pinned Gwen beneath him.

Breathless, Gwen could still not stop laughing. Water dripped from Luke's hair onto her face, and she shook her head as it tickled her skin. A smile lurked in Luke's eyes as he looked down on her.

"I should have known better, I suppose," he commented. "But you have such an innocent face."

"You don't." Gwen took deep gulps of air in a fruitless effort to control her giggles. "Yours isn't innocent at all."

"Thank you."

Abruptly, the heavens opened and rain fell, warm and wild. "Oh!" Gwen began to push against him. "It's raining."

"So it is," Luke agreed, ignoring her squirms. "We might get wet."

The absurdity of his statement struck her suddenly. After staring up at him a moment, Gwen began to laugh again. It was a young sound, appealing and free. Gradually, Luke's expression sobered. In his eyes appeared a desire so clear, so unmistakable, that Gwen's breath caught in her throat. She opened her mouth to speak, but no words came.

"My God," he murmured. "You are exquisite."

His mouth took hers with a raw, desperate hunger. Her mouth was as avid as his, her blood as urgent. Their wet clothing proved no barrier as their bodies fused together in ageless intimacy. His caress was rough, and she reveled in the exquisite pain. The soft moan might have come from either of them. He savaged the vulnerable curve of her neck, tasting, arousing, demanding. His quick, desperate loving took her beyond the edge of reason and into ecstasy.

She felt no fear, only excitement. Here was a passion that sought and found her hidden fires and set them leaping. Rain poured over them unfelt, thunder bellowed unheard. His hands were possessive as they moved over her. Through the clinging dampness of her blouse, his mouth found the tip of her breast. She trembled, murmuring his name as he explored the slender smoothness of her thigh. She wanted him as she had never wanted anyone before.

"Luke?" His name was half question, half invitation.

Lightning flashed and illuminated the bayou. Just as swiftly they were plunged again into gloom.

"We'd better get back," Luke said abruptly, rising. "Your mother will be worried."

Gwen shut her eyes on a sudden stab of hurt. Hurriedly, she scrambled to her feet, avoiding Luke's outstretched hand. She swayed under a dizzying onslaught of emotions. "Gwen," Luke said, and took a step toward her.

"No." Her voice shook with the remnants of passion and the beginning of tears. Her eyes as they clung to his were young and devastated. "I must be losing my mind. You had no right," she told him shakily, "you had no right."

"To what?" he demanded roughly and grasped her shoulders. "To begin to make love with you or to stop?" Anger crackled in his voice.

"I wish I'd never seen you! I wish you'd never touched me."

"Oh, yes." Temper whipped through Luke's voice as he pulled her close to him again. "I can only say I wish precisely the same, but it's too late now, isn't it?" She had never seen his eyes so lit with fury. "Neither of us seems pleased with what's been started, but perhaps we should finish it." Rain swept around them, slicing through the trees and battering the ground. For a moment, Gwen knew terror. He could take her, she knew, even if she fought him. But worse, she knew he would need no force, no superior strength, after the first touch. Abruptly, he released her and stepped away. "Unless that's what you want," he said softly, "you'd best get out of here."

This time Gwen took his advice. Sobbing convulsively, she darted away among the moss-draped trees. Her one thought…to reach the safety of home.

5

The rain had awakened the garden. Twenty-four hours later it was still vibrant. Rose petals dried lazily in the sun while dew clung tenaciously to the undersides of leaves. Without enthusiasm, Gwen moved from bush to bush, selecting firm young blooms. Since the day before, she had avoided Luke Powers. With a determination born of desperation, she had clung to her mother's company, using Anabelle as both a defense and an offense. If, she had decided, *she* was always with Anabelle, Luke could not be. Nor could he take another opportunity to confuse and humiliate Gwen herself.

The basket on her arm was half filled with flowers, but she felt no pleasure in their colors and scents. Something was happening to her—she knew it, felt it, but could not define it. More and more often, she caught her thoughts drifting away from whatever task she was performing. It is, she reflected as she snipped a slender, thorny rose stem with Anabelle's garden shears, as if even my thoughts aren't wholly mine any longer.

When she considered her behavior over the past two days, Gwen was astounded. She had come to warn her mother about her relationship with Luke Powers and instead had found herself responding to him as she had never responded to Michael or any other man. But then, she admitted ruefully, she had never come into contact with a man like Luke Powers. There was a basically sensual aura about him despite his outward calm. She felt that he, like the bayou, hid much below the surface. Gwen was forced to admit that she had no guidelines for dealing with such a man. Worse, he had kindled in her a hitherto-buried part of her nature.

She had always thought her life and her needs simple. But suddenly, the quiet dreams inside her had risen to the surface. She was no longer the uncomplicated, controlled woman she had thought herself to be. The somewhat volatile temper she possessed had always been manageable, but in just two days the reins of restraint had slipped through her fingers.

His fault, Gwen grumbled to herself as she glared at a pale pink peony. He shouldn't be here—he should be in his beach house in California. If he were in California, perhaps battling an earthquake or hurricane, I'd be having a nice, uncomplicated visit with Mama. Instead he's here, insinuating himself into my life and making me feel… Gwen paused a moment and bit her lip. How does he make me feel? she thought. With a sigh, she let her gaze wander over the variety of colors and hues in the garden. I'm not sure how he makes me feel. He frightens me. The knowledge came to her swiftly, and her eyes reflected her surprise. Yes, he frightens me, though I'm not altogether sure why. It's not as if I thought he'd hurt me physically, he's not that sort of man, but still… Shaking her head, Gwen moved slowly down the walkway, digesting the new thought. He's a man who controls people and situations so naturally you're hardly aware you've been controlled.

Unconsciously, Gwen lifted her finger and ran it along her bottom lip. Vividly she remembered the feel of his mouth on hers. Its touch had ranged from gentle and coaxing to urgent and demanding, but the power over her had been the same. It was true—there was something exhilarating about fencing with him, like standing on the bow of a ship in a storm. But no matter how adventurous she might be, Gwen was forced to concede that there was one level on which she could not win. When she was in his arms, it was not surrender she felt, but passion for passion, need for need. Discovering this new facet of herself was perhaps the most disturbing knowledge of all.

I won't give up. Gwen lifted her chin and straightened her shoulders. I won't let him intimidate me or dominate my thoughts any longer. Her eyes glittered with challenge. Luke Powers won't control me. He'll find out that Gwen Lacrosse is perfectly capable of taking care of herself *and* her mother.

"Just a minute longer." Bradley Stapleton held up a pencil briefly, then continued to scrawl with it on an artist's pad. He sat crosslegged in the middle of the walkway, his feet sandaled, wearing paint-spattered carpenter's pants, a checked sport shirt unbuttoned over his thin chest and a beige fisherman's cap on his head. Surprised and intrigued, Gwen stopped in her tracks.

"Wonderful!" With surprising agility, Bradley unfolded himself and rose. His eyes smiled with genuine pleasure as he strolled over to Gwen. "I knew you'd be a good subject, but I didn't dare hope you'd be spectacular. Just look at this range of emotions!" he commanded as he flipped back several pages in his pad.

Gwen's initial amusement altered to astonishment. That the pencil sketches were exceptionally good was obvious, but it was not his talent as much as the content of the sketches that surprised her. She saw a woman with loose, curling hair and a coltish slenderness. There was a vulnerability she had never perceived in herself. As Gwen turned the pages, she saw herself dreaming, pouting, thinking and glaring. There was something disturbing about seeing her feelings of the past half hour so clearly defined. She lifted her eyes to the artist.

"They're fabulous," she told him. Bradley's face crinkled into a grin. "Bradley," she searched for the right words. "Am I really...so, well...artless as it seems here?" She looked back down at the sketches with a mixture of conflicting emotions. "What I mean is, are my thoughts, my feelings, so blatantly obvious? Am I so transparent?"

"That's precisely what makes you such a good model," Bradley said. "Your face is so expressive."

"But—" With a gesture of frustration, Gwen ran a hand through her hair. "Do they always show? Are they always there for people to examine? I feel defenseless and, well, naked somehow."

Bradley gave her a sympathetic smile and patted her cheek with his long, bony fingers. "You have an honest face, Gwen, but if it worries you, remember that most people don't see past the shape of a nose or the color of eyes. People are usually too busy with their own thoughts to notice someone else's."

"Yet you certainly did," Gwen replied, but she felt more comfortable.

"It's my business."

"Yes." With a smile, Gwen began flipping through the pages again. "You're very good..." She stopped, speechless as the pad fell open to a sketch of Luke.

It was a simple sketch of him sitting on the rail of the veranda. He was dressed casually, and his hair was tousled, as though he had been working. Bradley had captured the strength and intelligence in his face, as well as the sensual quality she had not expected another man to notice. But it was Luke's eyes, which seemed to lock on to hers, that impressed her. The artist had caught the strange melding of serenity and power that she had felt in them. Gwen was conscious of an odd quickening of her breath. Irresistibly, she was drawn to the picture just as she was drawn to the man.

"I'm rather pleased with it." Gwen heard Bradley's voice and realized with a jolt that he had been speaking for several seconds.

"It's very good," she murmured. "You understand him." She was unaware of the wistfulness and touch of envy in her voice.

After a brief, speculative glance at her lowered head, Bradley nodded. "To an extent, I suppose. I understand he's a complicated man. In some ways, he's much like you."

"Me?" Genuinely shocked, Gwen lifted her eyes.

"You're both capable of a wide range of emotions. Not everyone is, you know. The main difference is, he channels his, while yours are fully expressed. Will you sit for me?"

"What?" Gwen tried to focus on him again. The question was out of context with the rest of his statement. She shook her head to clear it of the disturbing thoughts his words had aroused in her.

"Will you sit for me?" Bradley repeated patiently. "I very much want to do you in oils."

"Yes, of course." She shrugged and conjured up a smile to dispel her own mood. "It sounds like fun."

"You won't think so after a couple of hours of holding a pose," Bradley promised good-naturedly. "Come on, we'll get started now, before you change your mind." Taking her hand, he pulled her up the walkway.

Several hours later, Gwen clearly understood the truth of Bradley's statement. Posing for a temperamental artist, she discovered, was both exhausting and demanding. Her face had been sketched from a dozen angles while she stood or sat or twisted in accordance with his commands. She began to feel more sympathy for the models at *Style*.

She had been amused at first when Bradley rooted through her wardrobe in search of attire suitable to sitting for the portrait. When he selected a thin white silk robe, she had taken what she considered a firm stand against his choice. He ignored her objections and, to her amazement, Gwen found herself doing exactly as he instructed.

Now, tired and alone, Gwen stretched out on her bed and relaxed her muscles. A smile lurked at the corners of her mouth as she recalled how Bradley had gently steamrolled her. Any embarrassment she had felt about wearing only the robe while he studied her or moved her this way and that had been swiftly eradicated. She might as easily have been an interesting tree or a fruit bowl. He had not been interested in the body beneath the robe but in the way the material draped.

I don't have to worry about fending off a passionate attack, Gwen reflected as she shut her eyes, only about stiffening joints. With a deep sigh, she snuggled into the pillow.

Her dreams were confused. She dreamed she was roaming through the bayou picking roses and blueberries. As she passed through a clearing, she saw Luke chopping down a thick, heavy tree. The sound of the ax was like thunder. The tree fell soundlessly at her feet. As Luke watched, she walked to him and melted into his arms. For an instant she felt violent joy, then, just as suddenly, she found herself hurled into the cool stream.

From behind a curtain of water, Gwen saw Anabelle, a gentle smile on her lips as she offered her hand to Luke. Gwen struggled for the surface but found it just beyond her reach. Abruptly she was standing on the bank with Bradley sitting at her feet sketching. Ax in hand, Luke approached her, but Gwen found her arms and legs had turned to stone. As he walked, he began to change, his features dissolving, his clothing altering.

It was Michael who came to her now, a practical brief-case taking the place of the ax. He shook his head at her stone limbs and reminded her in his precise voice that he had told her she was cold. Gwen tried to shake her head in denial, but her neck had turned to stone, as well. When Michael took her by the shoulders and prepared to carry her away, she could only make a small sound of protest. From a distance, she heard Luke call her name. Michael dropped her, and as her stone limbs shattered, she awoke. Dazed, Gwen stared into blue-gray eyes. "Luke," she murmured, "I'm not cold."

"No." He brushed the hair from her cheek, then let his palm linger. "You're certainly not."

"Kiss me again, I don't want to turn to stone." She made the request petulantly. Amusement touched Luke's mouth as he lowered it to hers.

"Of course not, who could blame you?"

Sighing, Gwen locked her arms around his neck and enjoyed the warm gentleness of the kiss. Her limbs grew warm and fluid, her lips parted and begged for more. The kiss deepened until dream and reality mixed. A sharp stab of desire brought Gwen crashing through the barriers of lingering sleep. She managed a muffled protest against his mouth as she struggled for release. Luke did not immediately set her free but allowed his lips to linger on hers until he had had his fill. Even then, his face remained dangerously close. His mouth was only a sigh away.

"That must've been some dream," he murmured. With easy intimacy, he rubbed his nose against hers. "Women are so irresistibly soft and warm when they've been sleeping."

Cheeks flaming, Gwen managed to struggle up to a sitting position. "You have a nerve," she flared. "What do you mean by coming into my bedroom and molesting me?"

"Take a guess," he invited with a wolfish grin. Her color grew yet deeper as she gripped the V of her robe. "Relax," Luke continued. "I didn't come to steal your virtue, I came to wake you for dinner." He ran a fingertip along her jawline. "The rest was your idea."

Indignation stiffened Gwen's spine but muddled her speech. "You—you…I was asleep, and you took advantage…"

"I certainly did," Luke agreed, then pulled her close for a hard, brief kiss. "And we both enjoyed every second of it." He rose gracefully. "White suits you," he commented, his gaze wandering over the soft folds of the robe, "but you might want to change into something a bit less informal for dinner, unless your object is to drive Bradley into a frenzy of desire."

Gwen rose, wrapping the robe more tightly about her. "Don't worry about Bradley," she said icily. "He spent all afternoon sketching me in this robe."

The humor disappeared so swiftly from Luke's face, Gwen wondered if she had imagined its existence. His mouth was grim as he stepped toward her. "What?" The one word vibrated in the room.

"You heard me. I've agreed to let Bradley paint me."

"In that?" Luke's eyes dropped the length of the robe, then returned to her face.

"Yes, what of it?" Gwen tossed her head and turned to

walk away from him. The silk of her robe floated around her legs and clung to her hips as she moved. When she reached the window, she turned and leaned back against the sill. Her stance was at once insolent and sensual. "What business is it of yours?"

"Don't play games unless you're prepared to lose," Luke warned softly.

"You're insufferable." The brown of her eyes grew molten.

"And you're a spoiled child."

"I'm not a child," Gwen retorted. "I make my own decisions. If I want to pose for Bradley in this robe or in a suit of armor or in a pair of diamond earrings and nothing else, that's nothing to do with you."

"I'd consider the diamond earrings carefully, Gwen." The soft tone of Luke's voice betrayed his rising temper. "If you try it, I'd have to break all of Bradley's fingers."

His calm promise of violence added fuel to Gwen's fire. "If that isn't typical male stupidity! If something doesn't work, kick it or swear at it! I thought you were more intelligent."

"Did you?" A glimmer of amusement returned to Luke's eyes. Reaching out, he gave her hair a sharp tug. "Too bad you were wrong."

"Men!" she expostulated, lifting her palms and eyes to the ceiling. "You're all the same."

"You speak, of course, from vast personal experience."

The sarcasm in his voice did not escape Gwen. "You're all arrogant, superior, selfish—"

"Beasts?" Luke suggested amiably.

"That'll do," she agreed with a nod.

"Glad to help." Luke sat back on the edge of the bed and watched her. The flickering lights of the setting sun accentuated the hollows and shadows of her face.

"You always think you know best and that women are too muddleheaded to decide things for themselves. All you do is give orders, orders, orders, and when you don't get your own way, you shout or sulk or, worse, patronize. I hate, loathe and despise being patronized!" Balling her hands into fists, Gwen thrust them into the pockets of her robe. "I don't like being told I'm cute in a tone of voice that means I'm stupid. I don't like being patted on the head like a puppy who can't learn to fetch. Then, after you've finished insulting my intelligence, you want to breathe all over me. Of course, I should be grateful for the attention because I'm such a sweet little simpleton." Unable to prevent herself any longer, Gwen gave the bedpost a hard slap. "I am not," she began, and her voice was low with fury, "I am *not* cold and unresponsive and sexually immature."

"Good Lord, child." Gwen, jolted by Luke's voice, blinked as she refocused on him. "What idiot ever told you that you were?"

Gwen stared at Luke in frozen silence.

"Your opinion of men obviously comes from the same

source," he continued. "Your Michael must have been really convincing." Embarrassed, Gwen shrugged and turned back to the window. "Were you in love with him?"

The question caught her so off balance that she answered automatically. "No, but I thought I was, so it amounts to the same thing, I imagine."

"Bounced around a bit, were you?" His tone was surprisingly gentle as were the hands that descended to her shoulders.

"Oh, please." Quickly, Gwen moved away as she felt a strange, sweet ache. "Don't be kind to me. I can't fight you if you're kind."

"Is that what you want to do?" Luke took her shoulders firmly now and turned her around to face him. "Do you want to fight?" His eyes dropped to her lips. Gwen began to tremble.

"I think it's better if we do." Her voice was suddenly breathless. "I think fighting with you is safer."

"Safer than what?" he inquired. He smiled, a quick, flashing movement that was both charming and seductive. The room grew dim in the dusk, silhouetting them in the magic light of a dying day. "You are beautiful," he murmured, sliding his hand along the slope of her shoulders until his fingers traced her throat.

Mesmerized, Gwen stared up at him. "No, I—I'm not. My mouth's too wide, and my chin's pointed."

"Of course," Luke agreed as he drew her closer. "I

see it now, you're quite an ugly little thing. It's a pity to waste velvet eyes and silken skin on such an unfortunate-looking creature."

"Please." Gwen turned her head, and his mouth brushed her cheek rather than her lips. "Don't kiss me. It confuses me—I don't know what to do."

"On the contrary, you seem to know precisely what to do."

"Luke, please." She caught her breath. "Please, when you kiss me, I forget everything, and I only want you to kiss me again."

"I'll be happy to do so."

"No, don't." Gwen pushed away and looked at him with huge, pleading eyes. "I'm frightened."

He studied her with quiet intensity. He watched her lip tremble, her teeth digging into it to halt the movement. The pulse in her neck throbbed under his palm. Letting out a long breath, he stepped back and slipped his hands into his pockets. His look was thoughtful. "I wonder, if I make love to you, would you lose that appealing air of innocence?"

"I'm not going to let you make love to me." Even to herself, Gwen's voice sounded shaky and unsure.

"Gwen, you're much too honest to make a statement like that, let alone believe it yourself." Luke turned and walked to the door. "I'll tell Anabelle you'll be down in a few minutes."

He closed the door behind him, and Gwen was left alone with her thoughts in the darkening room.

6

Gwen endured Bradley's sketching for nearly an hour. His eyes were much sharper in his plain, harmless face than she had originally thought. And, she had discovered, he was a quiet tyrant. Once she had agreed to pose for him, he had taken over with mild but inescapable efficiency. He placed her on a white wrought-iron chair in the heart of the garden.

The morning was heavy and warm, with a hint of rain hovering despite the sunshine. A dragonfly darted past, zooming over a rosebush to her right. Gwen turned her head to watch its flight.

"Don't do that!" Bradley's beautifully modulated voice made Gwen guiltily jerk her head back. "I'm only sketching your face today," he reminded her. She murmured something unintelligible that had him smiling. "Now I understand why you work behind the scenes at *Style* and not in front of the camera." His pencil paused in midair. "You've never learned how to sit still!"

"I always feel as though I should be doing something," Gwen admitted. "How does anyone ever just sit like this? I had no idea how difficult it was."

"Where's your Southern languor?" Bradley asked, sketching in a stray wisp of hair. She would sit more quietly if he kept up a conversation, he decided, even though he did not particularly care for splitting his concentration between sketching and talking.

"Oh, I don't think I ever had it," Gwen told him. She brought up her foot to rest on the chair and laced her hands around her knee. Enjoying the heady perfumes of the garden, she took a deep breath. "And living in New York has made it worse. Although…" She paused, looking around her again, though this time remembering to move only her eyes. "There is something peaceful here, isn't there? I'm discovering how much I've missed that."

"Is your work very demanding?" Bradley asked, perfecting the line of her chin with a dash of his pencil.

"Hmm." Gwen shrugged and longed to take a good stretch. "There's always some deadline that no one could possibly meet that, of course, we meet. Then there are the models and photographers who need their artistic egos soothed—"

"Are you good at soothing artistic egos?" Bradley narrowed his eyes to find the perspective.

"Surprisingly, yes." She smiled at him. "And I like the challenge of meeting deadlines."

"I've never been good with deadlines," he murmured. "Move your chin, so." He gestured with a fingertip, and Gwen obeyed.

"No, some people aren't, but I have to be. When you're a monthly publication, you have no choice."

For a moment, Gwen fell silent, listening to the hum of bees around the azalea bushes in back of her. Somewhere near the house, a bird sent up a sudden, jubilant song. "Where are you from, Bradley?" she asked at length, turning her eyes back to him. He was a strange man, she thought, with his gangly body and wise eyes.

"Boston." His eyes went briefly to her, then back to his sketch pad. "Turn your head to the right a bit… There, good."

"Boston. I should have guessed. Your voice is very… elegant." Bradley chuckled. "How did you decide to become an artist?"

"It's my favorite mode of communication. I've always loved sketching. In school my teachers had to confiscate my sketchbooks. And some people are very impressed when they hear you're an artist."

Gwen laughed. "The last's not a real reason."

"Don't be too sure," Bradley murmured, involved with the curve of her cheek. "I enjoy flattery. Not everyone is as self-sufficient as you."

Forgetting his instructions, Gwen turned to him again. "Is that the way you see me?"

"Sometimes." He lifted a brow and motioned for her to turn away again. For a moment he studied her profile before beginning to draw again. "To be an artist, a good one, without the driving passion to be a great one, suits me perfectly." He smiled at her thoughtful expression. "It wouldn't suit you at all. You haven't the patience for it."

Gwen thought of the brisk, no-nonsense Gwen Lacrosse of *Style* magazine—a practical, efficient woman who knew her job and did it well, a woman who knew how to handle details and people, who was good at facts and figures. And yet...there was another Gwen Lacrosse who loved old, scented gardens and watched weepy movies on television, who hopped into hansom cabs in the rain. Michael had been attracted to the first Gwen but despaired of the second. She sighed. Perhaps she had never understood the mixture herself. She had not even questioned it. At least not until she had met Luke Powers.

Luke Powers. She didn't want to think about him. Things were not working out quite the way she had planned in that department. Worse yet, she wasn't at all sure they ever would.

Gwen tilted her head up to the sky. Bradley opened his mouth to remonstrate, then finding a new angle to his liking, continued sketching. The sun lit reddish sparks in her hair. She noticed that the clouds were rolling in from the west. A storm was probably brewing, she thought. It was still far off, hovering, taking its time. She had a feeling that it would strike when least expected. Though the day appeared to be sunny and pleasant, she felt the passion there, just below the surface. The air throbbed with it. In spite of the heat, Gwen shivered involuntarily. Irresistibly, her eyes were drawn to the house and up.

Luke was watching her from the window of his room. She wondered how long he had been there, looking down with that quiet, direct expression that she had come to expect from him. His eyes never wavered as hers met them.

He stared without apology, without embarrassment. For the moment, Gwen found herself compelled to stare back. Even with the distance between them, she could feel the intrusion of his gaze. She stiffened against it.

As if sensing her response, Luke smiled…slowly, arrogantly, never shifting his eyes from hers. Gwen read the challenge in them. She tossed her head before turning away.

Bradley cocked a brow at Gwen's scowling face. "It appears," he said mildly, "that we're done for the day." He rose from his perch on a stone, unexpectedly graceful. "Tomorrow morning, I want you in the robe. I've a pretty good idea on the pose I want. I'm going in to see if I can charm Tillie out of a piece of that chocolate cake. Want some?"

Gwen smiled and shook her head. "No, it's a bit close

to lunch for me. I think I'll give Mama a hand and do some weeding." She glanced down at the petunia bed. "She seems to be neglecting it a bit."

"Busy lady," Bradley said and, sticking the pencil behind his ear, sauntered down the path.

Busy lady? Gwen frowned after him. Her mother did not seem preoccupied...but *what* precisely was she doing? Perhaps it was just her way of intimating to Gwen that she, too, had a life, just as important as Gwen's big-city profession. Moving over to the petunia bed, Gwen knelt down and began to tug at stray weeds.

Anabelle had developed a habit of disappearing from time to time—that was something new. Unable to do otherwise, she glanced up at Luke's window again. He was gone. With a scowl, she went back to her weeding.

If only he would leave, she thought, everything would be fine. Her mother was a soft, gentle creature who trusted everyone. She simply had no defenses against a man like Luke Powers. And you do? she mocked herself. Swearing, Gwen tugged and unearthed a hapless petunia.

"Oh!" She stared down at the colorful blossom, foolishly guilty. A shadow fell across her, and she stiffened.

"Something upsetting you?" Luke asked. He crouched down beside her; taking the blossom from her hand, he tucked it behind her ear. Gwen remembered the rose and blushed before she could turn her face away.

"Go away. I'm busy," she said.

"I'm not." His voice was carelessly friendly. "I'll help."

"Don't you have work to do?" She shot him a scornful glance before ripping savagely at another weed.

"Not at the moment." Luke's tone was mild as he felt his way among the flowers. His fingers were surprisingly deft. "The advantage of being self-employed is that you make your own hours—at least most of the time."

"Most of the time?" Gwen queried, curiously overcoming her dislike for this annoying man.

"When it works, you're chained to the typewriter, and that's that."

"Strange," Gwen mused aloud, forgetting to ignore him. "I can't picture you chained to anything. You seem so free. But it must be difficult putting all those words on paper, making the people inside your head walk and talk and think. Why did you decide to become a writer?"

"Because I have an affection for words," he said. "And because those people in my head are always scrambling to get out. Now I've answered your question frankly." Luke turned to her as he twirled a blade of grass between his fingers. "It's my turn to ask one. What were you thinking of when you were watching the sky?"

Gwen frowned. She wasn't at all sure she wanted to share her private thoughts with Luke Powers. "That we're in for some rain," she compromised. "Must you watch me that way?"

"Yes."

"You're impossible," she told him crossly.

"You're beautiful." His look was suddenly intense, shooting a quiver up her spine. He cupped her chin before she could turn away. "With the sunlight on your hair and your eyes misty, you were all I have ever dreamed of. I wanted you." His mouth drew closer to hers. His breath fluttered over her skin.

"Don't!" Gwen started to back away, but his fingers on her chin held her steady.

"Not so fast," Luke said softly.

His kiss was surprisingly gentle, brushing her mouth like a butterfly's wing. Instinctively, she parted her lips to receive his probing tongue. With a sigh, she succumbed to the mood of the waiting garden. Her passion had lain sleeping, like the threatened storm behind the layer of soft clouds. She trembled with desire as his fingers carefully traced the planes of her face. They caressed her cheekbones, the line of her jaw, the thick tousle of her hair at her temples, before he kissed her again. His tongue teased and tasted with only the slightest pressure. She gripped his shirt front tightly and moaned his name. Her skin was alive with him. Wanting, needing, she twined her arms around his neck and pulled him against her. Her mouth was avid, seeking.

For one blazing moment, the flame rose and consumed them both, as they embraced in the fragrant morning heat. Then he had drawn her away, and Gwen was staring up at him, trying to catch her breath.

"No." She shook her head, pressing her hands to her temples as she waited for her thoughts to steady. "No." Before she could turn and flee, Luke had sprung up, grabbing her wrist.

"No what?" His voice was deeper, but still calm.

"This isn't right." The words tumbled out of her as she tried to find reason. "Let me go."

"In a minute." Luke kept his hand on her wrist and stepped toward her. A sweeping gaze took in her frantic color and widened eyes. "You want it, and so do I."

"No, no, I don't!" She shot out the fierce denial and jerked her arm. Her wrist stayed in his grip.

"I don't remember your protesting too much!" he said mildly. She was annoyed to recognize amusement in his eyes. "Yes, I distinctly recall it was you who took matters to the boiling point."

"All right, all right. You win." She took a breath. "I did. I forgot, that's all."

He smiled. "Forgot what?"

Gwen narrowed her eyes at his amusement. It fanned her temper more than his anger would have. "Forgot that I don't like you," she tossed out. "Now let me go, my memory's back."

Luke laughed a joyous masculine laugh before he pulled Gwen back into his arms. "You tempt me to make you forget again, Gwenivere." He kissed her again, a hard and possessive kiss. It was over almost before it had begun, but her senses were already reeling from it. "Shall we go back to weeding?" he asked pleasantly, as he released her.

She drew herself straight, indignant, furious. "You can go…"

"Gwen!" Anabelle's soft voice cut off Gwen's suggestion. Her mother had drifted into the garden. "Oh, here you are, both of you. How nice."

"Hello Anabelle." Luke gave her an easy smile. "We thought we'd give you a hand with the garden!"

"Oh?" She looked vaguely at her flowers, then her face brightened with a smile. "That's sweet, I'm sure I haven't been as diligent as I should be, but…" She trailed off, watching a bee swoop down on a rosebud. "Perhaps we can all get back to this later. Tillie's got lunch ready and insists on serving right away. It's her afternoon off, you know." She turned her smile on Gwen. "You'd better wash your hands, dear," she looked anxiously at Gwen, "and perhaps you should stay out of the sun for a while, you're a bit flushed."

Gwen could feel Luke grin without looking at him. "You're probably right," she mumbled. Detestable man! Why did he always succeed in confusing her?

Unaware of the fires raging in her daughter, Anabelle smilingly laid a hand on Gwen's cheek, but whatever she planned to say was distracted by the drone of a furry bee. "My, my," she said, watching it swoop greedily down on an azalea blossom. "He's certainly a big one." Having forgotten Tillie's instructions, she glanced back up at Gwen.

"You were sitting for Bradley this morning, weren't you, dear?"

"Yes." Gwen made a face. "For almost two hours."

"Isn't that exciting?" Anabelle glanced up at Luke for his confirmation, then continued before he could comment. "A portrait painted by a real artist! I can hardly wait to see it when it's all finished! Why, I'll have to buy it, I suppose." Her blue eyes brightened. "Perhaps I'll hang it right over the mantel in the parlor. That is…" Another thought intruded, and she stopped her planning and rearranging to look at her daughter. "Unless you want it for you and your Michael."

"He isn't *my* Michael, Mama, I told you." Gwen stuck her hands in her pockets, wishing Luke would say something instead of simply watching her with those cool blue-gray eyes. Why was it never possible to tell what he was thinking? "And in any case, he'd never buy a painting from an unknown. He wouldn't be assured of the investment value," she added. She was sorry that a note of rancor slipped into her voice.

Luke's eyes remained cool, but Gwen saw his brow lift fractionally. He doesn't miss anything, she thought with a stab of resentment. Turning, she began to pull loose petals from an overbloomed rose.

"Oh, but surely, if it were a portrait of you…" Anabelle began. Observing her daughter's expression, she hastily changed her course. "I'm sure it's going to be just beautiful," she said brightly. She turned to Luke. "Don't you think so, Luke?"

"Undoubtedly," he agreed as Gwen gave the rose her fiercest attention. "Bradley has the raw material to work with. That is…" He paused and, unable to resist, Gwen looked over her shoulder to meet his eyes again. "If Gwenivere manages to hold still until it's finished."

Gwen's spine stiffened at the amusement in his voice, but before she could retort, Anabelle laughed gaily. "Oh, yes, Gwen's a ball of fire, I declare," she emoted. "Even as a youngster, flitting here and there, quicker than a minute. Why, I'd have to nearly chain her to a chair to braid her hair." She smiled in maternal memory, absently fluffing her own hair. "Then, at the end of the day, or most times long before, it looked as though I had never touched it! And her clothes!" She clucked her tongue and rolled her eyes. "Oh, what a time I used to have with torn knees and ripped seams."

"Mama." Gwen interrupted before Anabelle could launch into another speech on her girlhood. "I'm sure Luke's not interested in the state of my clothes."

He grinned at that, widely, irreverently. Gwen blushed to the roots of her hair. "On the contrary," he said as she groped around for something scathing and dignified to say. "I'm extremely interested." His eyes softened as he smiled at Anabelle. "It's all grist for my mill—just the sort of background material a writer needs."

"Why, yes, I suppose so." Gwen saw that her mother

found this extremely profound. Anabelle lapsed into silence again, dreaming off into the middle distance. Luke grinned at Gwen over her head.

"And I've always had a fondness for little girls," he told her. "Particularly ones whose braids won't stay tied, and who regularly scrape their knees." He glanced down, letting his eyes run over Gwen's French-cut T-shirt and cinnamon-colored shorts. "I imagine over the years Anabelle was pretty busy administering first aid." His eyes traveled up on the same slow, casual journey before meeting hers.

"I didn't make a habit of falling down," Gwen began, feeling ridiculous.

Anabelle came out of her trance for a moment. "Oh, yes." She picked up on Luke's comment. "I don't think a day went by when I wasn't patching up some hurt. A fishhook in your hand one day…" She shuddered at the memory. "And a lump the size of a goose egg on your forehead the next. It was always one thing or another."

"Mama." Gwen crushed what was left of the rose between her fingers. "You make it sound as if I had been a walking disaster."

"You were just spirited, darling." Anabelle frowned a bit at the damaged rose, but made no comment. "Though there were times, I admit, I wasn't certain you'd live to grow up. But, of course, you have, so I probably shouldn't have worried so much."

"Mama." Gwen was suddenly touched. How difficult

it must have been, she reflected, for such a young, dreamy woman to raise a lively youngster all on her own! How many sacrifices Anabelle must have made that Gwen had never even considered. Stepping over, Gwen put her hands on Anabelle's soft rounded shoulders. "I love you, and I'm terribly glad you're my mother."

With a sound of surprised pleasure, Anabelle framed Gwen's face and kissed both her cheeks. "What a sweet thing to hear, and from a grown daughter, too." She gave Gwen a quick, fragrant hug.

Over her mother's shoulder, Gwen saw that Luke was still watching them. His direct intensity made her feel self-conscious.

How do I really feel about him? she asked herself. And how can I feel anything, anything at all, when the woman I love most in the world stands between us? She felt trapped, and something of her panic showed in her eyes.

Luke tilted his head. "You're very fortunate, Anabelle." He spoke to the mother, though his eyes remained on the daughter. "Love is very precious."

"Yes." She kissed Gwen's cheek again, then linked her arm through her daughter's. "I'm in a festive mood," she told them both, glowing. "I think we should be daring and have some wine with lunch." Her eyes widened. "*Lunch!* Oh, dear, Tillie will be furious! I completely forgot." She rested a hand against her heart as if to calm it. "I'll go smooth things along. Give me a minute." She assumed a businesslike air. "Then come right in. And see that you make a fuss over whatever she's fixed. We don't want to hurt her feelings any more than we have." She gave the final instructions as she swept back up the path and disappeared.

Gwen started to follow. Luke neatly cut off her retreat by taking her hand. "You'd better let her play diplomat first," he told her.

Gwen swung around to face him. "I don't want to be here with you."

Luke lifted a brow, letting his eyes play over her face. "Why not? I can't imagine more attractive circum-stances. This lovely garden… A beautiful day… Tell me something," he continued, interrupting whatever retort she might have made. Casually, he tangled the fingers of his other hand in her hair. "What were you thinking of when you hugged your mother and looked at me?"

"That's none of your business." Gwen jerked her head, trying to free her hair from his curious fingers.

"Really?" He lifted and stroked a straying lock of her hair. Somewhere in the distant west, she heard the first rumbles of thunder. "I had the impression whatever was going through your mind at that moment was very much my business." He brought his eyes back down to hers and held them steady. "Why do you suppose I did?"

"I haven't the faintest idea," Gwen returned coolly. "Probably an author's overheated imagination."

Luke's smile moved slowly, touching his eyes seconds

before it touched his lips. "I don't think so, Gwen. I prefer thinking of it as a writer's intuition."

"Or a man's overinflated ego," she shot back, lifting her hand to her hair in an attempt to remove his exploring fingers. "Would you stop that!" she demanded, trying to ignore the dancing of nerves at the back of her neck.

"Or a man's sensitivity to a woman," he countered, bringing her hand to his lips. He kissed her fingers one at a time until she regained the presence of mind to try to jerk free. Instead of releasing her, Luke simply laced fingers with hers. They stood, joined as carelessly as schoolchildren, while she frowned at him. The thunder came again, closer. "Sensitive enough to know when a woman who is attracted to me," he went on lazily, "is not willing to admit it."

Her eyes narrowed. "You're impossibly conceited."

"Hopelessly honest," he corrected. "Shall I prove it to you?"

Gwen lifted her chin. "There's nothing to prove." She knew the hopelessness of attempting to pull her hand from his. Casually, she looked past him to the sky. "The clouds are coming in. I don't want to get caught in the rain."

"We've got a minute," he said, without even glancing at the sky. He smiled. "I believe I make you nervous."

"Don't flatter yourself," she tossed back, and kept her hands calm in his.

"The pulse in your throat is hammering." His eyes dropped and lingered on it, further increasing its pace. "It's strangely attractive—"

"It always does when I'm annoyed," she said, fighting for poise as the sweep of his eyes from her throat to her face threatened to destroy her composure.

"I like you when you're annoyed. I like to watch the different expressions on your face and to see your eyes darken…but…" He trailed off, slipping his hands to her wrists. "At the moment, I believe it's nerves."

"Believe what you like." It was impossible to prevent her pulse from pounding against his fingers. She tried to calm her rebel blood. "You don't make me the least bit nervous."

"No?" His grin turned wolfish. Gwen braced for a struggle. "A difference of opinion," he observed. "And one I'm tempted to resolve." He drew her closer, letting his eyes rest on her mouth. Gwen knew he was baiting her and held her ground. She said nothing, waiting for him to make his move.

"At the moment, however, I'm starved." Luke grinned, then gave her a quick, unexpected kiss on the nose. "And I'm too much of a coward to risk Tillie's bad temper." He dropped one of her hands, but kept the other companionably linked with his. "Let's eat," he suggested, ignoring Gwen's frown.

7

Gwen noticed several small changes in Anabelle. There was an air of secrecy about her that Gwen found out of character. *She disappears so often,* Gwen thought as she seated herself in front of the vintage Steinway in the parlor. *She's here one minute and gone the next. And she spends too much time with Luke Powers. There are too many discussions that stop abruptly when I walk in on them. They make me feel like an intruder.* With little interest, she began to pick out a melody. The breeze came softly through the window, barely stirring the curtain. The scent of jasmine was elusive, teasing the senses.

I'm jealous, Gwen realized with a jolt of surprise. *I expected Mama's undivided attention, and I'm not getting it.* With a rueful laugh, Gwen began to play Chopin. *Now when have I ever had Mama's undivided atten-*

tion? She's always had her "visitors," her antiques, her flowers.

Thinking back over childhood memories, Gwen played with absentminded skill. She had forgotten how soothing the piano was to her. I haven't given myself enough time for this, she reflected. I should take a step back and look at where my life is going. I need to find out what's missing. Her fingers stilled on the last note, which floated quietly through the air and then vanished.

"Lovely," Luke said. "Really lovely."

Gwen suppressed the desire to jump at the sound of his voice. She forced herself to raise her eyes and meet his, struggling to keep the color from tinting her cheeks. It was difficult, after what she had said the evening before, to face him. She felt her defenses were shaky, her privacy invaded. He knew more of her now than she wanted him to.

"Thank you," she said politely. "I am, as Mama always said I would be, grateful for the music lessons she forced me to take."

"Forced?" To Gwen's consternation, Luke sat down on the stool beside her.

"As only she can." Gwen relieved a portion of her tension by giving her attention to another melody. "With quiet, unarguable insistence."

"Ah." Luke nodded in agreement. "And you didn't want to study piano?"

"No, I wanted to study crawfishing." She was stunned

when he began to play along with her, picking out the melody on the treble keys. "I didn't know you played." The utter disbelief in her voice brought on his laugh.

"Believe it or not, I, too, had a mother." He gave Gwen his swift, conspiratorial grin. "I wanted to study rock skipping."

Totally disarmed, Gwen smiled back at him. Something passed between them. It was as strong and as real as the passion that had flared with their kiss, as gentle and soothing as the music drifting from the keys.

"Isn't that sweet." Anabelle stood in the doorway and beamed at both of them. "Duets are so charming."

"Mama." Gwen was relieved her voice did not tremble. "I looked for you earlier."

"Did you?" Anabelle smiled. "I'm sorry, dear, I've been busy with...this and that," she finished vaguely. "Aren't you sitting for Bradley today?"

"I've already given him his two hours this morning," Gwen answered. "It's lucky for me he wants the early light, or I'd be sitting all day. I thought perhaps you had something you'd like me to do or someplace you'd like me to take you. It's such a lovely day."

"Yes, it is, isn't it?" Anabelle agreed. Her eyes drifted momentarily to Luke's. Abruptly, her cheeks dimpled and her lips curved. "Why, as a matter of fact, darling, there *is* something you could do for me. Oh—" She paused and shook her head. "But it's so much trouble."

"I don't mind," Gwen interrupted, falling into a child-hood trap.

"Well, if it really isn't a bother," Anabelle continued, beaming again. "I especially wanted some embroidery thread, very unusual shades, difficult to find, I'm afraid. There's a little shop in the French Market that carries them."

"In New Orleans?" Gwen's eyes widened.

"Oh, it is a bother, isn't it?" Anabelle sighed. "It's not important, dear. Not important at all," she added.

"It's not a bother, Mama," Gwen corrected, smiling at the old ruse. "Besides, I'd like to get into New Orleans while I'm home. I can be a tourist now."

"What a marvelous idea!" Anabelle enthused. "Wouldn't it be fun? Roaming through the Vieux Carré, wandering through the shops, listening to the music in Bourbon Street. Oh, and dinner at some lovely gallery restaurant. Yes." She clapped her hands together and glowed. "It's just the thing."

"It sounds perfect." Anabelle's childlike enthusiasm caused Gwen to smile. Shopping, she remembered, had always been Anabelle's favorite pastime. "I can't think of a better way to spend the day."

"Good. It's settled, then." She turned to Luke with a pleased smile. "You'll go with Gwen, won't you, dear? It wouldn't do for her to go all alone."

"Alone?" Gwen cut in, confused. "But, Mama, aren't you—?"

"It's such a long drive, too," Anabelle bubbled on. "I'm sure Gwen would love the company."

"No, Mama, I—"

"I'd love to." Luke easily overruled Gwen's objections. He gave Gwen an ironic smile. "I can't think of a better way to spend the day."

"Gwen, dear, I'm so glad you thought of it." The praise was given with a sigh as Anabelle moved over to pat Gwen's cheek.

Looking up into the ingenuous eyes, Gwen felt the familiar sensations of affection and frustration. "I'm very clever," she murmured, moving her lips into a semblance of a smile.

"Yes, of course you are," Anabelle agreed, and gave her a quick, loving hug. "I would change, though, darling. It wouldn't do to go into the city in those faded old jeans. Didn't I throw those out when you were fifteen? Yes, I'm sure I did. Well, run along and have fun," she ordered as she began to drift from the room. "I've just so much to do, I can't think of it all."

"Mama." Gwen called after her. Anabelle turned at the door, lifting her brows in acknowledgement. "The thread?"

"Thread?" Anabelle repeated blankly. "Oh, yes, of course. I'll write down the colors and the name of the shop." She shook her head with a self-deprecating smile. "My, my, I'm quite the scatterbrain. I'll go in right now and tell Tillie you won't be here for dinner. She gets so annoyed with me when I forget things. Do change those pants, Gwen," she added as she started down the hall.

"I'd hide them," Luke suggested confidentially. "She's liable to throw them out again."

Rising with what she hoped was dignity, Gwen answered, "If you'll excuse me?"

"Sure." Before she could move away, Luke took her hand in a light but possessive grip. "I'll meet you out front in twenty minutes. We'll take my car."

A dozen retorts trembled on Gwen's tongue and were dismissed. "Certainly. I'll try not to keep you waiting." She walked regally from the room.

The weather was perfect for a drive—sunny and cloudless, with a light breeze. Gwen had replaced her jeans with a snowy crepe de chine dress. It had a high, lacy neck and pleated bodice, its skirt flowing from a trim, tucked waist. She wore no jewelry. Her hair lay free on her shoulders. Hands primly folded in her lap, she answered Luke's easy conversation with polite, distant monosyllables. I'll get Mama's thread, she determined, have a token tour of the city and drive back as quickly as possible. I will be perfectly polite the entire time.

An hour later, Gwen found that maintaining her aloof sophistication was a difficult task. She had forgotten how much she loved the Vieux Carré. It was not just the exquisite iron grillwork balconies, the profusion of flowering plants, the charm of long wooden shutters and buildings that had stood for centuries. It was the subtle magic of the place. The air was soft and seemed freshly washed, its many scents ranging from flowery to spicy to the rich smell of the river.

"Fabulous, isn't it?" Luke asked as they stood on the curb of a street too narrow for anything but pedestrian traffic. "It's the most stable city I know."

"Stable?" Gwen repeated, intrigued enough to turn and face him directly.

"It doesn't change," he explained with a gesture of his hand. "It just continues on." Before she realized his intent, he laced his fingers with hers and began to walk. She tugged and was ignored.

"There's no reason to hold my hand," Gwen told him primly.

"Sure there is," he corrected, giving her a friendly smile. "I like to."

Gwen subsided into silence. Luke's palm was hard, the palm of a man used to doing manual labor. She remembered suddenly the feel of it caressing her throat. He sighed, turned and pulled her hard against him, covering her mouth in an unexpected and dizzying kiss. Gwen had no time to protest or respond before she was drawn away again. Along the crowded street, several people applauded.

Gwen and Luke walked past the many street artists in Jackson Square. They paused briefly to admire the chalk portraits of tourists, the oils of city scenes and the mysterious studies of the bayous. Gwen was torn between her desire to share her pleasure at returning to the city of her childhood and the feeling that she should ignore the dominating man by her side. She was not here to have a good time, she reminded herself sternly. She was here to do an errand. It was on the tip of her tongue to remind Luke of the purpose of their trip when she saw the magician. He was dressed in black, with spangles and a rakish beret and a flowing moustache.

"Oh, look!" Gwen pointed. "Isn't he wonderful?" She moved closer, unconsciously pulling Luke along by tightening her grip on his hand.

They watched brilliantly colored scarves appear from nowhere, huge bouquets of paper flowers grow from the magician's palm and coins sprout from the ears of onlookers. Two young clowns in whiteface entertained the stragglers by twisting balloons into giraffe and poodle shapes. Some distance away, guitarists sold their songs to passing tourists. Gwen could just hear their close-knit harmony.

Forgetting all her stern resolutions, she turned to grin at Luke. He dropped a bill into the cardboard box that served as the portable cash register for the magician. Reaching out, he pinched her chin between his thumb and forefinger. "I knew it wouldn't last too long."

"What wouldn't?" She brushed the hair from her eyes in a habitual gesture.

"You enjoy things too much to remain cool for long," he told her. "No, now don't do that," he ordered, running a finger down her nose as she frowned. He smiled, then brushed his lips over her fingertips. "Shall we be friends?"

Her hand, already warm from his, grew warmer at the kiss. She knew his charm was practiced, his smile a finely tuned weapon. She forced herself to be cautious.

"I don't know that I'd go as far as that," she replied, studying him with eyes that were warily amused.

"Fellow tourists?" he suggested. His thumb moved gently across her knuckles. "I'll buy you an ice cream cone."

Gwen knew she was losing to the smile and the persuasive voice. "Well…" It would do no harm to enjoy the day. No harm in enjoying the city, the magic…in enjoying him. "Two scoops," she demanded, answering his smile with her own.

They moved at an easy pace through the park, enjoying both shade and sun. All around was the soft, continuous cooing from hundreds of pigeons. They flocked along the ground, scattered when chased by children, sunned atop the statue of Andrew Jackson on a rearing horse. Here and there people sat or slept on curved black benches. A young girl sat in a patch of shade and played softly on a recorder.

They walked along the levee and looked at the brown waters of the Mississippi. Lazy music from calliopes

provided a pleasant background as they talked of everything and of nothing. The bells of Saint Louis Cathedral
chimed the hour. They laughed at the toddler who escaped from his mother and splashed in the cool waters of
a fountain.

They walked along Bourbon Street, listening to the
tangled, continuous music that poured from open doors.
Jazz and country and rock merged into one jumbled,
compelling sound. They applauded the old man who
danced in the street to the demanding strains of "Tiger
Rag." They listened to the corner saxophone player
whose lonely song brought Gwen to tears.

On a gallery overlooking a narrow street surging with
people, they ate shrimp gumbo and drank cold, dry wine.
They lingered over the leisurely meal, watching the sun
slowly disappear. Pleasantly weary, Gwen toyed with
the remains of her cheesecake and watched the first stars
come out. Laughter rose from the street below. When she
turned, she found Luke studying her over the rim of his
glass.

"Why do you look at me like that?" Her smile was
completely relaxed as she rested her chin on her palm.

"A remarkably foolish question," Luke answered as he
set down his glass. "Why do you think?"

"I don't know." She took a deep breath. The scent
of the city assailed her senses. "No one's ever looked
at me quite the way you do. You can tell too much

about people. It's not fair. You study them and steal their thoughts. It's not a very comfortable feeling."

Luke smiled, and his fingers were light on the back of her hand.

Gwen lifted an eyebrow, then strategically moved her hand out of reach. "You also have a way of making people say things. Yesterday I…" Gwen hesitated and twisted the stem of her glass between her fingers. "I said things to you I shouldn't have. It's disturbing to know you've revealed your emotions to someone else." She sipped her wine. "Michael always says I'm too open."

"Your emotions are beautiful." Gwen looked up, surprised at the tenderness in his voice. "Michael is a fool."

Quickly she shook her head. "Oh, no, he's really quite brilliant, and he never does anything foolish. He has an image to maintain. It's just that I was beginning to feel as if I were being molded into his conception of a proper attorney's wife."

"He asked you to marry him?" Luke asked, as he poured wine into both glasses.

"He was sure that I would. He was furious when I didn't jump at the offer." Gwen sighed and made a restless movement with her shoulders. "I kept seeing a long, narrow tunnel, very straight, no curves, no detours, no surprises. I guess I developed claustrophobia." She made a frustrated sound, wrinkling her nose. "There, you've done it again."

"I have?" He smiled as he leaned back in his seat. Moonlight spilled over her hair.

"I'm telling you things…things I've barely told myself. You always manage to find out what's in a person's mind, but you keep your own thoughts all tidy and tucked away."

"I put them in print," he corrected. "For anyone who cares to read them."

"Yes," she said slowly. "But how does one know if they're your real thoughts? Your books are interesting, but how do I know who you really are?"

"Do you want to?" There was a soft challenge in his voice.

Gwen hesitated, but the answer was already moving to her lips. "Yes, I do."

"But you're not quite sure." He rose, then held out his hand to her. "The wine's made you sleepy," he said, looking down into her heavy eyes. "Shall I take you home?"

"No." Gwen shook her head. "No, not yet." She slipped her hand back into his.

Luke drove down the magnolia-lined lane. The scent of the night was delicate, mixing with the fragrance of the woman who slept on his shoulder. After stopping the car, he turned his head and looked down at her. Gwen's mouth was soft and vulnerable in sleep. There was a moment's hesitation before he lifted her chin and drew away from her.

"Gwen." He moved his thumb gently over her lips. She gave a soft, pleased sigh. "Gwen," he said again with more firmness. Her lashes fluttered and opened. "We're home." He massaged her shoulders lightly, and she stretched under his hands.

"Did I fall asleep?" Her eyes were huge and dark as she smiled at him. "I didn't mean to."

"It's late."

"I know." She smiled sleepily. "I had fun. Thank you." On impulse, she bent forward and brushed her lips over his. His fingers tightened on her shoulders as he pulled away from her sharply. Gwen blinked in confusion. "Luke?"

"I have my limits," he said tersely. He made a quick, impatient sound as her face registered consternation. "I told you once, women are very soft and warm when they've been sleeping. I have a weakness for soft, warm women."

"I didn't mean to fall asleep," she murmured as his hand slipped around to cradle the back of her neck. Her head felt light, her limbs heavy.

A cloud drifted over the moon. The light shifted, dimmed and glowed again. He was watching her, studying each feature with absorption. She could feel his fingers on the base of her neck. They were hard and long, their strength obvious even in the gentle touch. She whispered, "What do you want?"

In answer, he bent slowly toward her. His mouth was easy, teasing the corners of hers, drifting to her closed lids, exploring the hollows of her cheeks. Passion lay simmering beneath the surface as he began to caress her body with slow, patient hands. He traced her parted lips with the tip of his tongue. "Beautiful," he murmured, moving his mouth to her ear. She shivered with pleasure as his thumb lingered on the point of her breast. "When I touch you, I feel your body melt under my hands." He met her mouth with a long, tender kiss. "What do I want?" he answered as he tasted the heated skin of her throat. "What I want more than anything at this moment is to make love with you. I want to take you slowly, until I know all of you."

She felt her body growing fluid, and her will flowed with it. "Will you make love with me?" She heard herself ask, heard the tone that was request rather than question. Luke's mouth paused on her skin. Slowly he tightened his grip on her hair, then drew her head back until their eyes met. For a moment, they hung suspended in silence with only the echo of her voice between them.

"No." His answer was cool and quick as a slap. Gwen jerked away from it and him and fumbled with the handle of the door. She stumbled out of the car, but before she could escape into the house, Luke captured her arms in a firm grip. "Wait a minute."

Shaking her head, Gwen pushed against him. "No, I want to go in. I didn't know what I was saying. It was crazy."

"You knew exactly what you were saying," Luke corrected, tightening his grasp.

Gwen wanted to deny it, but found it impossible. She had wanted him, she knew she still wanted him. "All right, I knew what I was saying. Now will you let me go?"

"I won't apologize for touching you," he said.

"I'm not asking for apologies, Luke," she told him evenly. "I'm simply asking for my freedom." She realized uncomfortably that it was not freedom from his arms that she meant, but freedom from the power he held over her. The struggle inside her was reflected briefly in her face. Luke's frown deepened before he released her arms. "Thank you," she said.

She walked quickly inside the house before he could say another word.

8

A yellow butterfly fluttered delicately over a pot of white impatiens. From the veranda, Gwen watched its dance until it skimmed away, light as the air. Sitting in the white porch rocker, dressed in a yellow sundress, Anabelle looked as fragile as the butterfly. Gwen studied her mother's soft pink cheeks and gentle blue eyes. Anabelle's small hands were busy with the domestic task of shelling peas, but her eyes were, as always, dreamy. Watching her, Gwen was swamped with waves of love and helplessness.

Who am I? she demanded of herself. Who am I to advise anyone on men? For a moment, Gwen wished desperately that she could seek from Anabelle advice for herself. Her own emotions were chaotic. She was terrified that her own feelings for Luke were approach-

ing a dangerous level. Falling in love with a man like
Luke was courting disaster. And yet, Gwen wondered
unhappily, is it really possible for the mind to control the
heart? In this case it must...there's no choice. I have to
forget about last night. The sigh escaped before she could
stop it. Priorities, she reminded herself. Gwen watched
a bumblebee dive into a cluster of wisteria, then took a
deep breath and turned to Anabelle. "Mama." Anabelle
went on shelling peas, a misty smile on her lips. "Mama,"
Gwen repeated more sharply, placing a hand over her
mother's.

"Oh, yes, dear?" Anabelle looked up with the open,
expectant look of a child. "Did you say something?"

For an instant, Gwen teetered on the brink, then
plunged. "Mama, don't you think twelve years is a terribly big gap?"

Gravely, Anabelle considered. "Why, I suppose it could
be, Gwenivere, but then, as you grow older, twelve years
is hardly any time at all." Her momentary seriousness
vanished with a fresh smile. "Why, it seems like yesterday
that you were twelve years old. I remember quite clearly
when you fell out of that old cypress in the backyard and
broke your arm. Such a brave child..." She began shelling peas again. "Never shed a tear. I cried enough for
both of us, though."

"But, Mama." Valiantly Gwen tried to keep Anabelle's
thoughts from straying. "Twelve years, when you're
speaking of a man and a woman...." Anabelle failed to

respond to the prompting, only nodding to indicate she was listening. "The age difference, Mama," Gwen blurted out. "Isn't twelve years a terribly wide age gap?"

"Sally Deumont's girls are nearly twelve years apart," Anabelle stated with another series of nods. "I suppose having children that far apart has its drawbacks."

"No, Mama." Gwen ran both hands through her hair.

"And its advantages, certainly," Anabelle said soothingly, not wanting to be critical of an old friend.

"No, Mama, I don't mean that at all. I'm speaking of men and women...of relationships. Romantic relationships."

"Oh!" Anabelle blinked in surprise and smiled. "That's a different matter altogether, isn't it?" Gwen resisted grinding her teeth as her mother continued to shell peas for a moment in silence. "I'm surprised," Anabelle said at length, giving Gwen a look of gentle curiosity. "I'm surprised you would think that age and love had anything to do with each other. I've always thought of the heart as ageless."

The words caused Gwen to falter a moment. Slowly she leaned forward and took both her mother's hands in hers. "Mama, don't you think, sometimes, that love can blind people to what's right for them? Don't people often put themselves into a position where getting hurt is the only possible outcome?"

"Yes, of course." Anabelle shook her head, as if startled

by the question. "That's part of life. If you never open yourself for pain, you never open yourself for joy. How empty life would be then. This Michael of yours," Anabelle continued with a light of concern in her eyes, "did he hurt you terribly?"

"No." Gwen released her mother's hands and rose to walk the length of the veranda. "No, basically only my pride."

"That can happen by a fall off a horse," Anabelle stated. Abandoning her peas, she moved to join Gwen. "Darling, how young you are." She turned to face her, studying her with rare total concentration. "I sometimes forget that, because you're so much more practical and organized than I am. I suppose I always let you take care of me, much more than I took care of you."

"Oh, no, Mama," Gwen protested, but Anabelle placed a finger on her lips.

"It's true. I never like to look at the unpleasant side of things. I'm afraid I've always let you do that for me. In some ways you matured so quickly, but in others…" Anabelle sighed and slipped an arm around Gwen's waist. "Perhaps at last we've found something I can help you with."

"But, Mama, it's not me…" Gwen began, only to be ignored.

"Did you know I was only eighteen when I first saw your father? I fell instantly, wildly in love." The soft look in Anabelle's eyes halted Gwen's interruption. "Who would have thought his life would be so short? He never even got to see you. I always thought that the greatest tragedy. He would have been so proud to see himself in you." She sighed, then smiled at Gwen. "Ours was a first love, a desperate love, and often I've wondered if it would have withstood all the tests of time. I'll never know." Gwen remained silent, fascinated by a side of her mother she was seeing for the first time. "I learned so many things from that short, crowded marriage. I learned you must always accept love when it's offered, always give it when it's needed. There might not be a second chance. And I know, too, that until your heart's been broken, you never know the full beauty of love."

Gwen watched a squirrel dart across the lawn and scurry up a tree. It was an odd feeling, hearing her mother speak of being in love. She wondered if their relationship had blinded her from seeing Anabelle as a woman with needs and desires. Looking down, Gwen saw the smooth, untroubled skin of a woman at the peak of her beauty. There was still a youthful sweetness in the shape of the mouth, an impossible air of innocence in the eyes. Impulsively, Gwen asked the question that had lurked in her mind for years.

"Mama, why haven't you ever gotten married again?"

"I haven't wanted to," Anabelle answered instantly. She moved away with a swish of her skirts. "At first, I was too much in love with your father's memory, and later I was

having too much fun raising you." She plucked a with-
ered fuchsia bloom from a hanging basket and dropped
it over the railing of the veranda. "I'm quite good with
babies, you know. Later you became more and more in-
dependent, so I moved on to the next stage. I've had
some admirers." She smiled, pleased with the thought.
"I've simply never had the urge to settle down with any
of them." In silence, Gwen watched Anabelle move from
flower to flower. It occurred to her for the first time that
her mother had probably enjoyed love affairs over the
past twenty years. She had not been exclusively Gwen's
dreamy, gentle mother but Anabelle Lacrosse, a lovely,
desirable woman. For one brief moment, Gwen felt ridiculously like an orphan.

I'm being a fool, Gwen told herself, resting her head
against the rail post. She's still the same person—I'm the
one who's changing. I grew up, but I've kept her locked
in a childhood image. It's time I let her out. But I can't
bear to see her hurt, and I'm so afraid Luke will leave her
wounded. He can't love her, not when he can kiss me the
way he does. No... She closed her eyes. He wants me,
but it has nothing to do with his heart. He wants me,
but he turned away from me. Why else would he have
done that, if not for her? A bright flash of jealousy both
stunned and shamed her. With a shuddering sigh, she
turned to find Anabelle studying her.

"You're not happy," her mother said simply.

"No." Gwen shook her head with the word.

"Confused?"

"Yes." Quickly she swallowed the tears that threatened to come.

"Men do that to us so easily." Anabelle smiled as if the prospect was not altogether unappealing. "Try a rare piece of advice from your mother, darling. Do nothing." With a little laugh, she tossed back a stray wisp of golden hair. "I know how difficult that is for you, but do try. Just let the pieces fall into place around you for a time. Sometimes doing nothing is doing everything."

"Mama." Gwen was forced to smile. "How can something so silly make so much sense?"

"Luke says I've an intuitive understanding," Anabelle replied with a glow of pride.

"He has a way with words," Gwen muttered.

"Tools of the trade." Luke spoke as the screen door swung shut behind him. His eyes met Gwen's. There was something intimate in the glance, something possessive. Even as the stirring began inside her, she lifted her chin in defense. A smile teased his mouth. "Guns primed, Gwenivere?"

"I'm a dead shot," she returned evenly.

"Oh dear." Anabelle moved lightly across the veranda and began to gather her peas. "You didn't tell me you were going hunting. I hope Tillie packed you a lunch."

Luke grinned over her head with such easy boyish charm, Gwen was helpless to resist. Her eyes warmed and her mouth softened as they shared the intimacy of a joke.

"Actually, I had fishing in mind," Luke countered, keeping his eyes on Gwen's. "I thought I'd walk down to Malon's cabin."

"That's nice." Anabelle straightened and smiled. "Malon still brings up fresh fish," she told Gwen. "You run along, too, darling. You know he would be hurt if you didn't visit."

"Oh, well, I…" Seeing the amusement on Luke's face, Gwen continued smoothly, "I'll visit him, Mama, another time. I told Tillie I'd help her do some canning."

"Nonsense." Anabelle flitted to the screen door, beaming at Luke as he held it open for her. "Thank you, darling," she said before giving Gwen a look over her shoulder. "You're on vacation. That's no time to be standing in a hot kitchen over boiling tomatoes. Run along and have fun. She's always loved to fish," she added to Luke before she stepped inside. "Tell Malon I'd adore some fresh shrimp." The door closed behind her. Gwen had the odd feeling that she had just been pushed gently out of the way. Luke gave her slim blue jeans and plain white T-shirt a cursory glance.

"Looks like you're dressed for fishing," he said with a nod. "Let's go."

"I have no intention of going anywhere with you." Gwen dusted her hands on her hips and started to move by him. She was brought up short by his hand on her arm. They stood side by side. Gwen let her eyes rest on his imprisoning hand and then slid them slowly to meet his. It was her most disdainful stare. "I beg your pardon?" she said icily. To her dismay, Luke burst out laughing. The warm, deep tones of it caused a bird to dart from the lawn to the shelter of a tree. "Let me go, you...you..."

"Wasn't it 'beast' before?" he asked as he began to assist her down the stairs.

"You are the most outrageous man." She continued to struggle as she trotted to keep pace.

"Thanks."

Gwen dug in her heels and managed to persuade Luke to stop. Staring up at him, she took a long, deep breath. "You are the most arrogant, officious, egotistical, thick-skinned man I have ever met."

"You forgot unreasonable, tyrannical and incredibly attractive. Really, Gwen, you surprise me. I thought you had more imagination. Are those your best insults?"

"Off the cuff, yes." She sniffed and tried not to respond to the humor in his eyes. "If you'll give me a little time, I can be more articulate."

"Don't trouble, I got the idea." He released her arm, held up one hand in the air, and the other out to her. "Truce?"

Gwen's guard relaxed before she realized it. Her hand moved to meet his.

"Truce," she agreed, with only a token trace of reluctance.

"Until…?" he asked as he rubbed his thumb lightly across the back of her hand.

"Until I decide to be annoyed with you again." Gwen smiled, tossing back her curls as she enjoyed his laugh. It was, she decided, the most pleasing, infectious laugh she had ever heard.

"Well, will you fish with me?" he asked.

"Perhaps I will." For a moment she pursed her lips in thought. When she smiled again, it was the smile of challenge. "Ten bucks says I catch a bigger fish than you."

"Done." Casually, Luke laced his fingers through hers. This time Gwen made no objection.

Gwen knew every twist of the river and every turn of the paths in the bayou. Automatically, she moved north toward Malon's cabin. They walked under cascading moss and filtered sunlight.

"Do you really know how to can tomatoes, Gwenivere?" Luke asked as he bent under a low-hanging branch.

"Certainly, and anything else that comes out of a garden. When you're poor, a garden can mean the difference between eating or not."

"I've never known poor people who eat with Georgian silver," Luke commented dryly.

"Heirlooms." Gwen gave a sigh and a shrug. "Mama

always considered heirlooms a sacred trust. One can't sell a sacred trust. Nor," she added with a wry smile, "can one comfortably wear or eat a sacred trust. Mama loves that house, it's her Camelot. She's a woman who needs a Camelot."

"And Gwenivere doesn't?" A great egret, startled by their intrusion, unfolded himself from the water and rose into the sky. Gwen felt an old, familiar stir of pleasure as she watched.

"I suppose I've always wanted to find my own. Heirlooms belong to someone else first. I'd nearly forgotten the scent of wild jasmine," she murmured as the fragrance drifted to her.

There was a dreamlike stillness around them. Beside them, the stream moved on its lackadaisical journey to the Gulf. Its water mirrored the moss-dripping trees. Gwen tossed a pebble and watched the ripples spread and vanish. "I spent most of my leisure time out here when I was younger," she said. "I felt more at home here than inside my own house. There was never any real privacy there, with strangers always coming and going. I never wanted to share my kingdom with anyone before...."

She could feel Luke's big hand tighten his grasp on hers. He met her eyes with perfect understanding.

9

Malon's cabin hung over the water. It was built of split logs with a low, wide A roof and a porch that doubled as a dock for his pirogue. On a small, spare patch of grass beside the cabin, half a dozen chickens clucked and waddled. Somewhere deep in the marsh, a woodpecker drummed. A scratchy recording of music by Saint-Saëns came from the cabin to compete with the drumming and clucking. Stretched lengthwise on a narrow railing above the water, a tabby cat slept.

"It's just the same," Gwen murmured. She was unaware of the relief in her voice or the pleasure that lit her face. She smiled up at Luke and pulled him quickly across the lawn and up the three wooden steps. "Raphael," she said to the snoozing cat. Lazily he opened one eye, made a disinterested noise and shut it again. "Affectionate as ever," Gwen remarked. "I was afraid he'd forget me."

"Raphael is too old to forget anything."

Gwen turned quickly at the sound of the voice. Malon stood in the cabin doorway, a mortar and pestle in his hand. He was a small man, barely taller than Gwen herself, but with powerful arms and shoulders. His middle had not gone to flesh with age, but remained as flat as a boxer's, as he had indeed once been. His hair was white, thick and curly, his face brown and lined, his eyes were a faded blue under dark brows. His age was a mystery. The bayou had been his home for an unspecified number of years. He took from the stream what he needed and was content. He had both a passionate love and a deep respect for the bayou. These he had passed on to the young girl who had found his cabin more than fifteen years before. Gwen checked the impulse to run into his arms.

"Hello, Malon. How are you?"

"Comme ci, comme ça." He gave a tiny shrug, then set down his mortar and pestle. He nodded a greeting to Luke before concentrating on Gwen. For a full minute she stood silent under his scrutiny. At length he said, "Let me see your hands." Obediently, Gwen held them out. "Soft," Malon said with a snort. "Lady's hands now, *hein?* Why didn't you get a lady's figure in New York, too?"

"I could only afford the hands. I'm still saving up for the rest. And Tillie's still pressing your shirts, I see," Gwen ran an experimental finger over the faded but crisp material of his cotton shirt. "When are you going to marry her?"

"I'm too young to get married," he said. "I have not finished sowing wild oats."

Gwen laughed and laid her cheek against his. "Oh, I've missed you, Malon." He answered her laugh and gave her one quick, bruising and unexpected hug. From the outset, they had spoken in Cajun French, a dialect that Gwen used again without the slightest thought. She closed her eyes a moment, enjoying the strength in his burly arms, the feel of his leathery cheek against hers, the scent of woodsmoke and herbs that was his personal cologne. She realized suddenly why she had not come to see him earlier. He had been the one constant male figure in her life. She had been afraid she would find him changed.

"Everything's the same," she murmured.

"But you." There was a smile in his voice, and she heard it.

"I should have come sooner." For the first time since she had known him, Gwen dared kiss his cheek.

"You are forgiven," he said.

Gwen was suddenly conscious of Luke beside her. She flushed. "I'm sorry," she said to him, "I—I didn't realize that we were rambling on in French."

Luke smiled while absently scratching Raphael's ears. "You don't have to apologize—I enjoyed it."

Gwen forced her thoughts into order. She would not

fall under the charm of that smile again. "Do you speak French?" she asked with casual interest.

"No. But I still enjoyed it." She had the uncomfortable feeling he knew precisely how deeply his smile affected her. He turned his clear, calm eyes to Malon. "Anabelle says she'd like some shrimp."

"I go shrimping tomorrow," Malon answered with an agreeable nod. "Your book goes well?"

"Well enough."

"So, you take the day off, *hein?* You take this one fishing?" A jerk of his thumb in Gwen's direction accompanied the question.

"Thought I might," Luke replied without glancing at her.

Malon shrugged and sniffed. "Use t'be she knew which end of the pole to hold and which to put in the water, but that was before she went up there." A snap of his head indicated "up there." Even a town twenty miles from Lafitte was regarded with suspicion.

"Perhaps she remembers," Luke suggested. "She seems reasonably intelligent."

"She was raised good," Malon added, softening a bit. "Her papa was a good boy. She has his face. She don't favor her mama."

Gwen straightened her shoulders and raised her brows ever so slightly. "*She* remembers *everything*. My mother can outfish both of you in her sleep."

"Poo-yie!" Malon shook his hand and wrist as if he

had touched something hot. "This city girl, she scare me out of my shoe. You take her. Me, I'm too old to fight with mean women."

"A minute ago you were too young to get married," Gwen reminded him.

"Yes, it's a good age I have." He smiled contentedly. "*Allez,* I have medicine to make. Take the poles and the pirogue and bring me a fish for my dinner." Without another word, he walked into the cabin, letting the screen door slam shut behind him.

"He hasn't changed," Gwen stated, trying to sound indignant.

"No," Luke agreed, taking two fishing poles and putting them across his shoulder. "He's still crazy about you." After stepping into the pirogue, he held out a hand to her. With the ease of experience, Gwen settled into the canoe. Soundlessly, Raphael leaped from rail to boat and fell instantly back to sleep.

"He doesn't want to miss the fun," Gwen explained.

Luke poled away from the dock. "Tell me, Gwenivere," he asked, "how do you come to speak the dialect so fluently? Anabelle can barely read a French menu." Sunshine dappled their heads as they passed under a canopy of trees.

"Tillie taught me." Gwen leaned her head back and let the warm sunlight play on her face. She remembered Malon saying long ago that his pirogue could ride on a film of dew. "I've spoken the coastal dialect for as long as

I can remember. For the most part, the people here treat outsiders as beneath their notice; it's a very closed society. But I speak Cajun—therefore, I *am* Cajun. I'm curious, though, why Malon accepts you. It's obvious that you're on easy terms."

"I don't speak Cajun." Luke stood in the pirogue and poled down the river as if born to it. "But we speak the same language nonetheless."

They cleared the trees and drifted into a ghost forest shadowed by stumps of cypress. The boat moved through floating mats of hyacinths. Tiny baby crawfish clung to the clumped roots, while a fat cottonmouth disappeared into the lavender blooms. The winding river was teeming with life. Gwen watched a marsh raccoon fishing from the sloping bank.

"How is it," Gwen mused aloud, "that a Pulitzer Prize winner speaks the same language as a Louisiana *traiteur?*"

"Traiteur?" Luke repeated, meeting the frank curiosity in her eyes.

"Folk doctor. Malon fishes and trades and lumbers sometimes, but primarily he's the local *traiteur*. He cures snakebites, illness and spells. Spells are his specialty."

"Hmm. Did you ever wonder why he lives here, alone with his cat, his music and his books?" Gwen did not answer, content to watch Luke pole through the scattered stumps. "He's been to Rome and London and Budapest, but he lives here. He's driven tanks, broken horses, boxed and flown planes. Now he fishes and cures spells. He knows how to fix a carburetor, how to play classical guitar and how to cure snakebites. He does as he pleases and no more. He's the most successful man I know."

"How did you find out so much about him in such a short time?"

"I asked," Luke told her simply.

"No. No, it's not as easy as that." Gwen made a frustrated gesture with her hand. "People tell you things, I don't know why. I've told you things I have no business telling you, and I tell you before I realize it." She examined his face. "And worse, you don't always need to be told, you know. You see people much too clearly."

He smiled down at her. "Does it make you uncomfortable that I know who you are?"

The river widened. Gwen's pout became a frown. "Yes, I think it does. It makes me feel defenseless, the same way I felt when I first saw Bradley's sketches."

"An invasion of privacy?"

"Privacy's important to me," Gwen admitted.

"I understand," Luke leaned on the pole. "You grew up having to share your home with strangers, having to share Anabelle. The result is a desire for privacy and independence. I apologize for invading your privacy, but, after all, it's partly my profession."

"Are we all characters to you?" Gwen asked as she baited her hook and cast her line.

"Some more than others," he returned dryly, casting his line on the opposite side of the boat from hers.

Gwen shook her head. "You know," she began, then settled back, stretching her legs and crossing them, "I'm finding it very hard not to like you."

At the other end of the canoe, Luke mirrored her position. "I'm a very charming person."

"Unfortunately, that's true." With a contented sigh, Gwen closed her eyes. "You're not at all how I pictured you."

"Oh?"

"You look more like a woodchopper than a world-renowned writer."

Luke grinned. "And how should a world-renowned writer look?"

"Several different ways, I suppose. Intellectual, with small glasses and narrow shoulders. Or prominent..."

"Heaven forbid."

"Or prominent," Gwen continued, ignoring him. "Wearing a well-cut suit and with just a hint of a paunch. Dashing, maybe, with a faint scar along the jawline. Or Byronic..."

"Oh, good Lord."

"With a romantic pallor and tragic eyes."

"It's difficult to maintain a pallor in California."

"The trouble is, you're too physical." Gwen was enjoying the gentle drift of the boat and the warm fingers of sun. "What's your new book about?"

"A man and a woman."

"It's been done before," Gwen commented as she opened her eyes.

Luke smiled. His legs made a friendly tangle with hers. "It's *all* been done before, child. It's simply that each person believes his is a fresh experience."

Gwen tilted her head, waiting for his explanation.

Luke obliged. "Endless numbers of symphonies are composed on the same eighty-eight keys." He closed his eyes, and Gwen took the opportunity to study him.

"Will you let me read it?" she asked suddenly. "Or are you temperamental and sensitive?"

"I'm only temperamental when it's to my advantage," Luke told her lazily, opening one eye. "How's your spelling?"

"Comme ci, comme ça," Gwen grinned across at him.

"You can proof my rough draft, my spelling's only half that good."

"That's generous of you." Abruptly she let out a cry. "Oh, I've got one!" Instantly she was sitting up, giving all her attention to the fish on the end of her line. Her face was animated as she tossed her hair back with an impatient jerk of her head. There was competence in her hands and a gleam of challenge in her eyes. "Eight pounds easy," she announced as she plopped the defeated fish on deck. "And that was just for practice." Raphael roused himself to inspect the first catch, then curled up beside Gwen's hip and went back to sleep.

The silence lay comfortably between them. There was no need for conversation or small talk. Dragonflies streaked by now and then with a flash of color and a quick buzz. Occasionally birds called to each other. It seemed natural to Gwen to loll drowsily across from Luke under the hazy sun. Her legs crossed over his with absent camaraderie. The shadows lengthened. Still they lingered, drifting among the stumps of once-towering cypress.

"The sun'll be gone in a couple of hours," Luke commented. Gwen made an unintelligible sound of agreement. "We should be heading back." The boat rocked gently as Luke got to his feet.

Under the cover of gold-tipped lashes, Gwen watched him. He stretched, and muscles rippled. His eyes were clear and light, an arresting contrast to the burnished tone of his skin. They flicked over her as she lay still, too comfortable to stir herself. She knew that he was aware of her scrutiny.

"You owe me ten dollars," she reminded him smiling.

"A small price to pay for the afternoon." The water sighed as the boat glided over it. "Did you know you have five pale gold freckles on your nose?"

Gwen laughed as she stretched her arms luxuriously over her head. "I believe you're quite mad."

He watched her as the lashes shadowed her cheeks and

her mouth sweetened with a smile. "I begin to be sure of it," he murmured.

It wasn't until the pirogue bumped noiselessly against its home dock that Gwen stirred again. The thin wisps of clouds were pink now with the setting sun, and there was a coolness in the air.

"Mmm." Her sigh was filled with the simple pleasure of the moment. "What a lovely ride."

"Next time, you pole," Luke stated. He watched Raphael stand, stretch and leap nimbly onto the dock and then joined him. After securing the boat, he offered a hand to Gwen.

"I suppose that's only fair." Gwen stood in one fluid movement. As nimbly as Raphael, she leaped onto the dock. She tilted back her head to give Luke a flippant grin, but found her lips captured by his.

One hand tangled in her hair while his other pressed into the small of her back, demanding she come closer. His mouth was desperate in its need for possession. There was a tension in him, a whisper of power held tightly in check. Gwen's pulses hammered at the thought of it unleashed. There was no gentleness in the mouth that claimed hers nor in the arms that held her, and she asked for none. There was a wild, restless thing in her that cried for release. She explored the strength of his arms, then the softness of his hair, as she plunged deeper into sensations she could no longer measure. Touching him, she felt there were no limits to the power flooding her. What filled her was more than the quick heat of passion, more than a transient surge of desire. It was an all-consuming need to be his. She wanted to travel where only he could take her and to learn what only he could teach her. Then Luke's hands were on her shoulders, pushing her away.

"Gwen," he began in a voice roughened with desire.

"No, don't talk," she murmured, and pulled his mouth back to hers. It was his taste, and his taste only, that could satisfy her growing hunger. She was famished, only now aware that she had fasted all her life. For a soaring, blinding moment, his mouth bruised hers; then he wrenched away. He held her shoulders in a crushing grip, but Gwen felt no pain as his eyes met hers. She could only stare. Her confusion, her need, her willingness, were plain on her face. Luke's oath was savage and swift as he turned away.

"You should know better than to look at a man like that."

Gwen heard the harsh journey of air in and out of his lungs. Her fingers shook as she ran them nervously through her hair. "I—I don't know how I looked."

"Malleable," Luke muttered. He stared down at the sluggish river before turning back to her. "Pliant, willing and outrageously innocent. Do you know how difficult it is to resist the untouched, the uncorrupted?"

Helplessly, Gwen shook her head. "No, I…."

"Of course you don't," Luke cut in sharply. She winced

at his tone, and he let out a long breath. "Good heavens, how easy it is to forget what a child you are."

"I'm not, I…" Gwen shook her head in mute denial. "It happened so fast, I didn't think. I just…"

"I can hardly deny that it's my fault." His tone had cooled, and its marked disinterest had the edge of a knife. "You're an extraordinary creature, part will-o'-the-wisp, part Amazon, and I have a problem keeping my hands off you. Knowing I can have you is not exactly an incentive to restrain myself."

His matter-of-fact tone scraped at Gwen's raw pride, even as it tripped her temper. "You're hateful."

"Agreed," Luke said with a brief nod. "But still, I think, civilized enough not to take advantage of an innocent girl."

"I am not…" Gwen managed before she felt the need to swallow. "I am not an innocent girl, I'm a grown woman!"

"As you wish. Do you still want me to take advantage of you?" Luke's tone was agreeable now.

"No!" Impatiently, she brushed at the hair on her forehead. "I mean, it wouldn't be… Certainly not!"

"In that case…" Taking her arm, Luke firmly guided Gwen inside Malon's cabin.

10

Knocking on Luke's door was not the easiest thing Gwen had ever done, but it was necessary. She felt it necessary to prove to herself that she would not succumb to a newly discovered weakness again. She was a grown woman, capable of handling herself. She had asked to read Luke's manuscript, had agreed to proof it. She would not back down because of a kiss or a moment of madness. Still, Gwen braced herself as she lifted her knuckles to the wood. She held her breath.

"Come in."

These simple, ordinary words from inside the room caught at her heart. Letting out her breath slowly, she arranged her features in casual, almost indifferent lines and opened the door. Luke did not even bother to look up.

Reference books were piled on the table and scattered over the floor. Papers—typewritten, handwritten, crumpled and smooth—were strewn everywhere. On the table in the midst of the chaos was a battered portable typewriter. There sat the creator of the havoc, frowning at the keys while he pounded on them. The curtains were still drawn, closing out the late-morning sun, and the bed was a tangle of sheets. Everywhere were books, papers, folders.

"What a mess," Gwen murmured involuntarily. At her voice, Luke glanced up. There was at first a crease of annoyance between his brows, then a look of mild surprise before all was smoothed away.

"Hello," he said easily. He did not rise, but leaned back in his chair to look at her.

Gwen advanced, stepping over books and around papers on the journey. "This is incredible." She lifted her hand to gesture around the room, then dropped it to her side. "How do you live like this?"

Luke looked around, shrugged and met the curiosity in her eyes. "I don't, I work like this. If you've come to tidy up, I'll tell you the same thing I told the girl Anabelle used to send up here. Mess with my papers, and I'll toss you out the window."

Amused, Gwen stuck her hands in her pockets and nudged a book out of her way with her toe. "So, you're temperamental after all." This, she felt, was a trait she could understand and deal with.

"If you like," he agreed. "This way, if I lose some-thing, I can only swear at myself, not at some hapless maid or well-meaning secretary. I have an aversion for well-meaning secretaries. What can I do for you? I'm afraid the coffee's cold."

The formality in his tone made it clear this was his domain. Gwen schooled her voice to sound briskly pro-fessional. "You said yesterday you'd like me to proof your manuscript. I'd be glad to do it. If," she added with a glance around the room, "you can find it."

He smiled his charming, irresistible smile. Gwen hardened herself against it. "Are you an organized soul, Gwenivere? I've always admired organization as long as it doesn't infringe on my habits. Sit," he invited with a gesture of his hand.

Gwen stepped over two dictionaries and an encyclope-dia. "Would you mind if I opened the drapes first?" she asked.

"If you wish," he answered as he reached for a pile of typewritten pages. "Just don't get domestic."

"Nothing could be further from my mind," she as-sured him, and had the pleasure of seeing him wince at the brilliance of the sunlight that streamed into the room. "There," she said, adopting the tone of a nursery school teacher, "isn't that better?"

"Sit."

Gwen did so after removing a pile of magazines from the chair across from him.

"You look older with your hair up," Luke commented mildly. "Nearly sixteen."

A fire lit in her eyes, but she managed to keep her voice cool. "Do you mind if I get started?"

"Not at all." Luke handed her a stack of typewritten material. "You'll find a pencil and a dictionary some-where. Do as much as you like, just be quiet about it."

Gwen's mouth opened to retort, but as he was typing again, she closed it. After locating a pencil under a pile of discarded magazines, she picked up the first page. She refused to admit that the project excited her, that she wanted the job because it meant sharing something with him. Dismissing such thoughts, she resolved to read with objective professionalism. Minutes later, her pencil was forgotten—she was enthralled.

Time passed. Gwen no longer heard the clicking of the typewriter. Dust motes danced in the insistent sunlight, but Gwen was unaware of them. Luke's characters were flesh and blood to her. She felt she knew them, cared about them. She was even unaware that her eyes had filled with tears. She felt as the woman in Luke's story felt; des-perately in love, confused, proud, vulnerable. She wept for the beauty of the words and the despair of the heroine. Suddenly, she lifted her eyes.

Luke had stopped typing, but for how long, she did not know. She blinked to clear her vision. He was watch-ing her. His eyes were intent and searching, his mouth unsmiling. Helplessly Gwen stared back, letting the tears fall freely. Her weakness frightened her. He was not touching her, not speaking to her, yet her whole body felt attuned to him. She opened her mouth, but no words came. She shook her head, but he neither moved nor spoke. Knowing her only defense was escape, Gwen stood and darted from the room.

The bayou offered a haven, so she abandoned the house and fled toward it. She had calmed herself considerably by the time she neared Malon's cabin. Taking long, deep breaths, Gwen slowed her steps. It would not do to have Malon see her out of breath and distressed. As she rounded the last bend in the path, she saw Malon stepping from his pirogue onto the dock. Already, she felt reason returning.

"A good catch?" she asked, grateful she could smile at him without effort.

"Not bad," he answered with typical understatement. "Did you come for dinner?"

"Dinner?" Gwen repeated, glancing automatically at the sun. "Is it so late?" Could the afternoon have gone so swiftly? she wondered.

"It is late enough because I'm hungry," Malon replied. "We'll cook up some shrimp and eat, then you can take your mama her share. Can you still make coffee?"

"Of course I can still make coffee—just don't tell Tillie." Gwen followed him inside, letting the screen door slam behind them.

Before long the cabin was filled with the pungent

scent of shrimp gumbo cooking and the quiet strains of Chopin. Raphael sunned on the windowsill, leaving the humans to deal with the domestic chores. Gwen felt the tension draining from her system. She ate, surprised at her appetite until she recalled she had eaten nothing since breakfast.

"You still like my cooking, *hein?*" Pleased, Malon spooned more gumbo onto her plate.

"I just didn't want to hurt your feelings," Gwen told him between bites. Malon watched her clean her plate and chuckled. With a contented sigh, Gwen sat back. "I haven't eaten that much in two years."

"That's why you're skinny." Malon leaned back, too, and lit a strong French cigarette. Gwen remembered the scent as well as she remembered the tastes. She had been twelve—curious and ultimately sick—when she persuaded Malon to let her try one. He had offered no sympathy and no lecture. Grinning at the memory, Gwen watched the thin column of smoke rise.

"Now you feel better," Malon commented. At his statement, she shifted her eyes back to his. Instantly, she saw he was not referring to her hunger. Her shoulders lifted and then fell with her sigh.

"Some. I needed to come here—it's helped. I'm having trouble understanding myself, and there's... well, there's this man."

"There is bound to be," Malon agreed, blowing a series of smoke rings. "You are a woman."

"Yes, but not a very smart one. I don't know very much about men. And he's nothing like the men I've known in any case." She turned to Malon. "The trouble is…" She made a small, frustrated sound and walked to the window. "The trouble is, I'm becoming more involved, more emotionally involved with…this man than I can afford to."

"'Afford to,'" he repeated with a snort. "What do you mean, 'afford to'? Emotions cost you nothing."

"Oh, Malon." When she turned back to him, her eyes were unhappy. "Sometimes they cost everything. I'm beginning to need him, beginning to feel an—an attachment that can lead nowhere."

"And why can it lead nowhere?"

"Because I need love." After running a hand through her hair, Gwen paced the width of the cabin.

"So does everyone," Malon told her, carefully crushing out his cigarette.

"But he doesn't love me," she said miserably. Her hands made a futile gesture. "He doesn't love me, yet I can't stop thinking about him. When I'm with him I forget everything else. It's wrong, he's involved with someone else, and… Oh, Malon, it's so complicated." Her voice faltered away.

"Life is not simple, little girl," he said, reverting to her childhood title, "but we live it." Rising, he moved toward her, then patted her cheek. "Complications provide spice."

"Right now," she said with a small smile, "I'd rather be bland."

"Did you come for advice or for sympathy?" His eyes were small and sharp, his palm rough. He smelled of fish and tobacco. Gwen felt the ground was more solid where he stood.

"I came to be with you," she told him softly, "because you are the only father I have." Slipping her arms around his waist, she rested her head on one of his powerful shoulders. She felt his wide hand stroke her hair. "Malon," she murmured. "I don't want to be in love with him."

"So, do you come for an antilove potion? Do you want a snakeskin for his pillow?"

Gwen laughed and tilted back her head. "No."

"Good. I like him. I would feel bad putting a hex on him."

She realized Malon had known all along she had been speaking of Luke. Always she had been as clear as a piece of glass to him. Still, she was more comfortable with him than with anyone else. Gwen studied him, wondering what secrets he held behind the small blue eyes. "Malon, you never told me you'd been to Budapest."

"You never asked."

She smiled and relaxed. "If I asked now, would you tell me?"

"I'll tell you while you do the dishes."

★ ★ ★

Bradley frowned at his canvas, then at his model. "You're not giving me the spark," he complained as he pushed the fisherman's cap further back on his head.

Three nights of fitful sleep had dimmed Gwen's spark considerably. She sat, as Bradley had directed her, in the smoothly worn U formed by two branches of an ancient oak. She wore the robe he had chosen, with a magnolia tucked behind her ear. Following his instructions, she had left her hair free and kept her makeup light. Because of their size and color, her eyes dominated the picture. But they did not, as Bradley had anticipated, hold the light he had seen before. There was a listlessness in the set of her shoulders, a moodiness in the set of her mouth.

"Gwen," Bradley said with exaggerated patience, "depression is not the mood we're seeking."

"I'm sorry, Bradley." Gwen shrugged and sent him a weary smile. "I haven't been sleeping well."

"Warm milk," Monica Wilkins stated from her perch on a three-legged stool. She was painting, with quiet diligence, a tidy clump of asters. "Always helps me."

Gwen wanted to wrinkle her nose at the thought, but instead she answered politely. "Maybe I'll try that next time."

"Don't scald it, though," Monica warned as she perfected her image of a petal.

"No, I won't," Gwen assured her with equal gravity.

"Now that we've got that settled…." Bradley began, in such a martyrlike voice that Gwen laughed.

"I'm sorry, Bradley, I'm afraid I'm a terrible model."

"Nonsense," Bradley said. "You've just got to relax."

"Wine," Monica announced, still peering critically at her asters.

"I beg your pardon?" Bradley turned his head and frowned.

"Wine," Monica repeated. "A nice glass of wine would relax her beautifully."

"Yes, I suppose it might, if we had any." Bradley adjusted the brim of his cap and studied the tip of his brush.

"I have," Monica told him in her wispy voice.

"Have what?"

Gwen's eyes went back to Bradley. I'm beginning to feel as though I was at a tennis match, she thought, lifting a hand to the base of her neck.

"Wine," Monica answered, carefully adding a vein to a pale green leaf. "I have a thermos of white wine in my bag. It's nicely chilled."

"How clever of you," Bradley told her admiringly.

"Thank you." Monica blushed. "You're certainly welcome to it, if you think it might help." Carefully she opened a bulky macramé sack and pulled out a red thermos.

"Monica, I'm in your debt." Gallantly, Bradley bowed

over the thermos. Monica let out what sounded suspiciously like a giggle before she went back to her asters.

"Bradley, I really don't think this is necessary," Gwen began.

"Just the thing to put you into the mood," he disagreed as he unscrewed the thermos lid. Wine poured, light and golden, into the plastic cup.

"But Bradley, I hardly drink at all."

"Glad to hear it." He held out the cup. "Bad for your health."

"Bradley," Gwen began again, trying to keep her voice firm. "It's barely ten o'clock in the morning."

"Yes, drink up, the light will be wrong soon."

"Oh, good grief." Defeated, Gwen lifted the plastic cup to her lips and sipped. With a sigh, she sipped again. "This is crazy," she muttered into the wine.

"What's that, Gwen?" Monica called out.

"I said this is lovely," Gwen amended. "Thank you, Monica."

"Glad to help." As the women exchanged smiles, Bradley tipped more wine into the cup.

"Drink it up," he ordered, like a parent urging medicine on a child. "We don't want to lose the light."

Obediently, Gwen tilted the cup. When she handed it back to Bradley, she heaved a huge sigh. "Am I relaxed?" she asked. There was a pleasant lightness near the top of her head. "My, it's gotten warm, hasn't it?" She smiled at no one in particular as Bradley replaced the lid on the thermos.

"I hope I haven't overdone it," he muttered to Monica.

"One never knows about people's metabolisms," Monica said. With a noncommittal grunt, Bradley returned to his canvas.

"Now look this way, love," he ordered as Gwen's attention wandered. "Remember, I want contrasts. I see the delicacy of your bone structure, the femininity in the pose, but I want to see character in your face. I want spirit—no, more—I want challenge in your eyes. Dare the onlooker to touch the untouched."

"Untouched," Gwen murmured as her memory stirred. "I'm not a child," she asserted, and straightened her shoulders.

"No," Bradley agreed as he studied her closely. "Yes, yes, that's perfect!" He grabbed his brush. Glancing over his shoulder, he caught sight of Luke approaching, and then he gave his full attention to his work. "Ah, the mouth's perfect," he muttered, "just between sulky and a pout. Don't change it, don't change a thing. Bless you, Monica!"

Bradley worked feverishly, unaware that the wine was a far less potent stimulant to his model than the man who now stood beside him. It was his presence that brought the rush of color to her cheeks, that brightened her eyes with challenge and made her mouth grow soft, sulky and inviting. Luke's own face was inscrutable as he watched. Though he stood in quiet observation, there was an air of alertness about him. Bradley muttered as he worked. A crow cawed monotonously in the distance.

A myriad of thoughts and feelings rushed through Gwen's mind. Longing warred fiercely with pride. Luke had infuriated her, charmed her, laughed at her, rejected her. I will not fall in love with him, she told herself. I will not allow it to happen. *He won't make a fool of me again*.

"Magnificent," Bradley murmured.

"Yes, it is." Luke slipped his hands into his pockets as he studied the portrait. "You've caught her."

"It's rare," Bradley muttered, touching up the shadows of Gwen's cheeks in the portrait. "Her looks are just a bonus. It's that aura of innocence mixed with the hint of banked fires. Incredible combination. Every man who sees this portrait will want her."

A flash of irritation crossed Luke's face as he lifted his eyes to Gwen's. "Yes, I imagine so."

"I'm calling it *The Virgin Temptress*. It suits, don't you think?"

"Hmm."

Taking this as full agreement, Bradley lapsed back into unintelligible mutters. Abruptly, he put down his brush and began packing his equipment. "You did beautifully," he told Gwen. "We're losing the morning light. We should start a bit earlier, I think. Three more good sittings should do it now."

"I'll walk back with you, Bradley." Monica rose. "I've done about all I can do on this one." Gathering up her paints, easel and stool, she started after Bradley.

Gwen slipped down from her seat in the fork of the tree with a quick flutter of white. As her bare feet touched the grass, the wine spun dizzily in her head. Instinctively she rested her hand against the tree for support. Watching her, Luke lifted a brow in speculation. With exaggerated care, she straightened, swallowed the odd dryness in her throat and started to walk. Her legs felt strangely weak. It was her intention to walk past Luke with icy dignity, but he stopped her easily with a hand on her arm.

"Are you all right?"

The sun had the wine bubbling inside her. Clearing her throat, Gwen spoke distinctly. "Of course. I am just fine."

Luke placed two fingers under her chin and lifted it. He studied her upturned face. Humor leaped into his eyes. "Why, Gwenivere, you're sloshed."

Knowing the truth of his statement only stiffened her dignity. "I have no idea what you are talking about. If you would kindly remove your hand from my face, I would greatly appreciate it."

"Sure. But don't blame me if you fall on it once the support's gone." Luke dropped his hand, and Gwen swayed dangerously. She gripped Luke's shirt to right herself.

"If you will excuse me," she said regally, but neither moved nor dropped her hand. Heaving a deep sigh, Gwen raised her face again and frowned. "I'm waiting for you to stand still."

"Oh. Sorry. May one ask how you came to be in this condition?"

"Relaxed," Gwen corrected.

"I beg your pardon?"

"That's what I am. It was either wine or warm milk. Monica's a whiz at these things. I'm not too fond of warm milk, and there wasn't any handy in any case."

"No, I can see it might be difficult to come by," Luke agreed, slipping a supporting arm around her waist as she began to weave her way across the lawn.

"I only had a topful, you know."

"That should do it."

"Oh, dear." Gwen stopped abruptly. "I've stepped on a bee." She sat down in a floating film of white. "I suppose the poor little thing will go off and die." Lifting her foot, she frowned at the small welt on the ball of her foot.

"Happily bombed, I should think." Luke sat down and took her foot in his hand. "Hurt?" he asked as he drew out the stinger.

"No, I don't feel anything."

"Small wonder. I think it might be wise to tell Bradley

you don't want to be quite so relaxed at ten in the morning."

"He's very serious about his art," Gwen said confidentially. "He believes I'll become immoral."

"A distinct possibility if you continue to relax before noon," Luke agreed dryly. "But I believe you mean 'immortal.'"

"Do you think so, too?" Gwen lifted her face to the sun. "I really thought he and Monica were macadamias."

"What?"

"Nuts." Gwen lay back in the grass and shut her eyes. "I think it would be rather sweet if they fell in love, don't you?"

"Adorable."

"You're just cynical because you've been in love so many times."

"Have I?" He traced a finger over her ankle as he watched the sun highlight her hair. "Why do you say that?"

"Your books. You know how women think, how they feel. When I was reading yesterday, I hurt because it was too real, too personal." The robe shifted lightly with her sigh. "I imagine you've made love with dozens of women."

"Making love and being in love are entirely separate things."

Gwen opened her eyes. "Sometimes," she agreed. "For some people."

"You're a romantic," Luke told her with a shrug. "Only a romantic can wear floating white or toss flowers to the stars or believe a magician's illusions."

"How odd." Gwen's voice was genuinely puzzled as she closed her eyes again. "I've never thought of myself as a romantic. Is it wrong?"

"No." The word was quick and faintly annoyed. Luke rose and stared down at her. Her hair was spread out under her, glinting with golden lights. The robe crossed lightly over her breasts, making an inviting shadow. Swearing under his breath, he bent and scooped her into his arms.

"Mmm, you're very strong." Her head spun gently, so she rested it against his shoulder. "I noticed that the first day, when I watched you chop down the tree. Michael lifts weights."

"Good for Michael."

"No, actually, he strained his back." With a giggle, Gwen snuggled deeper into the curve of his shoulder. "Michael isn't very physical, you see. He plays bridge." Gwen lifted her face and smiled cheerfully. "I'm quite hopeless at bridge. Michael says my mind needs discipline."

"I simply must meet this Michael."

"He has fifty-seven ties, you know."

"Yes, I imagine he does."

"His shoes are always shined," Gwen added wistfully, and traced Luke's jawline with her fingertip. "I really must try to be more tidy. He tells me continually that the image a person projects is important, but I tend to forget. Feeding pigeons in the park isn't good for a corporate image."

"What is?"

"Opera," she said instantly. "German opera particularly, but I fall asleep. I like to watch murder mysteries on the late-night TV."

"Philistine," Luke concluded as his mouth twitched into a smile.

"Exactly," Gwen agreed, feeling more cheerful than she had in weeks. "Your face is leaner than his, too, and he never forgets to shave."

"Good for Michael," Luke mumbled again as he mounted the porch steps.

"He never made me feel the way you do." At these words Luke stopped and stared down into Gwen's eyes. Cushioned by the wine, Gwen met his look with a gentle smile. "Why do you suppose that is?"

Luke's voice was edged with roughness. "Can you really be so utterly guileless?"

She considered the question, then shrugged. "I don't know. I suppose so. Do you want me to be?"

For a moment, Luke's arms tightened, shifting her closer against him. In immediate response, Gwen closed her eyes and offered her mouth. When his lips brushed over her brow, she sighed and cuddled closer. "Sometimes you're a very nice man," she murmured.

"Am I?" He frowned down at her. "Let's say sometimes I remember there are a few basic rules. At the moment, I'm finding my memory unfortunately clear."

"A very nice man," Gwen repeated, and kissed a spot under his jaw. With a yawn, she settled comfortably against him. "But I won't fall in love with you."

Luke looked down at her quiet face with its aureole of soft curls. "A wise decision," he said softly, and carried her into the house.

11

It was dark when Gwen awoke. Disoriented, she stared at the dim shapes of furniture and the pale silver moonlight. It was a knock at the door that had awakened her, and it came again, soft and insistent. Brushing her hair from her face, she sat up. The room spun once, then settled. Gwen moaned quietly and swallowed before she rose to answer the knock. In the hallway the light was bright. She put her hand over her eyes to shield them.

"Oh, darling, I'm sorry to wake you." Anabelle gave a sympathetic sigh. "I know how these headaches are."

"Headaches?" Gwen repeated, gingerly uncovering her eyes.

"Yes, Luke told me all about it. Did you take some aspirin?"

"Aspirin?" Gwen searched her memory. Abruptly, color rushed to her cheeks. "Oh!"

Taking this as an affirmative response, Anabelle smiled. "Are you feeling better now?"

"I haven't got a headache," Gwen murmured.

"Oh, I'm so glad, because you have a phone call." Anabelle smiled more brightly. "It's from New York, so I really thought it best to wake you. It's that Michael of yours. He has a lovely voice."

"Michael," Gwen echoed softly. She sighed, wishing she could return to the comforting darkness of her room. She felt only weariness at the sound of his name. Glancing down, she saw she still wore the white robe. She could clearly remember her conversation with Luke and, more disturbing, the feel of his arms as he carried her.

"You really shouldn't keep him waiting, darling." Anabelle interrupted Gwen's thoughts with gentle prompting. "It's long-distance."

"No, of course not." Gwen followed her mother to the foot of the stairs.

"I'll just run along and have Tillie warm up some dinner for you." Anabelle retreated tactfully, leaving Gwen staring down at the waiting receiver. She took a deep breath, blew it out and picked up the phone. "Hello, Michael."

"Gwen—I was beginning to think I'd been left on hold." His voice was even, well pitched and annoyed.

"I'm sorry." The apology was automatic, and immediately, she swore at herself for giving it. Why does he always intimidate me? she demanded silently of herself. "I was busy," she added in a firmer voice. "I wasn't expecting to hear from you."

"I hope it's a pleasant surprise," he replied. From the tone of his voice, Gwen knew he had already concluded it was. "I've been busy myself," he went on without bothering to hear her answer. "Right up to my chin in a lawsuit against Delron Corporation. Tricky business. It's had me chained to my desk."

"I'm sorry to hear that, Michael," Gwen said. Glancing up, she saw Luke coming down the steps. *Oh, perfect,* she thought in despair. She feigned unconcern with a faint nod of greeting, but when he stopped and leaned against the newel post, she frowned. "Do you mind?" she whispered sharply to Luke.

"No, not a bit." He smiled but made no effort to move. "Say hello for me."

Her eyes narrowed into furious slits. "You're horrible, absolutely horrible."

"What?" came Michael's puzzled voice. "What did you say?"

"Oh, nothing," Gwen said sharply.

"For heaven's sake, Gwen, I'm simply trying to tell you about the Delron case. You needn't get testy."

"I am not testy. Why did you call, Michael?"

"To see when you'd be coming home, sweetheart. I

miss you." He was using his quiet, persuasive tone, and Gwen sighed. Closing her eyes, she rested the receiver against her forehead a moment.

"Does he always make you feel guilty?" Luke asked conversationally. Gwen jerked up her chin and glared.

"Shut up," she ordered, furious that he could read her so accurately.

"What?" Michael's voice shouted through the receiver. Luke gave a quick laugh at the outraged voice. "We must have a bad connection," he concluded.

"Must have," Gwen muttered. Taking a deep breath, Gwen decided to clear the air once and for all. "Michael, I…"

"I thought I'd given you enough time to cool off," Michael said pleasantly.

"Cool off?"

"It was foolish of us to fight that way, sweetheart. Of course I know you didn't mean the things you said."

"I didn't?"

"You know you have a tendency to say rash things when you're in a temper," Michael reminded her in a patient, forgiving tone. "Of course," he went on, "I suppose I was partially to blame."

"You were?" Gwen struggled to keep her voice quiet and reasonable. "How could you be partially to blame for my temper?" Glancing up, she saw Luke still watching her.

"I'm afraid I rushed you. You simply weren't ready for a sudden proposal."

"Michael, we've been seeing each other for nearly a year," Gwen reminded him, pushing her fingers through her hair in irritation. The gesture caused the V of her bodice to widen enticingly.

"Of course, sweetheart," he said soothingly. "But I should have prepared you."

"*Prepared me?* I don't want to be prepared, Michael, do you understand? I want to be surprised. And if you call me sweetheart again in that patronizing voice, I'm going to scream."

"Now, now, Gwen, don't get upset. I'm more than willing to forgive and forget."

"Oh." Gwen swallowed her rage. "Oh, that's generous of you, Michael. I don't know what to say."

"Just say when you'll be back, sweetheart. We'll have a nice celebration dinner and set the date. Tiffany's has some lovely rings. You can take your pick."

"Michael," Gwen said, "please listen to me. Really listen this time. I'm not what you want…. I can't be what you want. If I tried, I'd shrivel up inside. Please, I do care about you, but don't ask me to be someone I'm not."

"I don't know what you're talking about, Gwen," he interrupted. "I'm not asking you—"

"Michael," Gwen said, cutting him off. "I just can't go through all this again. I did mean the things I said, but I don't want to have to say them all again. I'm not good for you, Michael. Find someone who knows how to fix vodka martinis for twenty."

"You're talking nonsense." It was his cool attorney's voice, and Gwen closed her eyes, knowing arguments were futile. "We'll straighten all this out when you get home."

"No, Michael," she said, knowing he wouldn't hear.

"Give me a call and I'll meet your plane. Goodbye, Gwen."

"Goodbye, Michael," she murmured, even while she replaced the receiver. She felt a wave of sorrow and guilt. Lifting her eyes, she met Luke's. There was no amusement in them now, only understanding. She felt that amusement would have been easier to handle. "I'd appreciate it very much," she said quietly, "if you wouldn't say anything just now." She walked past him and up the stairs while he looked after her.

Gwen stood on her balcony under a moonlit sky. Moss-draped cypress trees appeared ghostly and tipped with silver. There was a bird singing in a sweet, clear voice, and she wondered if it was a nightingale. The time seemed right for nightingales. She sighed, remembering that Luke had called her a romantic. Perhaps he was right. But it was not the soft night or the song of a bird that kept her out of bed and on the balcony.

Of course you can't sleep, she berated herself silently. How can you expect to sleep at night when you slept all afternoon? Color rushed to her cheeks as she recalled the reason for her peaceful midday nap. I certainly managed to make a first-class fool of myself. Did he have to be there? Couldn't I have stumbled into the house without an audience? Why can I never be cool and dignified around him?

And then the call from Michael. Gwen lifted her hand to the base of her neck and tried to massage away the tension. Again she played over the telephone conversation in her mind, attempting to find some way she could have made her feelings clearer. It's all been said before, she reminded herself, but he doesn't listen. *He forgives me.* With a quiet laugh, Gwen pressed her fingers to her eyes. He forgives me but thinks nothing of the cruel things he said. He doesn't even love me. He loves the woman he'd like me to be.

As she watched, a star shivered and fell in a speeding arc of light. Gwen caught her breath at the fleeting flash from heaven. Abruptly her thoughts centered on Luke. With him, she had felt a meteoric intensity, a brilliant heat. But she knew she could not hold him any more than the night sky could hold the trailing shimmer of light. Feeling a sudden chill, Gwen slipped back into her room. The middle of the night's a bad time for thinking, she decided. I'd be much better off if I went downstairs and tried some of Monica's detestable warm milk.

Gwen moved quickly down the hall, not bothering to switch on a light. She knew her way, just as she knew

which steps creaked and which boards moaned. An unexpected sound made her whirl around as she reached the
head of the stairs.

"Mama!" Stunned, Gwen watched her mother creep
down the third-floor staircase. Anabelle started at Gwen's
voice, and her hand fluttered to her heart.

"Gwenivere, you scared the wits out of me!" Anabelle's
soft bosom rose with her breath. Her hair was charmingly
disordered around her face. The robe she wore was frilly,
pink and feminine. "Whatever are you doing out here in
the dark?"

"I couldn't sleep." Gwen moved closer and caught the
familiar scent of lilac. "Mama…."

"Of course, you're probably starving." Anabelle gave
a sympathetic cluck. "It doesn't do to miss meals, you
know."

"Mama, what were you doing upstairs?"

"Upstairs?" Anabelle repeated, then glanced back over
her shoulder. "Oh, why, I was just up with Luke." She
smiled, not noticing Gwen's draining color.

"W-with Luke?"

"Yes." She made a token gesture of tidying her hair.
"He's such a marvelous, generous man."

Gwen gently took her mother's hand. "Mama." She bit
her lip to steady her voice and took a deep breath. "Are
you certain this is what you want?"

"Is what what I want, darling?"

"This—this relationship with Luke," Gwen managed to get out, although the words hurt her throat.

"Oh, Gwen, I simply couldn't get along without Luke." She gave Gwen's icy hand a squeeze. "Goodness, you're cold. You'd best get back to bed, dear. Is there anything I can get for you?"

"No," Gwen answered quietly. "No, there's nothing." She gave Anabelle a quick, desperate hug. "Please, you go back to bed, I'll be fine."

"All right, dear." Anabelle kissed her brow in a way Gwen recognized from childhood. Satisfied that there was no fever, Anabelle patted her cheek. "Good night, Gwen."

"Good night, Mama," Gwen murmured, watching her disappear down the hall.

Gwen waited until the sound of the closing door had echoed into silence before she let out a shuddering breath. Face it, Gwen, you've been falling for your mother's man. For a moment, she merely stared down at her empty hands. Doing nothing wasn't enough, she reflected. I could have stopped it…. I didn't want to stop it. There's nothing to do now but get untangled while I still can. It's time to face things head-on. Lifting her chin, she began to climb the stairs to the third floor.

Without giving herself a chance to think any further, she knocked at Luke's door.

"Yes?" The reply was curt and immediate.

Refusing to give in to the urge to turn and run, Gwen

twisted the knob and pushed open Luke's door. He was, as he had been before, seated in the midst of his own disorder. He was hitting the keys of the typewriter in a quick, staccato rhythm, and his eyes were intent and concentrated. Faded, low-slung jeans were his only concession to modesty. The faintest hint of lilac drifted through the air. Moistening her lips, Gwen kept her eyes from the tousled sheets of the bed.

I am in love with him, she realized suddenly, and simultaneously remembered it was impossible for her to be so. I'll have to find a way to fall out of love with him, she told herself, warding off a brief stab of misery. I'll have to start now. Keeping her head high, she closed the door behind her and leaned against it.

"Luke?"

"Hmm?" He glanced up absently, his fingers still working the keys. His expression altered as he focused on her. His hands lay still. "What are you doing here?" There was such sharp impatience in his voice that Gwen bit her lip.

"I'm sorry to interrupt your work. I need to talk to you."

"At this hour of the night?" His tone was politely incredulous. "Run along, Gwen, I'm busy."

Gwen swallowed her pride. "Luke, please. It's important."

"So's my sanity," he muttered, without changing rhythm.

She ran a hand through her hair. *Sanity,* she thought desperately, *I must have lost mine the moment he put down that ax and walked toward me.* "You're making this very difficult."

"I?" he tossed back furiously. "I make it difficult? Do you know how you look at me? Do you know how many times I've found myself alone with you when you're half-dressed?" Instinctively, Gwen reached for the low neckline of her robe. "Contrary to popular opinion," he continued as he rose and strode to a small table across the room, "I am a mortal man given to normal instincts." There was a decanter of brandy on the table, and he poured himself a hefty glass. "Damn it, I want you. Haven't I made that clear enough?"

His tone was rough. Gwen felt the tears burn in her throat. When she spoke, her voice was thick with them. "I'm sorry, I didn't mean…" She broke off with a helpless shrug.

"For God's sake, don't cry," he said impatiently. "I'm in no mood to give you a few comforting kisses and send you along. If I touch you now, you won't leave here tonight." His eyes met hers. She swallowed even the thought of tears. "I'm not in a civilized mood, Gwen. I told you once that I know my limit. Well, I've reached it." He lifted the decanter and poured again.

Temptation fluttered along her skin. He wanted her, she could almost taste his desire. How easy it would be to take just one small step…to steal a night, a moment.

The night would be full and rich. *But the morning would be empty.* Gwen's eyes dropped, and she struggled with her own heart. When his passion was spent, she knew her love would starve. Love has found another fool, she thought resignedly. It's best to do this quickly.

"This isn't easy for me," Gwen told him quietly. Though she fought for calm, her eyes were tragic as they met his. "I need to talk to you about Mama."

Luke turned and walked to the French doors. Tossing them open, he stared out into the night. "What about her?"

"I was wrong to interfere." Gwen shut her eyes tight and struggled to strengthen her voice. "It was wrong of me to come here thinking I had any say in whom my mother becomes involved with."

Luke swore and whirled back to face her. She watched him struggle with temper. "You are an idiot. Anabelle is a beautiful woman—"

"Please," Gwen interrupted swiftly, "let me finish. I need to say this, and it's so difficult. I'd like to say it all at once." She still stood with her back to the door, poised for escape. Luke shrugged, dropped back into his chair and signaled for her to continue. "It isn't up to me to decide what's right for my mother, it's not my right to interfere. You're good for her, I can't deny it." Gwen's breath trembled before she could steady it. "And I can't deny I'm attracted to you, but it's nothing that can't be resolved by a bit of distance. I think—I think if you and

I just stay out of each other's way for the rest of my visit, everything will work out."

"Oh, do you?" Luke gave a quick laugh as he set down his glass. "That's an amazing piece of logic." He rubbed the bridge of his nose between his thumb and forefinger. Gwen frowned at the action, finding it somehow out of character.

"I'm leaving next week," Gwen told him. "There's no need for me to stay, and I've left several things undone back in New York." Hurriedly, she turned to the door.

"Gwen." Luke's voice stopped her, but she could not bear to turn and face him again. "Don't waste yourself on Michael."

"I don't intend to," she answered in a choked voice. Blind with tears, she opened the door and plunged into the darkness.

12

Gwen dressed with care. She stretched out the process, dawdling over the buttons of her pale lavender blouse. After another sleepless night, Gwen knew she could not survive even a few more days in the same house with Luke. She could not be sophisticated, mature or philosophical about love. She went to her closet and pulled out her suitcase.

When two women love the same man, she mused, one of them has to lose. If it were anyone else, I could fight her. She opened the first case. How does a daughter fight her own mother? Even if she wins, she loses. I haven't really lost, she reflected as she moved to her dresser and pulled open a drawer. You have to have something first to lose it. I never had Luke.

Gwen packed methodically, using the task as a diversion. She refused to speculate on what she would do when she returned to New York. While packing, she had no past and no future, only the present. She would have to face the shambles of her life soon enough.

"Gwen." Anabelle knocked quickly and stuck her head into the room. "I wonder if you've seen… Oh!" She opened the door all the way when she saw Gwen's half-packed cases. "What's this?"

Gwen moistened her lips and strove for casualness. "I've got to get back to New York."

"Oh." There was disappointment in the single syllable. "But you just got here. Are you going back to Michael?"

"No, Mama, I'm not going back to Michael."

"I see." She paused a moment. "Is there some trouble at your office?"

The excuse was so perfect, agreement trembled on Gwen's tongue. Regretably, the lie would not form on her lips. "No."

Anabelle tilted her head at her daughter's tone, then quietly closed the door at her back. "You know I don't like to pry, Gwen, and I know you're a very private person, but…" Anabelle sighed before she walked over to sit on Gwen's bed. "I really think you'd better tell me what this is all about."

"Oh, Mama." Gwen turned away and rested both palms on her dresser. "It's such an awful mess."

"It can't be as bad as all that." Anabelle folded her

hands neatly in her lap. "Just tell me straight out, it's the best way."

Gwen took a breath and held it. "I'm in love with Luke," she said quickly, then expelled the breath in one swift whoosh.

"And…" Anabelle prompted.

Gwen's eyes flew to the mirror in search of her mother's. "Mama, I said I was in love with Luke."

"Yes, darling, I heard that part. I'm waiting for the part about the dreadful mess."

"Mama." Gingerly, Gwen turned around. Anabelle smiled patiently. "It's not just an infatuation or a crush, I'm really in love with him."

"Oh, yes, well, that's nice."

"I don't think you understand." Gwen covered her face with her hands for a moment and then dropped them. "I even wanted him to—to make love with me."

Anabelle blushed a soft, gentle pink and brushed at her skirts. "Yes, well…I'm sure that's quite natural. I don't believe you and I ever had a talk about…ah, the birds and the bees."

"Oh, good grief, Mama," Gwen said impatiently. "I don't need a lecture on sex. I know all about that."

"Oh?" Anabelle lifted her brows in maternal censure. "I see."

"No, I don't mean…" Gwen stopped in frustration. How did this conversation get away from me? she wondered. "Mama, please, this is hard enough. I came home to get rid of the man, and before I knew it, I was involved with him. I didn't plan it, I didn't want it. I'd never, never do anything to hurt you, and I was wrong because years don't mean a thing, and no one has the right to choose for anyone else. Now I have to go away because I love you both so terribly, don't you see?" Gwen ended on a note of despair and dropped down at Anabelle's feet.

Anabelle stared down at the tragic face thoughtfully. "Perhaps I will in a minute," she answered, furrowing her brow. "No, actually, I don't think I will. Why don't you try again? Start with the part about your coming here to get rid of Luke. I believe that's where I got confused."

Gwen sniffled and accepted Anabelle's lace hankie. "I wanted to make him go away because I thought it was wrong for you to have an affair with him. But it was none of my—"

"A what?" Anabelle interrupted. Her hand paused on its journey to smooth Gwen's curls. *"An affair?"* she repeated, blinking rapidly. "An affair? Luke and I?" To Gwen's amazement, Anabelle tossed back her head and laughed. It was a young, gay sound. "How delightful! Darling, darling, how flattering. My, my." She smiled into space, her cheeks rosy with pleasure. "Such a handsome young man, too. He must be—" she stopped and fluttered her lashes "—well, a year or two younger than I." She laughed again and clapped her hands together as Gwen looked on. Bending down, she kissed her daughter soundly. "Thank you, sweet, sweet child. I don't know when I've had a nicer present."

"Now *I* don't understand." Gwen wiped a lingering tear from her lashes. "Are you saying you and Luke aren't lovers?"

"Oh, my." Anabelle rolled her eyes. "How very blunt you are."

"Mama, please, I'll go mad in a moment." Briefly, Gwen pressed her fingers to her eyes. Rising, she began to pace the room. "You talked and talked about him in all your letters. You said he'd changed your life. You said he was the most wonderful man you'd ever met. You couldn't get along without him. And just last night you were coming out of his room in the middle of the night. And you've been acting strangely." Gwen whirled around and paced in the other direction. "You can't deny it. Locking your door and practically pushing me out of the house on the flimsiest of excuses."

"Oh, dear." Anabelle clucked her tongue and touched a hand to her hair. "I begin to see. I suppose it was silly of me to keep it a secret." Standing, Anabelle took a blouse from Gwen's suitcase, shook it out and walked to the closet. "Yes, it's obviously my fault. But then, I wanted to surprise you. Poor darling, no wonder you've been so unhappy and confused. I'm afraid I thought you were brooding over Michael, but it wasn't him at all, was it? Luke makes much better sense, I'm sure." Carefully, Anabelle hung up the blouse. "Now, when I think back on it, I can see how you might think so." She moved back to the suitcase while Gwen prayed for patience. "Luke and I aren't having an affair, though I do thank you for the kind thought, dear. We are, however, collaborating in a sense. Why don't you sit down?"

"I think," Gwen said, "I'm going to scream any minute."

"Always so impatient," Anabelle sighed. "Well, this is a bit embarrassing. I feel so foolish." She placed her hands on her cheeks as they grew warm. "Oh, I do hope you won't laugh at me. I'm…I'm writing a book." The confession came out in a swift jumble of words.

"What?" Gwen exclaimed, touching her hand to her ear to check her hearing.

"I've always wanted to, but I never thought I could until Luke encouraged me." Excitement joined the embarrassment in Anabelle's voice. "I've always had such pretty stories in my head, but I never had the courage to write them down. Luke says—" Anabelle lifted her chin and glowed proudly "—he says I have a natural talent."

"Talent?" Gwen echoed as she sank onto the bed.

"Isn't that lovely of him?" Anabelle enthused. She shook out one of Gwen's packed dresses and moved toward the closet. "He's given me so much help, so much time and encouragement! He doesn't even mind if I pop up to his room and try out an idea! Why, just last night he stopped his own work to listen to me."

Remembering the conclusions she had drawn,

Gwen shut her eyes. "Oh, good grief! Why didn't you tell me?"

"I wanted to surprise you. And to be honest, I felt you'd think I was being silly." She began neatly to put away Gwen's lingerie. "My, what a pretty chemise. New York has such wonderful shops. Then there's the money."

"Money," Gwen repeated. Opening her eyes, she tried valiantly to follow her mother's winding train of thought. "What money?"

"Luke thinks I should sell the manuscript when I'm finished. It's—well, it's a bit crass, don't you think?"

"Oh, Mama." Gwen could only close her eyes again.

"I am sorry about not telling you and about locking my door so you wouldn't catch me writing. And about shooing you out of the house so that I could finish up. You aren't angry with me, are you?"

"No, no, I'm not angry." Gwen stared up at Anabelle's glowing face and then buried her own in her hands and laughed. "Oh, help! What a fool I've made of myself!" She rose quickly and embraced her mother. "I'm proud of you, Mama. Very proud."

"You haven't read it yet," Anabelle reminded her.

"I don't have to read it to be proud of you. And I don't think you're silly, I think you're marvelous." Drawing away slightly, she studied Anabelle's face. "Luke's right," she said, kissing both of her mother's cheeks. "You are a beautiful woman."

"Did he say that?" Anabelle dimpled. "How sweet." After patting Gwen's shoulder, she moved to the door. "I think we've solved everything nicely. Come down after you're unpacked, and I'll let you read my first chapters."

"Mama." Gwen shook her head. "I can't stay...."

"Oh, Luke." Anabelle beamed as she opened the door. "How lucky. You'll never believe the mess Gwen and I have just straightened out."

"Oh?" Luke looked past Anabelle to Gwen, then studied the open cases on her bed. "Going somewhere?"

"Yes."

"No," Anabelle said simultaneously. "Not anymore. She was going back to New York, but we solved everything nicely."

"Mama," Gwen said warningly, and stepped forward.

"I've confessed all," she told Luke with a bright smile. "Gwen knows all about my secret hobby. The poor darling thought you and I were having a romance."

"Weren't we?" Luke lifted her hand to his lips.

"Oh, you devil." Anabelle patted his cheek, highly pleased. "I must get along now, but I'm sure Luke will want to hear what you told me about being in love with him."

"Mama!" The sharp retort emerged as a tragic whisper.

"I'd close the door," Anabelle suggested to Luke. "Gwen favors her privacy."

"I'll do that," Luke agreed, and kissed her hand again. With a delighted blush and flutter, she disappeared.

"A truly marvelous woman," Luke commented, quietly closing the door and turning the key. He turned it over in his palm a moment, studying it, then slipped it into his pocket. Gwen decided it was better strategy not to comment. "Now, suppose you tell me what you told Anabelle about being in love with me."

Looking into his calm eyes, Gwen knew it wasn't going to be easy. Temper would not work as long as he had the key. It was vital that she remain as calm as he. "I owe you an apology," she said as she casually moved to her closet. Taking the dress Anabelle had just replaced, Gwen folded it and laid it back in the suitcase.

Luke continued to stand by the door, watching her movements. "For what, precisely?"

Gwen bit the underside of her lip hard and moved back to the closet. "For the things I said about you and Mama."

"You're apologizing for believing we were having an affair?" Luke smiled at her for the first time, and although she heard it in his voice, she did not turn to see it. "I took it as a compliment."

Turning slowly, Gwen decided to brazen it out. It was impossible, she decided, to be any more humiliated than she already was. "I'm well aware that I've made a fool of myself. And I know that I deserve to feel every bit as ridiculous as I feel. As I look back, I believe that you decided on the very first day to teach me a lesson. You never admitted you were having an affair with my mother, you simply told me it was none of my business. I felt differently at the time." Gwen paused to catch her breath, and Luke moved into the room to lean comfortably on one of the bedposts. "I was wrong and you were right. It wasn't any of my business, and you succeeded in teaching me a lesson just by letting me draw my own conclusions. These were helped along by Mama's unusual behavior and her affection for you. You could, of course, have saved me a great deal of anxiety and humiliation by explaining things, but you chose to make your point. Point taken, Mr. Powers," she continued as she worked herself up into a temper. "I've been put in my place by an expert. Now, I'd like you to get out of here and leave me alone. If there's one thing I want above all else, it's never to see you again. I can only be thankful we live on opposite ends of the continent."

Luke waited a moment while she tore two skirts out of her closet and heaved them into the case. "Can I get a copy of that speech for my files?"

Gwen whirled, eyes flaming. "You unfeeling, pompous boor! I've done all the groveling I'm going to do. What more do you want?"

"Was that groveling?" he asked, lifting a brow in interest. "Fascinating. What I want," he continued, "is for you to elaborate on the statement Anabelle made before she left the room. I found it very interesting."

"You want it all, don't you?" Gwen snapped, slamming the lid on her first case. "All right, then, I'll give it to you. It makes little difference at this point." She took a breath to help the words come quickly. "I love you. What will you do now that you know?" she demanded, keeping her head high. "Write it into one of your books for comic relief?"

Luke considered a moment and then shrugged. "No. I rather think I'll marry you."

In stunned silence, Gwen stared at him. "I don't think that's very funny."

"No, I doubt marriage is a funny business. I'm sure it has its moments, though. We'll have to find out." Straightening, he walked over and put his hands on her shoulders. "Soon."

"Don't touch me," she whispered, and tried to jerk out of his hold.

"Oh, yes, I'll touch you." He turned Gwen to face him. "I'll do much more than touch you. Idiot," he said roughly when he saw her tear-drenched eyes. "Are you so blind you can't see what you've put me through? I wanted you from the first moment I saw you. You stood there smiling at me, and I felt as though someone had hit me with a blunt instrument. I wanted to teach you a lesson, all right, but I didn't expect to learn one. I didn't expect some skinny kid to tangle herself up in my mind so that I couldn't get her out." He pulled her close as she stared up at him, dry-eyed and fascinated. "I love you to the edge of madness," he murmured before his mouth crushed hers.

It's a dream, Gwen thought dazedly as his mouth roamed her face, teasing her skin. It must be a dream. She threw her arms around his neck and clung, praying never to wake up. "Luke," she managed before her mouth was silenced again. "Tell me you mean it," she begged as he tasted her neck. "Please tell me you mean it."

"Look at me," he ordered, taking her chin in his hand. She did, and found her answer. Joy bubbled inside her and escaped in laughter. Laughing with her, Luke rested his brow against hers. "I believe I've surprised you."

"Oh, Luke." She buried her face in his shoulder, holding him as if she would never let him go. "I'm not surprised, I'm delirious." She sighed, weak from laughter, dizzy with love. "How did this happen?"

"I haven't the faintest idea." He brushed his lips over the top of her head. "Falling in love with you was not in my plans."

"Why not?" she demanded, rubbing her cheek against his. "I'm a very nice person."

"You're a child," he corrected, lost in the scent of her hair. "Do you realize what we were doing when I was your age?" He gave a quick, mystified laugh. "I was working on my second novel, and you were drawing pictures with your Crayolas."

"It's twelve years, not twenty," Gwen countered, slipping her hands under his shirt to feel the warmth of his back. "And you can hardly make an issue out of an age difference, particularly a twelve-year age difference, after all this. You don't have any double standards, do you?" she asked, lifting a brow.

Luke gave her hair a brief tug. "It's not just the years. You're so innocent, so unspoiled. Wanting you was driving me mad, then loving you only made it worse." He kissed her lightly behind the ear, and she shivered with pleasure. "Even up to last night I was determined not to take advantage of that innocence. Part of me still wants to leave you that way."

"I hope the rest of you has more sense," Gwen tossed back her head to look up at him.

"I'm serious."

"So am I." She ran a fingertip along his jawline. "Buy Bradley's portrait, if you want an image."

"I already have." He smiled, caught her fingers in his and kissed them. "You don't think I'd let anyone else have it, do you?"

"Have me, too." Amusement vanished from his face as she pressed against him. "I'm a woman, Luke, not a child or an image. I love you, and I want you." Rising on her toes, she met his mouth. His hands sought her, possessed her, while she trembled with excitement. Her love seemed to expand, surrounding her until there was nothing else. She pressed closer, offering everything. It was he who drew away.

"Gwen." Luke let out a long breath and shook his

head. "It's difficult to remember that you're Anabelle's daughter and that she trusts me."

"I'm trying to make it impossible," she countered. She could feel the speed of his heartbeat against hers, and reveled in a new sense of power. "Aren't you going to corrupt me?"

"Undoubtedly," he agreed. Framing her face with his hands, he kissed her nose. "After we're married."

"Oh." Gwen pouted a moment, then shrugged. "That's sensible, I suppose. Michael was always sensible, too."

Luke's eyes narrowed at the mischief in hers. "That," he said distinctly, "was a low blow. Do you know how very near I came to pulling the phone out of the wall last night when I heard you talking to him?"

"Did you?" Gwen's face illuminated at the thought. "Were you jealous?"

"That's one way of putting it," Luke agreed.

"Well," Gwen considered carefully, trying not to smile, "I suppose I can understand that. As I said, he's a very sensible man. It's all right, though, I'm sure you're every bit as sensible as Michael."

Luke studied her carefully, but Gwen managed to keep the smile a mere hint on her lips. "Are you challenging me to kiss you into insensibility?"

"Oh, yes," she agreed, and closed her eyes. "Please do."

"I never could resist a dare," Luke murmured, drawing her into his arms.

$$\star \star \star \star \star$$

Don't miss the next enthralling read from bestselling
author Nora Roberts!

Without a Trace

Coming next month.

Read on for a preview!

WITHOUT A TRACE

As dusk fell, the sky became quieter, and the cantina noisier. A radio played Mexican music interrupted by occasional bursts of static. Someone broke a glass. Two men started to argue about fishing, politics and women. Trace poured another shot.

He saw her the minute she walked in. Old habits had his eye on the door. Training had him taking in the details without seeming to look at all. A tourist who'd made a wrong turn, he thought, as he took in the ivory skin dashed with freckles that went with her red hair. She'd burn to a crisp after an hour under the Yucatán sun. A pity, he thought mildly, and went back to his drink.

He'd expected her to back out the moment she realized the type of place she'd wandered into. Instead, she went up to the bar. Trace crossed his ankles and whiled away the time by studying her.

Her white slacks were spotless despite the dusty heat of the day. She wore them with a purple shirt that was loose enough to be cool. Even so, he noted that she was slender, with enough curve to give the baggy slacks some style. Her hair, almost the color of the setting sun, was caught back in a braid, but her face was turned away, so he could see only her profile. Classic, he decided with out much interest. Cameo style. The champagne-and-caviar type.

He tossed back the rest of the drink and decided to get very drunk—for Charlie's sake.

He'd just lifted the bottle when the woman turned and looked directly at him. From the shadow of his hat, Trace met the look. Tensed, he continued to pour as she crossed the room toward him.

"Mr. O'Hurley?"

His brow lifted only slightly at the accent. It had a trace of Ireland, the same trace his father's had taken on in anger or in joy. He sipped his whiskey and said nothing.

"You are Trace O'Hurley?"

There was a hint of nerves in the voice, as well, he noted. And, close up, he could see smudges of shadows under what were extraordinary green eyes. Her lips pressed together. Her fingers twisted on the handle of the canvas bag slung over her shoulder. Trace set the whiskey down and realized he was just a bit too drunk to be annoyed.

"Might be. Why?"

"I was told you'd be in Mérida. I've been looking for you for two days." And he was anything but what she'd expected. If she wasn't so desperate, she'd already have fled. His clothes were dirty, he smelled of whiskey, and he looked like a man who could peel the skin off you with out drawing blood. She pulled in a deep breath and decided to take her chances.

"May I sit down?"

With a shrug, Trace kicked a chair back from the table. An agent—from either side—would have approached him differently. "Suit yourself."

She wrapped her fingers around the back of the chair and wondered why her father believed this crude drunkard was the answer. But her legs weren't as steady as they might be, so she sat down. "It's very important that I speak with you. Privately."

Trace looked beyond her to the cantina. It was

crowded now, and getting noisier by the minute. "This'll do. Now why don't you tell me who you are, how you knew I'd be in Mérida, and what the hell you want?"

She linked her fingers together because they were trembling. "I'm Dr. Fitzpatrick. Dr. Gillian Fitzpatrick. Charles Forrester told me where you were, and I want you to save my brother's life."

Passion. Power. Suspense.
It's time to fall under the spell of Nora Roberts.